NEVER

EVER

YOU

T0204938

NEVER EVER YOU

A Novel

SARAH ECHAVARRE

LAKE UNION
PUBLISHING

Published by Lake Union Publishing, Seattle

www.apub.com

Amazon, the Amazon logo, and Lake Union Publishing are trademarks of Amazon.com, Inc., or its affiliates.

ISBN-13: 9781662517815 (paperback)
ISBN-13: 9781662517808 (digital)

Cover design by Kathleen Lynch/Black Kat Design
Cover image: © Stephen Mulcahey / Arcangel

Printed in the United States of America

NEVER
EVER
YOU

Chapter 1

February 14, 2024

I wake to the smell of hazelnut coffee. It's my second favorite way to wake up, next to a kiss on the shoulder—never on the mouth because dear god, morning breath.

Thank goodness my husband understands this. And thank goodness he's a hard-core caffeine addict like me. It's a fact I don't take for granted seeing as he's English.

Not that English people don't drink coffee. Plenty of them do. But there's a fixation on tea here in England that I, as an American, didn't fully understand until I moved to London nine years ago. Tea in the morning. In the afternoon. In the evening. After dinner. Sometimes more. Tea all day, every day. Too bad just a whiff of Earl Grey makes me want to puke. It possesses a dank, faintly citrus smell with wet-dirt undertones. How can anyone ingest liquid that smells like mud multiple times a day, every day?

Thankfully, when I inhale, it's a rich, nutty, caramel aroma that slides through my nostrils. Eyes still closed, I smile as I roll from my back to my side on our pillow-top mattress. Because that's not the smell of brewed coffee wafting from our kitchen; that's the smell of a fresh cup nearby.

When I open my eyes and sit up, I'm greeted with the image of my husband, Tristan, walking toward me clad in rumpled boxers and yesterday's undershirt, wooden tray in hand. On it there's a blessedly huge cup of coffee that looks more like a bowl and a thin glass vase with a trio of daisies sprouting from the top. *Fake* daisies—my husband is allergic to flowers.

"You've made it a year being married to me. Congrats, love." The way his pet name for me rolls clipped off his tongue, like a soft growl, turns my sleepy smile into a grin.

Setting the tray on my lap, he leans down and dusts a kiss on my bare shoulder where my satin sleeping top has fallen off. I close my eyes, relishing the contrast of sensations on my skin. The wet heat of his breath against the crisp air in the bedroom. The softness of his lips paired with the scratch of his strawberry-blond stubble.

"Coffee in bed *and* a shoulder kiss. Is this some one-year-anniversary tradition I don't know about?"

He settles at the foot of the bed. "I reckon you'd like it more than the traditional gift for a first-year wedding anniversary: paper."

When he wrinkles his nose in mock disgust, I laugh. "You know me so well," I say before taking a long sip.

He flicks the stem of the daisies. "I tried to find fake peonies, since they're your favorite, but apparently those are impossible to procure. So daisies it is."

I tell him it's okay before taking another long sip of coffee. I reach my arm out to offer him some, but he shakes his head. "Already had a cup. That's all for you."

By "already had a cup," he means that he's drained almost an entire pot while fielding predawn work calls, his typical morning routine. As the co-owner of a half dozen upscale restaurants in London, Tristan works from the moment he wakes to the moment he crawls into bed. When he's not putting in fourteen hours a day at his various restaurants, he's on the phone negotiating with a produce supplier or planning a menu with one of his executive chefs or calling maintenance to handle a repair.

Tristan is a textbook workaholic whose lifeblood is the restaurant industry. That's why seeing him carve out time in his frantic morning schedule to bring me breakfast in bed is a moment worthy of a heart flutter. You have to be one hell of a special person in Tristan Chase's life to get him to interrupt his routine. Yeah, it's a strange thing to take pleasure in, but that sort of stuff is what counts for me. I'm one of the few people he disrupts his packed schedule for. And in the thirty-two years I've been on this planet, I've learned that if a guy as handsome, charming, and successful as Tristan is willing to disrupt his routine to accommodate you, it means he really does care.

Leaning forward, I grab his hand and lace my fingers with his. "This is the sweetest anniversary surprise. Thank you."

The corner of his mouth quirks up, and his crystal-blue eyes sparkle just before he captures my lips in a kiss. I laugh, shocked, and push him back.

"Morning breath!" I sputter against my hand as I cover my mouth.

But Tristan wraps his warm, thick fingers around my wrist and gently pulls my hand away from my face before kissing me again.

"I don't care," he says against my mouth.

I decide right then and there that I don't either.

We go at it like two hormone-crazed teenagers. We break apart just long enough for Tristan to move the tray to the floor and shed his shirt and boxers. Sunlight streams in from the nearby window, bathing his alabaster skin in an orange glow. The muscles in his tall, lean frame pulse as he pulls the fabric from his body. As soon as I peel off my shirt and panties, I reach up and pull him on top of me.

He lowers his mouth to the shell of my ear, his hot breath sheeting across my skin. It sends a shiver through me. I writhe underneath him and claw at his back.

"Happy anniversary, love."

~

"Riley, love, I've got a surprise for you," Tristan calls from the kitchen.

I smile at my reflection in the bathroom mirror. "Coming!"

I finish swiping on the last bit of my makeup. I take the extra few seconds to blot my lipstick on a square of toilet paper. Such an old-fashioned habit—I don't know anyone my age or younger who does this. But I can't help it. It's a holdover from my modeling days, when I'd have to do my own makeup sometimes. I'm a stickler for perfectly applied lipstick. Always have been and always will be. It just looks so polished and understated. I've dropped most of my other model habits, like the twice-monthly facials, crash dieting, religious waxing, and holding cold spoons to my under-eyes to reduce swelling. But this lipstick-blot technique dies with me.

I get dressed and grab Tristan's anniversary gift from the drawer next to my sink in our bathroom, since I assume that's what we're about to do. Normally when it's a special occasion, we make dinner reservations and exchange gifts at the restaurant or when we get home. But tonight that's not an option because it's Tristan's grandparents' sixtieth-wedding-anniversary party.

Today isn't their official anniversary—that was two months ago. But his grandmother got sick with pneumonia right before their actual anniversary, and the party had to be pushed back. Once she recovered, it was rescheduled for tonight at one of Tristan's restaurants. His whole family is attending.

When I walk into the kitchen, he's standing at the far wall, straightening the trio of small, framed black-and-white landscape photos that are the only pieces of decor in the room's minimalist aesthetic. He looks up, grins at me, and then walks over to the marble island, where a gift box the size of a microwave sits.

I waggle the long velvet box at him. "Ready to exchange?"

He tells me to open mine, but I shake my head. "You first."

He chuckles, then walks over to me. "You sure this morning wasn't my gift?" he says against the side of my neck. "You look incredible, by the way. This dress . . ."

The tips of his fingers skim the midthigh-length hem of my black Max Mara sweaterdress.

"Christ, is this dress painted on your body?" he murmurs against my skin.

"Pretty much."

"And it's so short. So gloriously, gloriously short."

I chuckle and give myself a mental high five. I knew chopping off six inches from the length of this vintage store find was a good idea.

My eyelids flutter as I savor the feel of his lips on that ultrasensitive patch of skin just above my shoulder. This is my favorite way he kisses me—and speaks to me: his mouth pressed along the side of my neck, his words a cross between a whisper and a grunt.

"I mean, that was quite the present you gave me in bed, Miss America."

I smile at the ridiculous nickname he's called me ever since the day we met three years ago. I playfully push him away, knowing that if his lips remain on me for one more second, we're going to end up fucking against the kitchen island and make ourselves late for work.

"I think you'll like this too." I press the velvet, rectangular box into his hand.

As he pries it open, I bite back what I'm certain is the cheesiest smile ever. It was by total accident that I found this vintage Cartier watch. I was with my best friend and business partner, Poppy, at an antique jewelry store in Bermondsey when I spotted it. The impossibly shiny exterior caught my eye. It was stainless steel, but it had been kept up so well that it shone like silver. It was exactly Tristan's style—simple, sleek, and understated, yet undeniably high end.

At just over £2,500, it wasn't cheap, but I didn't care. In the three years we've been together, he's showered me with countless expensive gifts. Every piece of valuable jewelry I own is from him, including my cushion-cut diamond engagement ring, which cost five times as much as this watch. Whatever he got me for my anniversary gift is likely more expensive as well—every gift he's ever given me has always been nicer and cost more than whatever I've given him. He deserves this watch.

His eyes go wide for a split second as he gazes at the open box. Then the corner of his mouth turns up. "Christ . . ."

"Do you like it?"

He grins at me, then gently grabs my chin and kisses me. "I love it."

I help him put it on, giddy at how he can't stop looking at it. He thanks me, then nods at my gift on the counter. "Your turn."

"Is it the kitten I've always wanted?" I tease.

Ever since I moved in with Tristan, I've been begging for a pet, but he isn't an animal guy. Every time we see a cat or a dog when walking through the city, while I run to pet it, he frowns and keeps his distance. Even as a kid, he said, he didn't care for pets.

"This is way, way better than a kitten."

Two decades of living in London has softened his West Yorkshire accent, but every once in a while it peeks through, like when he says "way" and it comes out more like "weh." It makes me melt every time. Everything about Tristan is proper and sophisticated. His Cambridge MBA, his wardrobe full of designer suits, his old-money background. So whenever I hear remnants of that West Yorkshire accent, it always makes me smile. My ultrapolished husband has got a slight bit of unexpected edge.

I tear through the gold wrapping paper and pull open the box flaps to reveal a smaller box wrapped in the same paper. I chuckle and shake my head. This is exactly how he wrapped my engagement ring when he proposed.

After unwrapping and opening four gift boxes in total, I finally make it to a palm-size black velvet jewelry box, which I assume holds a pair of very expensive earrings.

But when I open it and see a car key fob, I frown. "What is this?"

Instead of answering, Tristan grins and grabs my hand before leading me down the stairs and through the front door of his Marylebone walk-up. We step onto the porch, and he points to a brand-new white Audi parked on the street.

"That's yours."

All I can do for a few seconds is stare with my mouth wide open. I twist to look at him. "Tristan, what the . . . a car? That's too—"

His gentle grip finds my waist. He pulls me against him. "It's not too much. Remember when I asked if we could get married on Valentine's Day, which was a weekday, pretty much the least convenient day to get married? And you agreed."

I cup his cheek. "I agreed because it was insanely romantic that you wanted to get married on Valentine's Day."

He smiles at me. "You're spending your first wedding anniversary with your in-laws when you should be having a romantic night with your husband. On Valentine's Day, no less. The car is partly an apology for that."

Most of Tristan's family are kind to me—except his parents and grandparents. They've been frosty to me ever since I met them. I expect it's because they didn't think their beloved son and grandson would marry a half-Filipino, half-white American girl who peddles lingerie and makeup for a living.

To be honest, I'm perfectly fine with keeping my distance from them. I've never been one to beg people for their acceptance. But Tristan's family means the world to him. If I have to see them every once in a while at family events and maintain a surface-level politeness, I'll do it.

"Okay, yeah, I admit I didn't expect to be attending someone else's anniversary party on my own wedding anniversary. But come on, you didn't have to buy me a car."

I stare at the key fob in my hand. My memory slingshots to the day after he proposed, when he planned a similar surprise, only then it was the key to his flat. I chuckled when I opened the gift box.

"I already have a key to your place," I said. I had been living with him for almost a year at that point.

"Read the card," he said with a knowing smile.

This flat never felt like home until you moved in. It's my gift to you, Miss America.

He led me by the hand to the front door, revealing a giant red bow tied on the outside. And then he pulled out a folded stack of papers tucked in an envelope from his back trouser pocket and handed it to me. It was a copy of the deed.

"I'm adding your name to the deed," he said.

"Are you serious?" I asked, stunned. Tristan's flat was worth millions. I'd never be able to afford a place like this in London, not in a hundred years.

"Of course I'm serious. We're going to be married soon. My home is your home, Mrs. Chase."

I kissed him breathless. "Mrs. Ricci-Chase."

He flashed a half smile. "I like the sound of that."

"Riley. You deserve this car," Tristan says, pulling me back to the present. The conviction in his low tone, combined with the way his hold turns firm against the curve of my hip, softens me.

I bite my lip as I look up at him, dizzy with disbelief. "You bought me a car."

"Guilty as charged, Miss America."

I squeal and jump up, wrapping my arms around his neck. He squeezes me tight against him. In this moment I know, without a doubt, I am the luckiest woman on the planet.

Chapter 2

"You lucky bitch." Poppy sits in the driver's seat of my brand-new car, shaking her head as she grips the steering wheel.

"I know, right?"

When I pulled up behind our brick storefront in Camden Town and parked, Poppy was making her way to the entrance with her Chihuahua, Gus, in tow, then stopped dead in her tracks when she saw me. Her jaw plummeted to the ground, as did the unlit cigarette from her crimson lips. She's a former pack-a-day smoker who's finally kicked the habit but says she misses the feel and taste of cigarettes, so she'll sometimes stick unlit ones in her mouth to satisfy the urge.

She sputtered "bloody fucking hell" before jogging over, flinging open the driver's-side door, and shooing me over to the passenger side so she could sit behind the wheel.

She scans the leather interior, tiny Gus sleeping in her purse, while I describe how Tristan surprised me this morning.

"Do you know what Desmond got me for our first wedding anniversary? An origami kit."

I try and fail to stifle a laugh. "Well, I mean, paper is the traditional first-year anniversary gift, right? So I guess that was kind of thoughtful of him."

Her raspy cackle ricochets in the car. "That's the year I started sending him my online shopping wish lists. Now I get exactly what I want for every birthday, Christmas, and anniversary. I no longer have to feign enthusiasm when he gifts me a brass bookend set or a dehumidifier or a crystal beer stein. Christ on a stick, I don't even drink beer."

I laugh. "Does this mean you'll be adding a car to your birthday wish list this year?"

She cackles. "Ha. You know, I jokingly told Desmond the other week that I wanted to upgrade our car, and he looked like he was going to pass out. And then he said we could maybe make it work if I'd be willing to sell our current car and take the tube and bus and walk instead of driving to save up the rest of the money." She makes a disgusted noise. "I told him no way in fucking hell would I ever do that, especially with the entire north section of the Northern line here in Camden Town being down until next year for repairs. Can you imagine me taking a fucking double-decker bus twice a day, crammed with all those tourists? Kill me."

I laugh even harder.

"So. Did Tristan like his watch?" she asks as we climb out of the car and open up Luscious, the lingerie and makeup store we co-own.

"He did, even though I felt like a bit of a wanker once I saw the car."

Poppy's ski-slope nose wrinkles as she flips on the lights, illuminating the small yet open space in the late-morning sun. "Never say 'wanker' again, Ri. You're far too American to pull it off."

I laugh while I walk to the checkout counter near the back of the store and set things up at the register. When Poppy walks over to replenish a stack of tissue paper and paper bags, she knocks me gently with her hip before setting Gus down on the floor.

"Hey. I'm just taking the piss. I know he loved it."

"He said he can't wait to show it off tonight at the anniversary party."

"Good man." Poppy winks at me. "By the way, love the outfit, you polished princess."

"Will you ever let that nickname die?" I ask.

"Only when you stop looking so put together all the time," she teases. "If Desmond had sprung a brand-new Audi on me, I'd be so shocked I'd have shown up to work naked. But here you are looking like you just strutted the runway. Quit making the rest of us look like slobs, will you?"

I roll my eyes and chuckle. "Poppy, there's no way you could ever be a slob. You look like a chic badass. Always."

She blows a kiss at me. "Seriously, though, when you die, you'd better leave that trench coat you're wearing to me. Stunning."

Through a laugh I tell her sure thing. I take off the Burberry trench I was gifted after a photo shoot years ago and hang it over the chair by the register.

"What's the dress code for the anniversary party this evening? Black tie optional? Or is it 'insufferable rich twat chic'?"

I force a smile at Poppy's joke even though I'm certain my best friend can spot my unease like a road flare. I lean down and give Gus a pat on his tiny head.

"You're wife of the year for agreeing to spend your first wedding anniversary—your Valentine's Day anniversary—with your in-laws," she says before walking over to the nearby rack of lace nighties and straightening out the hangers. "If Desmond tried that, I'd have his balls."

"It's one anniversary. In the grand scheme of things, it's not that big of a deal."

Poppy straightens up to her full five-foot-ten height. Her ice-blue eyes meet my gaze. "They're not here, Ri. You don't have to put it on and spout that bullshit."

I chuckle softly and scoop up Gus. I set him in his designated spot: on the counter next to the register on top of the plush pillow that serves as his bed whenever Poppy brings him in to work with her.

The bell above the glass-door entrance chimes and in walks Desmond, hair as rumpled as the plaid button-down and sable overcoat he wears. Poppy starts to ask what he's doing here, but she goes quiet when she sees the brown paper bag in his hand.

"You forgot your lunch," he says through an adorably crooked smile.

She walks up to him, and instead of taking the bag from him, she slinks her arms around his neck and kisses him. I turn away, smiling to myself as I give them a moment of privacy.

Behind me I hear Desmond utter a muffled protest, to which Poppy growls. A low, satisfied sigh is his response.

Poppy and her husband of four years, Desmond, are the dictionary definition of "opposites attract." She looks like Kate Moss raided a punk rocker's closet; Desmond looks every bit the computer programmer that he is: thick-rimmed glasses, disheveled chestnut hair, a consistent wardrobe of fraying button-ups and chinos. Her ideal night out is a bar crawl through Shoreditch and karaoke, while Desmond would rather binge his favorite sci-fi series with a glass of Scotch at home. Poppy can chat up anyone—drunk strangers, moody transit employees, celebrities. I've seen Desmond go beet red trying to get a bartender's attention in a crowded pub.

Despite these glaring differences, they work. He's the cuddly counter to her razor sharpness. Whenever she's stressed or upset, all it takes is one hug from him and she's calm. I've seen it more times than I can count, and it never ceases to blow me away. He happily does all the cooking and cleaning, things she hates, while she is more than willing to do all the things he loathes, like call up utility companies to argue about bills and verbally spar with car mechanics and salespeople. He's the calm to her storm, the nerdy sweetie pie to her badassery.

"Wrap it up, you two," I say while I organize the display of mini perfume bottles by the register. "You're in public."

Behind me I hear the sound of fabric rustling and shoes squeaking along the tile floor. I count to three after it ends and turn around to see Desmond wearing the most flustered smile along with a hefty smudge of his wife's lipstick.

He runs a hand through his mussed hair and looks over at me for exactly two seconds before his eyes dart to the floor. Poppy wipes her thumbs along his bottom lip, a devilish smirk tugging at her mouth.

"Well, um . . . I'd better get going." He clears his throat. "Nice to see you, Riley."

"You too, Desmond."

He heads for the door, and Poppy gives his backside a pat, causing him to yelp. I cover my mouth to stifle a laugh.

"See you at home, lover," she coos. He frowns, nods, and scurries off.

"That was both adorable and gross."

"You should greet Tristan that way tonight," Poppy says with a wag of her perfectly arched eyebrow.

"Maybe when we get home. Wouldn't want to give his mom or grandparents a heart attack with that level of PDA. I've never seen his parents or grandparents so much as hold hands. The make-out session you just had with Desmond would make their heads explode, I'm sure of it."

Two middle-aged ladies walk into the store, and Poppy asks if they need help before leaving them to browse.

"Sometimes I forget just how soul-sucking Tristan's family are, his mum especially," Poppy says when she sidles up next to me at the register. "You're an angel for tolerating her for as long as you have."

My chest warms at Poppy's fierce defense of me. She's met Tristan's family a dozen times and disliked them from the get-go.

"You'd think they were descendants of the royal family given how far up their own arses they are," she mutters.

"They're a rich, established, and proper family who hoped their precious baby boy would marry a rich, established, and proper English girl. And given that I'm pretty much the polar opposite of that, it's no surprise they're not fans of me."

Poppy tugs my hand, her nonverbal way of demanding I look at her. Even though we're the same height, I have to look up at her because she's wearing leather boots with three-inch heels that put her just past six feet.

"You say that like it's a bad thing," she chides. "Be proud that you're not like those insufferable twats. You worked for every single thing you had, Ri. You had no support and moved across the ocean and established a life for yourself."

"As a lingerie model," I say. "I may as well have 'whore' tattooed on my forehead. It's essentially the same thing to them."

Poppy rolls her eyes. "There's nothing wrong with being a lingerie model. That's how you nabbed the attention of their precious Tristan. Have they forgotten that?"

I think back to the day we met three years ago, when I was working as a live model during the grand opening of a La Perla store in Soho right before Christmas. I was posing in the shop window, decked out in a black lace bra, matching panties, hold-ups, and heels when Tristan walked by, cell phone clutched to his ear.

When our eyes locked, he stopped speaking and halted in front of the window. Even though I couldn't hear him, I could read his lips as he said, "I'll call you back," before slipping his phone in his coat pocket, never breaking eye contact with me. And then he smiled and walked off.

"Does that come in my size?" a low voice asked behind me a minute later.

I bit back a laugh before twisting around to look at the handsome man from the window, standing several feet behind me. "I don't think it does. Sorry."

"Your accent is lovely."

I chuckled out loud that time. "My accent is Californian. It's very boring."

"There is nothing boring about you, Miss America."

Another chuckle, followed by another charming line from Tristan. Five minutes of flirting later, he had my number, and I had a promise from him that he'd call me that night. He did. We went out for drinks the following day. We've been together since.

Poppy lets out a disgusted noise, pulling me back to the present. "You built a business with your friend from the ground up when you were twenty-seven, Ri. In one of the most expensive cities in the world. No help from anyone."

"I sell slutty underwear and makeup to tarts, according to Tristan's family."

Poppy's thick blonde eyebrows crash together. "Don't. You know that's not true."

"Of course I know that. But that's what they think. And no matter what I do, no matter what I say, that will always mark me as 'not good enough' to them."

My phone buzzes in my pocket with a text from my mom.

Anak! Happy anniversary to you and Tristan! Love you both!

A sad smile pulls at my mouth when I think about the difference between our families. My mom has been welcoming to Tristan since the day she met him, always greeting him with hugs and warm smiles, always genuinely happy to see him whenever he's visited her.

She sends another text.

Jordan sends his love too!

A sinking feeling in my stomach hits. Such a lie.

My little brother loathes Tristan, ever since the day he met him. I know for a fact that Jordan didn't tell our mom to wish me a happy anniversary and that she just sent that text to be nice. Never in a million years would Jordan think to wish Tristan a happy anything.

I push aside the unpleasant fact that my husband and brother don't get along and try to refocus on the moment with Poppy.

She shakes her head, her choppy, wheat-blonde bob swaying with the movement. "In addition to being a brilliant, self-made business-woman, you're also the kindest and funniest person I know. If Tristan's family refuses to see that, then they can get in the bin. I'd be happy to toss them in there myself if you'd like."

I wrap my arms around Poppy and hug her tight. "You're an angel." She squeezes me back. "Ha. Not even close. Even the devil won't have me."

The two customers bring a haul of makeup to the counter. After we check them out and they leave, she turns to me. "You sure you don't want me to come with you tonight? I'd be a buffer between you and Cruella."

I cackle at Poppy's nickname for my mother-in-law. "I appreciate the offer, but I'll be fine. Besides, you gotta go home and finish what you started with Desmond. You can't blow him off for Portia Chase of all people—you'll break his heart. And give him the worst case of blue balls."

Poppy chuckles before her expression turns pinched. "Fucking hell. Portia. With a name like that, I thought she'd be cool. Like Portia from *The Merchant of Venice*. Fuck, was I wrong," she mutters. "I will forever maintain that Cruella is an infinitely better moniker for her. It actually suits her. I mean, she hates dogs. How fitting."

The very first time Tristan introduced us, I wasn't prepared for the low-key hostility his mother threw like invisible daggers. Petite Portia Chase wore a pleasant expression when she first met me and even hugged me. But then we started talking.

"I'm afraid I've only ever met little boys with the name Riley, not lovely young ladies like yourself," she said to me while we shared tea at one of Tristan's restaurants.

I still remember the fake-as-hell smile she flashed, her thin lips shellacked in Charlotte Tilbury Pillow Talk. And the comments she made throughout that hour-long introduction, all delivered in a polite tone, with a racist undercurrent.

I don't think I've ever seen that shade of brown before in anyone's hair. It's quite . . . dark, isn't it?

Why, my dear, I think you're the tannest person in this room. A perk of your uniquely mixed heritage, I'd say. Must be nice not to have to encase yourself in sunblock all the time like us fair-skinned folks.

Ricci . . . that's quite an ethnic-sounding surname.

You're quite tall for a Filipino, aren't you?

Tristan prepped me beforehand, saying that his mother was an odd duck who never warmed up to most people.

"She barely tolerates me, love," he said after we left. Then he kissed my shoulder, whispering his apology against my skin. "I'm sorry. She's insufferable. Thank you for being so wonderful."

His empathetic words softened the scorch of her low-key insults. I can withstand her passive-aggressive comments the few times I see her every year for holidays and family gatherings, because I have Tristan. He's worth it.

"I know I'm not a psychologist, but I'm pretty sure she's a psychopath," Poppy says. She makes a kissing face at Gus as he peeks up from his dog bed. "I mean, she said to my face with Gus in my arms that she hates dogs. Who does that?"

"A psychopath."

She high-fives me before fishing a treat from her bag and feeding it to Gus.

"Maybe you'll get lucky tonight and the restaurant will flood or there'll be a blackout or some other disaster, and the anniversary party will be called off. Then you and Tristan can run home and spend your anniversary night fucking like rabbits as god intended."

I let out a laugh so loud poor Gus jolts in his plush pillow bed. "Here's hoping."

Chapter 3

"Are you trying to kill me, Miss America?"

Tristan's gaze catches on the hem of the tweed pencil skirt I'm wearing. It's nothing notable—it hits just above my knees, a perfectly respectable length for the family gathering we're currently at.

But I know it's not the hem he's fixated on. He's looking at that to keep his composure after what I just showed him, which was a peek of the red lace thong I'm wearing. When we walked through the doors of Last One Standing, the upscale pub he owns, I shed my trench coat, pulled up my blouse, tugged up the right strap of my thong, and winked at him.

"Part two of your anniversary gift," I whispered right before a gaggle of his relatives walked in. Tristan's eyes were as wide as saucers as he cleared his throat and said quick hellos to everyone, urging them in the direction of the party room in the back, where the anniversary party is.

When he takes my hand, I think he's going to lead us there, too, but he stays planted in that spot, his blue eyes on fire.

"We'll stay an hour, tops. Then we'll head straight home, and you're going to let me play with my gift," he growls against my mouth between kisses.

I bite back a giggle as he walks us into the private room. His grandparents sit at the head of the long mahogany table that is the center of the dimly lit space while a small group of relatives stands over them, chatting. I'm silently relieved that they're preoccupied and I don't have to stop and say hello. It doesn't matter how hard I've tried to be nice and engage them. They always offer a pinched expression and a polite "Hello, Riley," and then immediately focus their attention on Tristan. They pretty much pretend I don't exist. Even when Tristan tries to include me in the conversation, they always say, "Oh, that's nice" with a tight, fake smile and change the subject. It's so awkward, standing there and watching the three of them chat warmly while I look like a pathetic hanger-on.

I catch Tristan's grandmother's glance my way. Her scowl lands on the neckline of my blouse. Probably because the neckline dips lower than my throat and there's a delicate lace trim reminiscent of lingerie. I'm practically topless in her eyes, since I only ever see her wear turtlenecks and blouses that button all the way to her collarbone. I fuss with it for a split second before she looks away. I stop myself, my cheeks heating with embarrassment. I shouldn't let a mean look from his grandmother throw me off so much.

I look around and notice a mountain of gifts on the floor behind them, but it's the ice sculpture at the center of the table that I gawk at. It's two swans touching beaks, their profiles making a massive heart shape the size of a flat-screen TV. It rests on a silver tray that's lined with chocolate-covered strawberries along the perimeter.

"Um, wow."

Tristan sighs. "A bit over the top, I know. But my mum insisted. Said we needed a romantic touch to the centerpiece since it's Valentine's Day."

I silently reflect on the fact Portia has chosen swans as a symbol of love and affection, despite the fact that they're some of the meanest, most aggressive birds on the planet. I guess that's fitting.

One of Tristan's uncles pulls him away to ask a question about the wine they're serving tonight. I say hello to Tristan's cousin Nesta, who pulls me into a hug.

"My god, that blouse. Gorgeous. What is that color, emerald green?"

"More like kelly green, I think."

"Stunning. Is it from your boutique?"

I nod. "Just came in this week. We're trying out selling a few clothing items in addition to lingerie now. I'll set aside a blouse for you. Size medium?"

"You gem. Thank you. Though you'd better make it a large. I'm still pumping, and the girls are gigantic."

This is how Nesta greets me every time I see her at a family gathering—with a hug, a glowing compliment, and a promise to buy something from my shop. From the moment we met right after Tristan and I started dating, she was kind and welcoming to me. When she found out I ran a lingerie and makeup boutique, we became fast friends. Before she had her daughter, she would stop in almost every week to shop.

She smiles warmly at me. "How do you look so chic every time I see you? I'd be infuriated if I didn't adore you so much."

I chuckle as my cheeks flush. "You're sweet, Nesta. It's a holdover from my modeling days, I guess. I always had to look presentable."

"What a champ you are, coming to this tonight," she says in a hushed voice. She wrinkles her nose at the ice sculpture. "Say you're from a wanky rich white family from London without saying you're from a wanky rich white family from London. You'd think we've forgotten that half our family are from Leeds."

I snort a laugh. Her husband, Roland, walks up, their infant daughter snoozing against his chest.

"Hey, Riley," he says through a breath. "Brilliant anniversary gift you got for Tristan." He aims a tired stare at Nesta. "Vintage Cartier watch is on my Christmas list this year."

"Then you'd better steal Tristan's. Too rich for my personal assistant salary."

He chuckles before sobering slightly. "I've got good news and bad news," he tells Nesta.

"Bad news first. Always," she says without missing a beat.

"Molly had a blowout, and I had to throw away the onesie."

"And the good news?"

"She was so exhausted from unloading the biggest poo I've seen her make so far in her three months of life that she's now fast asleep. Finally."

Roland explains to me that Molly's been cranky most of the day and refused to nap.

Nesta shakes her head, her copper-red curls dancing around her face as she chuckles, then takes Molly into her arms. "Hallelujah. Go grab a pint. You deserve it."

Roland runs off to the bar, promising to bring back lemon drops for the both of us.

"You two are incredible parents," I say to Nesta.

Nesta makes a noise that sounds more like a scoff than a laugh. "You wouldn't have thought I was very incredible if you had witnessed me muttering every curse word in the book while this little princess was screeching like a demon at four in the morning a few nights ago. I didn't sleep a wink, and I was raging."

"Lack of sleep will make anyone rage," I say. "You're amazing, Nesta. Truly."

She starts to smile, but then she looks behind me. She frowns. "Oh fucking hell," she mutters.

"Nesta, darling. How are you?" Portia's shrill purr sounds from behind me.

"Just fine, Auntie Portia. You?"

Portia sidles up next to me, her gaze fixing on Nesta. Instead of answering Nesta, she squints at her. "You're looking quite buxom, my dear."

I hold back a wince. Typical Portia, offering a thinly veiled insult as a greeting to her own niece. The only person she seems to ever have kind words for is her son.

Nesta purses her lips. "Well, seeing as my tits are engorged with milk in order to feed my baby, I'd say you're stating the obvious, Auntie Portia."

I cover my mouth to muffle the chuckle that falls from my mouth, but it's too late. Portia's glare pivots from her niece to me.

"Good of you to make it, Riley." There's a bitterness in her tone, like she's trying to speak after swallowing a shot of vinegar.

"I'll say." Nesta rests her free hand on her hip. "She's here on her wedding anniversary. That's quite commendable. You've got a hell of a daughter-in-law."

"Commendable. Yes." Portia narrows her gaze at me before sipping from her martini glass. She does a seconds-long once-over of me. All the muscles in my neck and shoulders tense as she sizes me up. I brace myself for whatever insult she's about to lob at me, but she says nothing. She just keeps sipping her martini. I feel the slightest tinge of relief. Of all the low-key ways my mother-in-law has insulted me, she's surprisingly never said a word about my clothes. A nice difference from the way Tristan's grandmother glowered at my blouse minutes ago.

A beat later I notice the glassy stare in her eyes. All the muscles in my body tense now.

I've only ever seen Portia intoxicated once—at Christmas dinner last year, right after a very loud argument with Tristan's dad . . . that everyone in their massive Westminster home overheard, even though Portia and her husband were holed up in their bedroom on the third floor. It was one of the few times Tristan's dad, Weston, was home in England.

According to Tristan, even though his parents have been married close to four decades, they've spent the majority of their marriage apart, with Weston traveling for work. I had met him only a handful of times, and every time he seemed like he couldn't wait to leave. And when they were together and I happened to be around, I could feel the tension between them, like a thick fog hanging in the air. The way they barely looked at each other, how they never hugged or kissed, how they exchanged minimal words in every interaction I'd ever witnessed.

At that dinner, after several minutes of shouting and muffled arguing, there was a door slam and the sound of tires screeching. Tristan's dad was nowhere to be found. But Portia proceeded to make a beeline for the liquor cabinet and got progressively drunker as the day wore on, lobbing insults at whoever happened to walk into her line of view. Thankfully Tristan put her to bed before she could set her sights on me, but I don't think I'll make out as easily tonight.

Portia eyes Molly as she sleeps cradled in Nesta's arms. "Speaking of babies, you and my son should probably get started," Portia says.

My eyes bulge at her. She merely shrugs before sipping her martini. Nesta mutters a curse under her breath right as Roland walks up to us.

"Two lemon drops for—"

He freezes when his hazel gaze lands on Portia. He drops the drinks on the table next to us and scurries to the other side of the room. I don't blame him for running off. He was one of the unlucky souls Portia drunkenly unloaded on at Christmas. Even now I wince as I recall how she loudly complimented Roland's beard and proclaimed that if she were thirty years younger, she'd make a meal out of him.

"You really shouldn't be drinking if you're trying to get pregnant, Riley."

"Wh—I'm not trying to get pregnant."

"Well, you should be. Otherwise, what good are you?"

This time I can't think of a single thing to say in response. All I can do is stand there with my mouth still open and stare as she glares at me over the rim of her glass.

"Carly would have happily had my son's baby," she mutters.

Just the sound of Tristan's ex's name spilling from my mother-in-law's lips turns my skin ice cold.

"What did you just say?"

"They would have had the cutest babies. Blue-eyed ones for sure, given that both Tristan and Carly have blue eyes. Can't really guarantee that with you, can you? Yours are so brown," she mutters while glancing off to the side.

I always suspected from Portia's initial lukewarm-at-best feelings toward me that she would have rather Tristan marry his ex, Carly, who's a corporate lawyer and comes from a loaded English family. He ended things with her right before he met me, but Portia still kept framed photos of them as a couple displayed in her house until Tristan asked her to take them down as soon as he and I got serious. It's no surprise to know that she prefers her to me.

But to hear Portia say the words out loud—to hear her tell me to my face that she wishes another woman would have married her son and given her grandbabies—slices deep.

I can barely swallow past the boulder in my throat. My eyes burn as I blink, still robbed of anything I could possibly say in response to the way Portia just hacked me open.

The feel of Nesta tugging on my hand jerks me out of my stupor.

"Come on," she whispers, pulling me to walk away. "Before I cold-cock my own aunt. Christ."

We round the corner of the massive table and bump into Tristan.

"Running off somewhere?" He smiles, his gaze darting between us.

"Yes. From your racist bitch mum," Nesta says.

Tristan frowns at her. "What the hell, Nesta. Don't say that about—"

"I'll say whatever I want about that cow after the way she humiliated your wife. Where the hell have you been anyway? What are you doing leaving Riley alone in a room with your drunk mum?"

Tristan's face falls. "Fuck. What did she say?"

"That you should have married your ex, Carly," I say, my voice shaky. "That she'd love it if Carly were the one to give her grandkids and not . . . not . . ."

Tristan's eyes go wide. My throat aches as I struggle to get that final word out, but the sound of gleeful shouting and laughter interrupts me.

I glance behind Tristan to see his cousin Milo standing in the door-way of the room, one arm in the air, like he's presenting himself to the family. In his other arm is a gigantic bouquet of roses, like the kind that beauty queens are given when they win a pageant.

"Happy anniversary, Gran and Grandad!" His Southern California accent cuts through the murmur of conversation in the room.

Tristan's grandparents squeal and clap at the sight of Milo as he rushes up to them and tucks the bouquet in his gran's arms. Her perma-scowl is gone, replaced with a wide grin. She saves her smiles for Milo, I've noticed over the years. He's clearly the favorite grandkid, next to Tristan.

"Only the most stunning bouquet for the most stunning woman this side of the Atlantic."

His gran blushes and pats Milo's dark stubble–covered cheek before commenting on how handsome he looks, like she always does every time she sees him. As much as I dislike Milo, his boisterous entrance was jarring enough that now, instead of fighting back tears, I'm annoyed. Better than crying in front of my in-laws on my first wedding anniversary.

After hugging a handful of family members, Milo points to the paper gift bag he set on the table. "Brought some American candy from my work trip for anyone who's got a sweet tooth."

All of Tristan's younger cousins head straight for the bag.

Milo does a quick scan of the room. "Wow. Is this a funeral or an anniversary party?"

"Anniversary party. Obviously," Tristan says. Even in the dim mood lighting, I can tell his jaw muscles are on the verge of ripping through the stubbled skin on his face, he's biting down so hard.

Judging by that smug smile he flashes, Milo is unfazed by the irri-tation in his cousin's tone. He waltzes up to Tristan and offers his usual greeting of a slap on the back.

"You sure you weren't going for a funeral-chic ambiance, cuz? Because I gotta say, with the dim lighting and the vases of white roses along the table, I'm getting memorial service vibes. A bit morbid, don't you think?"

Behind me I hear Roland chuckle; then Nesta mutters something unintelligible before he clears his throat and goes quiet.

"I think it looks nice," I say, my annoyance clear in my pitchy tone. Milo raises a thick brow before smirking at me. "Of course you do, Miss America."

I place my hands behind my back and clasp them together to keep from slapping Milo. When Tristan told me about his cousin after we first started dating, I was excited. We're both Americans living in London and are around the same age. We were even from the same state, California. I thought we'd be fast friends, just like Nesta and me. And when I met Milo at a family dinner at one of Tristan's restaurants, he was charming and polite at first. But then I overheard him talking shit about me by the bathrooms right as I was walking out.

"She's pretty. Gorgeous, actually. Excellent trophy wife material, I'll give her that," he muttered into his phone. "But Jesus, what the hell is Tristan thinking? A guy like him and a girl like her? Gimme a break."

The words float back in stunning clarity every time I recall that moment, like I'm hearing them for the first time all over again. The only person I've ever told about what Milo said is Poppy, who now hates him with the fury of ten thousand suns, like any loyal best friend would. I thought about telling Tristan, but it was clear from watching the two of them interact that they loathe each other, always trading thinly veiled insults whenever they're together. When I asked Tristan why they don't get along, he said that they've always disliked one another, even as kids.

"He's always been so cocky and obnoxious. Always the loudest one in the room. Always trying to one-up me since we're the same age. Family or not, I've never been a fan of that bullshit," Tristan had said.

I decided to keep that ugly comment from Milo to myself. Tristan already hated him. No need to add fuel to the fire.

"You're always so supportive, Miss America." Milo wags his eyebrows at me, smirk still firmly in place. "My cousin's a lucky man." He glances down at Tristan's arm. "New watch, cuz?"

He whistles like he's impressed. I roll my eyes. "Yes. My anniversary gift to him."

Milo winks at me, that smug grin on display. "Damn. Nice work, Miss America."

"Call her Riley," Tristan bites.

Milo chuckles before aiming his taunting stare at Tristan. "Sorry. I should know better than to steal such a precious pet name."

The sarcasm in Milo's voice makes me want to snap at him, but I bite my tongue. I've already made a pseudo scene with Portia minutes ago. I need to just ignore Milo's usual bullshit and get through the rest of tonight.

Tristan steps forward so that he's fully in Milo's space. I start to reach for him, but he waves me off with a hand.

"Shit," Nesta mutters.

"You think you can waltz in here and act like an absolute tosser by insulting my work and taunting my wife? What the fuck's your problem, Milo?"

Tristan's blue eyes are wild, and for the second time tonight, my entire body is on edge. I've never seen him get physical with anyone, even when he's been irate, and now it looks like he's about to come to blows with his cousin in front of their entire family.

Milo's smirk is long gone, replaced by the straight line of his mouth. That look in his deep-brown eyes is still taunting, though.

"I don't have a problem, man. I was just kidding around."

Tristan moves forward, bumping Milo's chest. But Milo doesn't even budge, keeping his tall, steady stance.

Standing nearly nose to nose, their physical differences have never been so stark. They're both a few inches past six feet and boast that long, lean, broad build all the men in their family seem to have. They're even dressed similarly tonight: both of them donned dark trousers with matching jackets and dressy button-up shirts, no tie. But Milo is the dark-haired, dark-eyed, olive-skinned, ruggedly handsome counter to Tristan's fair and boyish good looks, thanks to Milo's Portuguese American mother's genes.

For a second I wonder if Portia secretly hates Milo because of his ethnicity, like she does me. If she does, she's never admitted it or been open about it. I've only ever seen her be cordial to Milo. Not ever warm, but never rude. Probably because he's her nephew—her family.

"You're not fucking funny," Tristan mutters.

Milo shrugs his blazer-clad shoulders. "I'm not everyone's cup of tea, that's for sure." His unblinking gaze comes off like a dare.

Tristan huffs a breath, but before he can move or say another word, I grab his arm. "Enough."

And that's when I notice the entire room has gone silent. I twist my head around and see their whole family witnessing their exchange.

Milo and Tristan seem to notice, too, at the same moment, because a beat later they finally break their staring contest and take dual steps back from each other.

"Gotta love these precious family moments, right?" Milo chuckles before running a hand through his thick waves of brown-black hair.

Out of the corner of my eye, I see Tristan tense.

"Brought to us by our most precious boy—Tristan." Milo points at him, like he's making finger guns. "You always bring us together in the most beautiful way. Always in one of your fabulous restaurants. Your generosity and integrity are unmatched, golden boy."

The way Milo emphasizes the word "integrity" makes me pause. What the hell is that about?

They exchange a look I can't quite decipher. Then a split second later Tristan punches Milo in the face.

Chapter 4

"What the fuck!"

"Tristan, darling!"

"Whoa . . ."

More cursing and a few shrieks follow. I'm too stunned to make a noise as I stand off to the side, watching Tristan shake out his hand as he looms over Milo, who's hunched over and cradling his jaw.

A couple of Tristan's aunts rush over to the kids and usher them out of the room. Nesta and Roland dart to Milo while I turn to Tristan. His mom starts to rush over to him, but he holds up a hand, stopping her just a few feet away from us.

"What the hell was that?" I bark above the wave of confused conversation that's getting louder by the second.

Tristan's blue eyes transition from focused to dazed. "I . . . I don't . . ."

I pull him by the arm out of the room and out the service entrance door at the back of the restaurant. A gust of cold air whips around us, and I start to shiver.

"Tristan. You just punched your cousin in front of your entire family."

He moves to lean against the brick wall. "I don't need a play-by-play, Riley. I know what I did."

I stand in front of him, mouth agape, stunned at the apathy in his voice.

"Look, I know that you and Milo have never liked each other. And I agree, he was being a total asshole tonight. But that's no excuse to hit him."

Tristan's face twists into the most incredulous frown. "It wasn't just me he was being a dick to. It was you too, Riley."

"So, what, I'm supposed to feel flattered that you punched your cousin in the face for insulting me? What are we, in high school? I don't find acts of violence attractive, Tristan. I never have."

For a long moment he doesn't say a word. He just looks at me. But then he tugs a hand through his hair, and it's like the movement shakes him out of whatever trance he was just in. He closes his eyes and shakes his head.

"You're right. I'm sorry, love."

When he reaches forward and slinks his arms around my waist, I stiffen. But then he pulls me against him, and I soften.

"I'm sorry," he murmurs. "I just can't fucking stand my cousin."

I hug him back. "I can't either. But you don't see me punching him in the face, do you?"

With his face pressed against the side of my neck, he makes a satisfied noise. "Fair point."

We break apart, and he looks toward the door. "I should run in and apologize to everyone. Then we should go."

I tell him I'll wait for him out here.

"Stay the hell away from your cousin."

"Promise I will."

While I wait for Tristan to return, I check my phone and see a text from Poppy.

Poppy: Need me to call with a fake emergency to get you away from your in-laws?

Me: No need. Your wish came true. Anniversary party was a disaster, we're headed home now.

Poppy: What?? Are you all right?

Me: Fine. I just wanna go home and go to bed. Promise I'll tell you everything tomorrow at work.

I'm slipping my phone back into my purse when I hear the door swing open. I look up, expecting Tristan, but instead I see Milo's swollen face.

I cross my arms over my chest, anticipating a goading comment or a smug look. But I don't get either. Instead, Milo's expression turns remorseful as he stands just a few feet away from me, cupping his hand over the left side of his face.

"I'm sorry."

His dejected tone is almost as shocking as the actual apology he's given me. I don't ever remember hearing him delivering a non-sarcastic "sorry." I don't ever remember him sounding so beaten down.

For a moment I feel the tiniest pang of sympathy. But when he starts to walk past me in the direction of the street, I remind myself of all the hurtful, dismissive things he's done and said—including tonight. One apology doesn't make up for the epic jerk he's always been.

"You were out of line, Milo."

He stops walking but doesn't turn to face me. "You're right. I was."

I don't know if it's his casual tone of voice, if it's the way he refuses to look at me when he speaks, or if it's the three years' worth of snide remarks aimed at me and my husband that finally gets to me. Whatever the reason, it causes a strange and sudden spike of adrenaline. Like lava bubbling in my chest. I dart over and stand in front of him.

"Why are you like this?"

"Like what?" Eyes closed, he dips his head back and breathes in, like he's summoning some inner reserve of patience to talk to me.

"A dick to Tristan. And to me. Almost every single time we see you, it's like this. You give him shit all the time. God, why . . . why can't you just . . . ?"

I tug both hands through my hair and let out a groan-yell that finally prompts him to look at me.

"Why can't I just what, Riley?"

The sincerity in his tone throws me off completely. So does the intensity of his stare.

I swallow. "Why can't you just be polite? And nice? To Tristan. And me."

The corner of his mouth tilts up in a smile that's all bitter, zero joy. But he doesn't answer. So I press on, three years' worth of frustration bubbling up inside me, like a soda bottle that's been shaken and lodged in my stomach.

"Do you have any idea how hard Tristan worked to put together the anniversary party for your grandparents? He's been planning this night for weeks, trying to make sure everything was perfect for them. He gave up spending his anniversary night with his wife to make his grandparents and his family happy. And you made fun of him for it. The moment you walked into the restaurant, you had a slew of insults ready to throw at him, for no reason. Why would you do that? To your own cousin?"

My hands are shaking as I catch my breath.

"Why couldn't you just smile and say hello? Or say nothing at all? Is it physically impossible for you to be anything other than a complete jackass?"

Still nothing from Milo. He's just standing there, staring at me with a bewildered expression, like he can't understand why I'm so upset.

And that turns the frustration inside me to anger.

"You're an asshole, Milo. I've always thought that. No, wait. That's not true," I quickly say. "When we first met, I thought you were polite and nice. I actually liked you . . ."

Milo's expression flips so quickly, I'm speechless once more. He looks so hopeful at what I've said. I'm so thrown off by that look on his face that I have to glance away.

"I've always liked you, Riley."

I sputter a laugh of disbelief. "Ha. Very funny."

"I'm serious." He stares at me, his gaze pointed and unblinking.

"Then why the hell are you such a dick to me? Why the hell did you make that shitty trophy wife comment about me the night we met?"

He blinks right before he frowns in confusion. "What are you talking about?"

"Don't act like you don't remember." I pause to swallow, to steady my voice, because the feelings of hurt and humiliation are still so raw. "I heard what you said on the phone that night by the bathrooms in the restaurant. 'Excellent trophy wife material, I'll give her that. But Jesus, what the hell is Tristan thinking? A guy like him and a girl like her? Gimme a break.'"

I manage to repeat his own words back to him without my voice going too shaky. But I'm certain he can tell just how hurt I am. My eyes are watery now, and I'm recalling in perfect detail some throwaway conversation he had about me three years ago.

He slumps forward and stares down at the wet concrete, shaking his head like he's in disbelief. "I didn't mean . . ." He scrunches his lips before exhaling, almost like he's frustrated.

"Stop. I'm not in the mood for your lies or your bullshit. You thought I was garbage from the get-go."

"I've never thought you were garbage, Riley. Not once."

Something about his tone and his gaze makes me think he's telling the truth, oddly enough.

"I'm an asshole because your husband is a prick."

Something between a groan and a bitter chuckle falls from my lips. "Wow. Real mature."

He shrugs. "It's true."

"First of all, grow up. Second, Tristan is not a prick. You are."

He bites his lips like he's frustrated, then rests his hands on his hips. He inhales, his chest heaving with the movement.

"Tristan is the most thoughtful and giving person I've ever met—"

"How well do you really know him, Riley?"

"What?"

"The guy you married isn't as wonderful as you think he is."

I must open and close my mouth a half dozen times in the seconds following Milo's ridiculous claim. "What is that supposed to mean?"

The edge of Milo's jaw bulges, like he's gritting his teeth to stop himself from speaking.

"I should go," he finally says. "Sorry I ruined tonight."

He steps around me and walks off, leaving me to quietly sort out what he's said.

I remind myself that Tristan just punched him in the face in front of their whole family. Milo is probably so pissed that he'll say anything to make him look bad.

The door swings open and out walks Tristan with my jacket. I thank him and quickly put it on even though my skin is now hot to the touch.

"You ready to head home?" he asks while frowning at his phone.

"Yeah."

I follow him to my car, which is parked in the alley behind the restaurant. He moves to open the passenger-seat door for me.

"I'll drive so you can rest."

I mumble a "thanks," my mind still a muddled mess. I quietly watch him as he rounds the front of the car to the driver's side. He starts the engine, and for the first few minutes of our journey, we're silent. I steal a glance of Tristan's profile, which is tinted red from the brake lights of the cars in front of us.

"Sorry again about tonight, about what my mum said to you, and about how I acted," he says quietly as he gazes forward at the now-stopped traffic. "I'm going to have a talk with her. She has no right to disrespect you like that."

I take in his white-knuckle grip on the steering wheel.

"I don't know what came over me earlier, but you're right. I was wrong to punch Milo. It won't happen again." He turns and offers a sad smile. "I'm so sorry I ruined our first wedding anniversary, Miss America."

I reach over and grab his hand. "It's okay. You didn't ruin it."

"I'll make it up to you, I swear." He brings my hand to his lips and dusts a soft kiss across my knuckles. "How would you feel about stopping by the animal shelter tomorrow?"

I gasp. "Are you serious?"

"Dead serious. I think I'm ready to pop my pet cherry."

Inside I go gooey. I squeal and lunge at him, hugging him tight. The low rumble of his laugh fills the car. I chatter about how he's gonna love having a cat.

"They're the best pets in the world, you'll see."

A car behind us honks, and I pull away so that Tristan can start driving again. It's barely two minutes before we're back to standstill traffic in Central London.

I yawn, the excitement and chaos of the evening finally catching up to me.

I peer ahead and spot the flashing lights of emergency vehicles. "I guess we're gonna be here awhile."

"Looks like it."

When I yawn again, I lower my seat. "Wake me when we're home."

I lie down, curl up on my side, close my eyes, and fall right to sleep.

Chapter 5

I wake to the smell of something dank and wet. And citrusy. And floral. No, wait, more like mud.

Eyes still closed, I wrinkle my nose. Is that tea?

When I try to open my eyes, I can only keep them open for a moment. My eyelids feel so heavy. Like wet cement is painted over them. Wow, I must have passed out hard during my car nap.

It takes a few seconds, but I finally manage to open my eyes. When I do, it takes another few seconds before the dark finish of the front passenger door comes into focus.

I shift to face forward, and that's when I take in the road ahead swathed in early-morning sunlight.

What the hell? How long was I asleep? Why aren't we home?

When I twist to Tristan to ask him what's going on, I do a double take. I open my mouth, but I can't speak. I'm too shocked. Because sitting next to me, driving my car, is Milo.

He turns to look at me and flashes that smirk I know so well. Only it's technically not a smirk. It's too affectionate, too warm to call it that. This is a genuine smile.

"Morning, Sleeping Beauty."

He gestures to the cup holder next to the center console before refocusing on the road. There sits a tall disposable cup of tea, steam wafting from the opening in the plastic lid.

"Stopped by the tea shop down the street from the flat while you were snoozing and got your favorite," he says. "Half–Earl Grey, half–hazelnut black tea. The tea smith working there actually scowled at me when I ordered it. Again. Does he do that to you, too, whenever you order from him?"

He chuckles. I don't utter a word. I can't. I'm too stunned, too confused to know what the hell to say in this moment where Milo is driving my car and fetching tea for me, chatting like we're old friends.

"Wh-where . . . what . . . ?" God, that's barely two words I can force out. I'm blank.

"Damn. You're usually chattier than this in the morning. Must have been an extra-hard sleep."

"Usually"? What does he mean by that? How does he know what I'm like in the morning?

"What are you doing?" I finally say after what feels like a minute of silence.

He laughs. "Yup. You definitely napped for too long."

"Why are you here? What are you doing driving my car?"

That smile drops from Milo's face. He turns to me, brow furrowed slightly, like he's the confused one now.

"What . . . are you okay?" His voice is soft with shock.

Now that he's facing me, I see it's not confusion on his face; it's pain.

What in the world is happening?

"This isn't funny, Milo. You need to tell me right now what's going on."

The feel of his hand gently grabbing mine is a shock to my system. Like a bucket of ice water tossed over me. I still instantly. Because this isn't a casual touch between two people who can barely stand each other; this is something more intimate. We've done this before; I can feel it in my skin and bones.

Only, how? We barely touch each other. We shook hands the night we met. That's it.

So why does his hand on mine feel so familiar?

He strokes the top of my right hand with his thumb, and I can't stop staring at the shock of contact. Why does he think he can touch me like this? This is how Tristan touches me: soft, gentle, familiar.

And then I notice my ring finger. It's bare. My engagement ring and wedding band are gone.

Heat flashes across my skin at the exact moment that I start to shiver. I yank my hand away. "Stop the car."

"What? Riley, I'm not gonna—"

"Stop the fucking car, Milo!"

He slows to a halt along the side of the road.

I yank off my seat belt and pivot my body to face him. "Explain. Now."

He's staring at me like I've sprouted another head. "Explain what, Riley?"

"Why you're driving my car! Why you think you can hold my hand! Why we're driving along the outskirts of London so early on a Thursday morning when I should be at work . . ."

He frowns, tilting his head. "Thursday . . . Riley, it's not Thursday."

I hold up a hand, cutting him off. "I don't have the patience for whatever you're trying to pull here, Milo."

His furrowed brow conveys utter confusion. "You took the day off, remember?" he finally says. "Because it's Valentine's Day and you wanted to get away from all the . . ."

I don't hear another word Milo says. I'm too busy riffling through my purse for my phone to check the date. No way—yesterday was Valentine's Day. What in the world is he . . . ?

I look at the date on my phone screen. He's right. It's Valentine's Day. Friday, February 14.

"What the fuck . . . ," I mutter to myself as I unlock the screen with trembling hands. I tap on my calendar and pull up the month and today's date. February 14. Friday. Valentine's Day.

Not possible. Yesterday was Valentine's Day—and Valentine's Day was on a Wednesday.

This has to be some sort of glitch in my phone. I'm about to turn it off and restart it when I spot the year at the top of the calendar: 2025.

How the hell is it February 14, 2025? Last night it was February 14, 2024—my one-year wedding anniversary with Tristan. And now somehow I jumped an entire year in one evening nap?

"Riley. Are you okay?"

It's not till Milo says my name that I notice just how hard and how fast I'm breathing—panting, actually. It feels like my lungs are on fire, like I'm sprinting even though I haven't moved from this car.

I press my eyes shut and cradle my face against my trembling hands. This isn't happening. This *can't* be happening. This must be a mistake or some sort of sick joke or . . .

"Sweetie. What's wrong? Please tell me."

Hearing that pet name roll off Milo's tongue, so gentle, so soft— and completely unearned—jolts me. It's like I've been shocked with a defibrillator. I stop panting instantly and stare at Milo.

Of course this is a joke. A sick joke that my husband's cousin some-how pulled off because he's upset at Tristan for punching him and upset at me for going off on him when he left the restaurant. Because he's conniving and cruel and always taking shots at me and Tristan for his amusement. That's the only explanation.

I glance down and realize I'm wearing clothes that are different from the outfit I fell asleep in. What the . . .

"This isn't fucking funny, Milo," I snap.

He stammers. His eyebrows crash together, painting his obnox-iously handsome face with concern. "Of course this isn't funny. You're clearly upset, and I just want to help—"

"Where is my husband?" My voice ricochets against the interior of the car. It's so loud, so sharp that Milo's shoulders jump up.

"What?" He's breathless when he speaks, like he's just been socked in the stomach.

"Where is Tristan?"

He glances off to the side, out his window, and doesn't say anything for a long moment.

"I should have known this would happen, that you'd come to your senses one day." He lets out a sad chuckle before looking back over at me. "I don't know where he is, Riley. We don't exactly keep in touch after what went down between the three of us."

"The three of us?" I finally say after stammering for a solid five seconds. Is he talking about the fight last night? How I lashed out at him afterward?

When he falls quiet again, I'm about to press him to explain, but then he speaks.

"My guess is that he's at home. Or at one of his restaurants, working."

Of course he is.

I jump out of the car before Milo even finishes speaking and sprint toward the city.

Chapter 6

Terrible fucking idea, sprinting while wearing d'orsay flats. The backs of my heels are raw, and the ball of my right foot now sports a blister.

In my panic haze, I wasn't thinking straight, not at first. If I had, I'd have just called Tristan the moment I stepped out of the car. But instead I ran. I blew by three tube stations, huffing and puffing before realizing I could just take the tube to Marylebone. That's exactly what I'm doing now. I'm sitting here, my sweater and jeans soaked through with sweat, my feet bloody and raw, stinking of BO, two stops from the tube station closest to our house.

Damn my brain. I should have just gotten off at the last stop and called him—I've got zero signal now that I'm underground.

I shake my head and force out a breath. It'll all be okay. Once I'm at my stop, I'll call Tristan while I run home and hug him the second I see him. Together we'll piece together how the hell Milo managed to pull such an elaborate prank on us in the span of a single night.

As the car whizzes along the track, I start to wonder myself how Milo did all this. I barely had a sip of alcohol last night at the disastrous anniversary party, so there's no way I was so drunk that I passed out and missed something. I remember everything—laughing and chatting with Nesta, the shitty comments from Portia, Milo's shitty comments to Tristan, the punch, the collective gasps and shrieks from everyone in the room . . .

The telltale squeal of the tube screeching to a halt jolts me to my feet. I'm the first person out of the car, the first person running up the stairs, the first person to emerge from the tube station. As I jog in the direction of Dorset Street, I go to pull up Tristan's number, then slow to a walk. I can't find him in my phone. I step off to the side so I don't block the people walking around me and scroll through my contacts over and over. He's not there.

"What the . . ."

Fucking hell, Milo was thorough with this prank bullshit.

I force another breath, this time through gritted teeth, and dial Tristan's number manually. It goes straight to voicemail. And goddamn it, it's full.

I mutter a curse as I dart around a slow-moving couple in front of me and run across the street before the light changes. His voicemail has never, not once, been full in the three years that I've known him.

As I round the corner to our block, I try him three more times. Voicemail again and again and again.

I give up and call Poppy instead. When I get her voicemail, I groan-shout so loudly that the guy walking by me jumps and nearly trips and falls into the street.

I offer a breathless "sorry" before leaving Poppy a message.

"Good god, is no one answering their phone today? Poppy, I need you to call me back as soon as you can, okay? I just . . . this morning has been an absolute mind-fuck. I woke up in the passenger seat of my car with Milo driving it. Milo! Can you freaking believe it? And I tried calling Tristan, but he's not in my phone, and I have no idea what's going on or how any of this happened. I feel like I'm losing my mind and I need to talk to you so can you please just call me? As soon as you get this, please."

I quickly dial my mom. She picks up after just a few rings.

"*Anak.* How are you? You okay?"

She sounds worried, like she was expecting me to call her.

"No, actually." I take a second to catch my breath and am about to ask her what in the world is going on, but she speaks first.

"Oh, *anak*. I'm so sorry. I knew today would be hard, what with it being your anniversary after you and Tristan split. I took it hard, too, when the first anniversary rolled around after your dad and I got divorced."

I trip on an uneven spot in the pavement. Dread singes through my stomach like a hot iron. Why does my mom think Tristan and I are split up too?

Anger flashes through me as I think of Milo and how somehow he must have roped my mom into this prank.

I stop walking. "Mom. Did someone named Milo call you and put you up to this? Did he tell you to pretend like Tristan and I aren't together anymore?"

Dead silence follows.

"I think he's pulled some cruel prank. I can't figure out how, but I'm pretty sure of it."

Still no answer from my mom. The silence lasts for so long that I wonder if we got disconnected. But then she finally speaks.

"*Anak.* 'Someone called Milo'? Why are you talking about him like he's a stranger? Of course I know him."

It feels like a record scratching to a halt in my head. How does my mom know Milo?

"And why in the world would you say all that about him? About Milo, of all people?"

She sounds shocked. And there's a bite to her tone that I recognize instantly. She's mad.

"That young man is a sweetheart. An absolute sweetheart. Goodness, what's gotten into you?"

I'm thrown so off-kilter by the sheer indignation in her tone that I'm dizzy. What the hell is going on? Why does my mom sound genuinely upset at me for what I've said about Milo? Why is she defending him? And why is she speaking like she knows him? They've never even met . . .

47

A fresh wave of frustration flashes through me as I steady myself and trudge ahead toward the flat. There's no way I can sort this out now, not when she's this upset and confused, not when I have no idea what's going on either.

"Never mind, Mom. Sorry, I didn't mean to upset you. I'll call you later, okay? Love you." I end the call, and for a second I think about calling my brother, but I don't. I already know what he'll say. He dislikes Tristan enough that I bet he'd be up for being part of an elaborate prank like this to make it seem like we've split. Maybe he was able to convince Mom, and that's why she sounded so upset when I asked her what was going on.

I shove my phone in my bag and turn the corner. When the red-orange stone exterior of our Georgian-style walk-up comes into view, I break into a slow jog. I'm too confused, too drained after all the panicked sprinting I've done this morning. My breath turns to mist in the cold, damp air each time I huff and puff. Despite the temperature, which is hovering right around freezing, I'm still a sweaty mess.

I clear the half dozen steps in a second and grab at the doorknob of the front door. When it doesn't budge, it takes me a few seconds to realize that it's because it's locked. I fumble through my purse for the key, unlock it, and throw open the door.

"Tristan!" I holler as I race to the living room. But there's no answer. I call his name as I run down the hall to our bedroom and the spare bedroom, then the hallway bathroom and the primary bathroom.

Nothing. He's not here.

My legs are heavy as I force myself to walk back to our bedroom. I try to breathe, but my lungs feel tight. My heart feels like it's going to rip through my chest, it's beating so fast. The base of my throat tightens. I suddenly feel dizzy. Shit. I'm going to pass out, aren't I?

I stumble to the bed and plop down, barely able to sit up straight. It feels like the adrenaline that's powered my body these past several minutes is disappearing. I feel wrung out, like a wet, used towel.

The bout of dizziness leaves my brain feeling foggy. I need to keep looking for Tristan. Of course he's not at home right now. It's a weekday, which means he's at one of his restaurants, working. I try to stand, but my legs are too shaky, and my head feels like a concrete block. I cradle my temple with my hand and close my eyes. That feels good. Maybe that's what I need, a quick nap so that I can rest up, find Tristan, and sort this mess out.

I shed my trench coat and toss it onto the floor. That's when I realize just how sweat-soaked my sweater is. Gross.

I rip it off along with my bra and jeans, and throw them aside. I don't even bother to crawl under the sheets; my limbs are too heavy, too tired. I can barely keep my eyes open as I grab the edge of the duvet and wrap it over me. As soon as I close my eyes, I'm asleep.

A sharp beeping noise cuts through my sleep haze. It feels like it takes forever to open my eyes again, I'm so exhausted. When I finally do, it's another several seconds before I'm able to sit up. The beeping persists. And then I realize that's the text-message alert on my phone.

My brain finally catches up, and I jolt into a sitting position. That must be Tristan trying to get a hold of me.

I almost fall off the bed as I scramble for my purse, which I dropped on the floor. When I finally dig my phone out and look at the screen, my heart sinks. It's not Tristan. It's Milo.

My eyes go wide at the screen. It's filled with missed texts and calls from Milo. I grit my teeth, frustrated. What the hell kind of messed-up game is he playing?

I don't even bother to read them. Instead, I hop out of bed and dart to my closet to grab some clean clothes to put on so I can head out and keep looking for Tristan.

My hands are shaking as I grab at the nearest clothing—I'm so jittery. It's almost noon, which means I was out cold for almost three hours, but that's done little to calm my nerves. Every muscle in my body is twitching with the need to find my husband and figure out what the hell is going on.

I'm tightening the drawstring on a pair of too-big plaid pajama pants as I dart back out the door. As I hurry down the porch steps, I register the cold wet pavement on my bare feet. I forgot to put on shoes.

I dart back up the stairs and through the front door, kick aside my d'orsay flats in favor of a beaten-up pair of tennis shoes. My poor feet have suffered enough.

As I run in the direction of Last One Standing, almost everyone passing by pauses to gawk at me. Everyone is looking at me like an alien has sprouted from my chest.

I skid to a halt when I reach a busy intersection. As I wait for the light to change, I glimpse my reflection in a nearby glass storefront. I flinch. I'm a fucking mess. My hair is a rat's nest. My eye makeup is so smeared from sweat and sleep that I look like a deranged raccoon. I'm wearing a long-sleeve T-shirt with a cartoon keg on it and the words I'D TAP THAT printed on it. It's splattered in red paint too. I blink at my image in the dingy glass. I look like a psychotic cartoon character.

I've never, ever allowed myself to go out in public looking like this before. I feel the heat of embarrassment burst across my cheeks.

"Oi, love. You all right?"

I look to my left and see an older couple frowning at me in concern. The woman elbows the man next to her, I assume her husband. He looks at her for a second before nodding and digging a tenner from his wallet. He reaches his hand out and tucks it into my palm.

"Get yourself home safely, all right?" he says before they walk off.

For several seconds, I stand there and stare at the cash in my hand, mystified as to what the hell just happened. And then it dawns on me: They thought I was lost. Or homeless.

I huff out a heavy sigh. To my surprise, the embarrassment fades. That panicked feeling is back in the form of tightness in my chest and my racing heartbeat. I don't have time to feel ashamed about my appearance. All I care about is finding Tristan.

The light changes and traffic stops. I'm the first one off the sidewalk and across the street, running as fast as I can toward Tristan's restaurant.

Chapter 7

I skid to a halt at the front of Last One Standing . . . or what used to be Last One Standing.

As I take in the sight of the charred front, my jaw drops. The gorgeous red brick is no longer. The large window at the front is cracked and streaked with smoke. Yellow caution tape and orange construction barricades surround the front. A sign plastered on the entrance reads CLOSED FOR REPAIRS. The pub must have caught on fire at some point last night . . . but how?

Last night it was completely fine. What in the world could have happened in the last fifteen hours to have made it look this way?

I start to wonder if Milo had something to do with it, but even thinking that makes my stomach churn. I can't stand Milo and how much of a jerk he is, but he's not an arsonist.

People walk around me, muttering annoyed comments as I stand in the middle of the sidewalk and gawk. I finally come to my senses and step off to the side so I'm not in the way anymore, still confused and dazed. It must have been an accident in the kitchen or a freak electrical problem that caused this.

"Riley?"

The sound of Tristan speaking my name jolts me out of my stupor. I look over at him standing a half dozen feet from me. Relief washes over me at the sight of him. I start to smile, but then I freeze as I take him in.

Something about his appearance is off—different. For a moment I just look at him, trying to decipher what exactly it is. He's wearing a suit I've seen a million times before—that light-gray one with a crisp white shirt. But something about it—something about him—is different. I can feel it, the hesitation inside me, seeping through my insides like a slow-moving wave.

I zero in on his hair. It's not the way it was last night. Last night it was longer, on the shaggy side of short, his strawberry-blond waves curling around his ears. But now it looks like he's had a fresh haircut. Did he just have it cut? Is that what he was off doing while Milo somehow got me in my car while I was sleeping and drove me out of London? Tristan didn't mention anything about a haircut appointment yesterday . . .

He blinks at me, and I notice something else. The strange look in his eyes. Like he's stunned and confused to see me. It takes a few seconds, but I finally process it. He's gazing at me like it's been forever since he's seen me—like he's shocked to be looking at me right now.

"Riley, what are you doing here?" he asks.

I push aside the uncertainty and start to walk toward him. I'm just disoriented from this mind-fuck prank Milo somehow managed to pull on us. And he's probably looking at me all mystified because I look like I dropped acid and got dressed in the dark.

I wrap my arms around him and hug him tight. "I've been looking for you all morning," I say in a shaky whisper.

"You have?" He sounds so shocked.

I wait for him to say more, to say that he's been looking for me, too, to explain what's going on, to call me "Miss America." But he doesn't. He's quiet.

I lean back and look at him, my hands gripping his shoulders. "Of course I've been looking for you. Look, I don't know if you know this, but I'm pretty sure Milo has pulled some sort of prank on us, and when I woke up today and you weren't there, I was out of my mind with panic and . . ."

I trail off when I realize that Tristan's arms are stiff and at his sides. And that's when I realize: he didn't hug me back. He hasn't returned my touch, my embrace.

I drop my hands to my sides and step back. "I know I must look like a basket case right now."

The corner of his mouth hooks up in a hesitant smile. "It's okay. It's just . . . honestly, I'm a bit surprised to see you here."

"You are?"

"Well, yeah." He chuckles, like he's flustered. He rubs the back of his neck, and I pause. He does that only when he's nervous. Uneasy. Uncomfortable.

He darts his eyes to the street and stares for a few seconds. I follow his gaze and see that he's glancing at his Land Rover, which is parked at the end of the block.

He clears his throat as he looks back at me, his eyes shy. "Riley, the last thing in the world I expected was to see you here. Especially after what happened at the pub."

We both look at the burned-out brick front.

"What happened?" I ask.

He frowns at me. And then he laughs. "You're kidding, right?"

I shake my head. "Tristan, I'm serious. I have no idea what is going on, or why the pub burned down."

His thick brows crash together as he studies me. Like he's trying to decide whether he believes me.

That confused, dizzy feeling hits, and I close my eyes, my head aching as I try to figure out what the hell is going on . . .

But then he grabs my hand in his, and the unsteady feeling stops instantly. I open my eyes, relieved to see that familiar tender look in his soft blue gaze.

"It doesn't matter," he says. "You're here now."

I smile at him. "I'm here now," I repeat.

He glances around us, almost like he's trying to see if anyone is looking at us. His gaze lands on his car once more for a long moment before he turns back to me. He leans his face closer to mine. "There's so much to talk about, so much to explain," he says, his voice low and soft. "I've got something I need to do at the moment, but can you meet me in an hour? At the Landmark hotel in Hampstead?"

"Of course I'll meet you there." I say it without even thinking. Because that's exactly what I want—I want to be with my husband, and I want to sort out this nightmare mess once and for all. I just don't know why he wants to go to a random hotel in Hampstead to do it. He hates Hampstead.

He leans in and kisses my cheek before letting go of my hand and walking off toward his car. He climbs in the driver's seat and speeds off. As I watch him drive away from me, that ease I felt fades away. I glance down at my disheveled state. I need to change. I want to look good the next time I see Tristan.

I run back home, willing my sore legs and lungs to keep up with the panicked urgency swirling inside me. If I make it home fast enough, I can grab a quick shower and swipe on a bit of makeup before I meet Tristan.

I make it to the front door, unlock it, and stumble into the entry-way. When I walk into the living room and look up, my jaw falls open. There's Milo, standing in front of the couch, staring at me.

"You're home."

The way the words fall from his mouth, breathy and laced with relief, stuns me silent. I'm still as he walks over to me and pulls me into his arms.

"I was so worried about you," he mumbles into my hair. I'm about to shove him away, but his embrace tightens, causing me to still. He's shaking.

"I was about to call you," he says. "But I . . . I didn't want to push you. I know you need your space today of all days."

Today of all days.

"What are you talking . . . ?"

And then he lowers his face to mine and tries to kiss me. For a split second my body goes rigid and unmoving, but then instinct takes over. I plant my hand on his face and shove him away from me so hard, he falls into the wall behind him. I'm shaking and panting, I'm so freaked out.

"What the hell do you think you're doing?" I snap at Milo.

He pushes himself up off the wall, a dazed frown on his face as he looks at me. He shakes his head. "Sorry, I guess I thought you'd be okay with that after everything we . . ."

He trails off as his gaze focuses on me. "I'm sorry. I shouldn't have done that, today of all days."

Today of all days. Why does he keep saying that?

I'm about to ask him when the faint sound of a bell pulls my attention to the darkened hallway leading to the bedroom. A fluffy white ragdoll cat trots into the living room, right up to Milo's socked feet.

He looks down at the cat with a slight smile on his face, bends down, and scoops the cat up. "Hey, sleepy girl."

He scratches under the cat's chin. She's wearing a collar with a tiny gold bell on it. A loud purr echoes in the room.

"Looks like Coco missed us."

"Us?" I sputter.

Milo either doesn't hear me or ignores my confusion, because he doesn't say a word. He walks over to the kitchen and sets the cat on the floor next to a silver dish. When he reaches for a treat bag on the counter, that's when I notice the stark difference in the decor.

Gone is the trio of small black-and-white framed photos of landscapes on the far kitchen wall that have been there ever since I moved in with Tristan. Instead, there hangs a bright-red sign.

Keep Calm and Drink Tea

I slow-blink while staring at the massive white letters and the illustration of a steaming teacup at the top of the sign.

Seeing that change in the decor is like a starting pistol for my observation skills. That's when I notice every single thing that's different in this space. Instead of the cream-hued sofa, there's a massive plush sectional with four fuzzy gray throw pillows on it. Like someone skinned a Muppet and made pillows out of it. The stone fireplace, which used to be painted stark white, is covered in dark Mediterranean-style tile. And the once-bare top of the fireplace is now cluttered with knickknacks. There's a vase of flowers on one end, a tall candle and a Himalayan salt lamp on the other. A haphazard stack of books takes up the middle.

A blue-and-white chevron-pattern rug covers the entire living room floor, obscuring the dark hardwood Tristan loves so much. And there's a karaoke machine next to the coffee table.

I must have been so exhausted, so throttled by adrenaline, when I walked in here this morning that I didn't even notice the change in decor.

"You changed everything," I mutter. "How did you do all this?" I shuffle my feet, pivoting slightly, and notice the neon-pink HELLO, BABES sign on the wall next to the dining table. Christ, that's tacky as hell. Tristan is gonna be so pissed when he sees it.

Milo doesn't answer. The only sound I hear is the soft pad of his footsteps. I look up right as he pulls me into another hug. My body tenses as I prep to push him away again, but then I look past his shoulder and my gaze catches on a glass vase of baby-pink peonies sitting in the middle of the table. My favorite flower. We never have flowers in the house. Tristan is allergic.

"Peonies?" I murmur in disbelief.

"I figured this day would be a little triggering. I thought the flowers would help," he says softly before letting out a weak laugh. "I guess that was a pretty terrible idea, huh?"

A quiet moment passes. He huffs out a breath. "I just thought that since this was your wedding anniversary, and given how things ended . . ."

Ended?

I lean away from Milo, but his hold on me remains. He cups my shoulders with his hands, his burnt-umber stare unblinking and focused and concerned all at once as he looks at me. Sunlight from the nearby window illuminates him from head to toe, and that's when I notice just how smooth and even the skin on the left side of his face is—not a trace of discoloration or bruising or swelling from where Tristan punched him last night.

"I thought taking you out of the city today, being away from all the reminders you're constantly surrounded by, would be a good idea. I was going to surprise you," he says. "I was wrong. Clearly it was too much. I'm sorry."

A dizzy spell hits and I start to wobble. I open my mouth to say something, anything, to gain some clarity about this impossible situation, but I can't. I'm thrown completely off-kilter right now—I've been launched into a stratosphere of confusion. If this is all a joke, if this is a performance he's putting on, he deserves an Oscar. Because he seems so sincere and honest, like he truly believes every single thing he's saying to me. I've never, ever seen him like this. He's normally joking and taking the piss out of whatever friends and relatives are in his vicinity. Not like this—not sweet and caring and concerned and gentle.

Witnessing this sudden contrast feels akin to being swirled around in a stand mixer. The harder I try and think about it, to try and make sense of this, the more disoriented I feel.

I finally manage to step out of his embrace. I hold up both hands at him so he doesn't try to hug or touch me again. "Milo. I'm going to ask you something, and I need you to be honest."

"You can ask me anything."

"How did you pull this off?" I gesture at the decor, the furniture, at Coco the cat, who's now lying in a sunbeam near the dining table. "How is it that I'm here with you and not Tristan?"

His shoulders fall forward. A sad chuckle falls from his lips as he stares at the floor. When he looks back at me, there's an edge of amusement to his smile despite his pained expression. He shrugs. "I've asked myself that question a million times. I still don't know. I guess I got lucky."

I grit my teeth so hard, my temples ache. Whatever Method acting he's committed to in order to pull off this prank has gone too far. I'm done trying to reason with him. I'm done trying to figure it out. Now all I want is to get the hell away from Milo and go back to Tristan.

I spot my car keys lying on the coffee table. Fuming and frustrated, I grab them and dart out of the house. I start pressing the unlock button as I wave my arm around, hoping the car is parked close enough to pick up the signal. I hear a faint beeping noise around the corner. I run over and see my white Audi parked there. I hop in the driver's seat and speed away.

A half hour later I'm stuck in stop-and-go traffic right on the edge of Hampstead. I huff out a breath and look in my rearview mirror to check the cars behind me. I fixate on my raccoon eyes. My grand plans for freshening up before seeing Tristan obviously didn't work out because of Milo's unexpected appearance in my home.

I dig through my purse for a face wipe and some makeup. I spend the next few minutes tidying up my face while inching forward in the traffic toward a roundabout. I may be dressed like a slob, but at least my face looks better. I've leaned over and am setting aside my purse on the passenger seat when I see a flash of black in the corner of my eye. It's Tristan's black Land Rover speeding into the lane ahead of me. He enters the roundabout and leaves it through the third exit.

I know he said to meet at the Landmark hotel, but curiosity and desperation take hold. I'm tired of being away from him. I need to know where he's going.

I enter the roundabout and exit the way he did. I sit up straighter to keep an eye on his Land Rover, which is a few cars ahead. It's a solid ten minutes of me tailing him before the cars between us disappear. We pass the hotel he mentioned meeting me at. He slows his car along a narrow street in the heart of Hampstead as I follow behind him. Well, this is a surprise. Tristan loathes coming to this neighborhood. Every time we've met a friend or family member for a drink or a meal here, he's always called it a haven for annoying hipsters and artist types. I wonder what work errand he's running here.

I tear my gaze away from his car in front of me and glance at the row of multicolored brick buildings lining this block. He turns left at a converted church at the corner, which houses a thrift store and gastropub, as far as I can tell, then slows to a halt in front of a white-brick house that stands two stories tall.

There's only room along the street for him to park, so I ease to a stop about a block from him, grateful there are no cars coming along this quiet road at the moment. I contemplate pulling up to him and double-parking right next to his car so I can get his attention, but I stop myself. He doesn't even know I'm following him. That might freak him out. So I stay back and wait for him to get out of the car. I'll roll down my window and holler at him. He's taking a while to get out of his car, and it's long enough that one of the cars near me drives off, leaving a spot open for me to park. I pull my car along the curb and shut it off, hop out, then jog in his direction.

I'm a half block away when he finally climbs out of his car and walks up to the wrought iron gate that lines the small front lawn of this mystery house. I rack my brain for any memory of this place but come up empty. Nothing about this neighborhood or this house is familiar. I'm certain I've never been here.

I'm about to call out to him, but I stay quiet as he says hello to someone ahead of him. I look over to see who it is, but with the way he's standing, he's blocking my view of the person he's talking to.

"Little man, did you miss me?" he says in a singsong voice.

I stop walking and watch Tristan as he closes the gate behind him and walks over to a blanket on the lawn in front of the house. I crane my neck to get a view of the person Tristan's talking to, but I still can't see from where I am.

Just then Tristan steps to the side, and I see someone sitting on the blanket, holding a baby. I can't see their face, though, because of the way they're holding the baby up toward Tristan. Tristan leans down and scoops up the baby. The baby laughs as Tristan sways back and forth while smiling and coddling him. He looks a few months shy of a year old. I stand there and stare, completely blown away at my husband cuddling this baby I've never seen before. He looks so . . . comfortable holding him. Never in the three years that we've been together have I seen him handle a baby with such ease and confidence. Every time a relative or friend has brought a baby around him, he's been pleasant and smiled at the little one, but he has never asked to hold them. And whenever anyone has insisted that he hold their baby, Tristan has been stiff and nervous.

"I'm scared I'll drop them," he's joked before quickly handing them back to their parents.

But as I watch Tristan coo at and tickle this baby in his arms, there's zero hesitation, zero discomfort. It's like he's done this a million times before.

How in the world did that change overnight too?

I squint to get a better look at the baby. He must be the child of a friend or relative . . . but I know all the kids of our friends and family. This baby isn't one of them.

And then I notice his hair color: strawberry blond. And his eyes. Blue. The same hair and eye color as Tristan. This must be one of his cousins' kids. Why have I never seen him before?

I glance back down at the person sitting on the blanket in the grass to see if I recognize them, but they're gone. I was so entranced at watching Tristan with this baby that I didn't even notice that person walk off.

After a minute, Tristan heads through the front door of the house, closing it behind him. I hurry to follow him, halting just in front of the wrought iron gate.

I start to step forward but stop myself when I see movement through the large window off to the side of the front door. There's Tristan standing in the kitchen, still holding the baby, smiling and chatting with someone I can't see.

A woman appears and stands in front of him so that her back is to me. She's short with a slight build; her blonde hair is in a messy bun. When he beams down at her, there's a look in his eyes that has every muscle inside me tense. I know that look—it's equal parts adoring and hungry. He looks at me like that.

When the woman pivots slightly and I see her face, my heart ceases beating.

Carly. His ex.

He leans forward and they kiss. I nearly choke. My jaw is on the ground, and I no longer know how to blink or breathe.

I watch as she reaches over and takes the baby from Tristan's arms. Tristan smiles as he tickles that chunky belly. Even though there's glass and brick separating us, I swear I hear the melodic sound of his laugh. He laughs, the baby laughs, Carly laughs. My eyes start to burn, but I can't blink. All I can do is stare.

I don't know how long I stand there, but it's long enough to take stock of the baby's physical features. I see now that he's the spitting image of Tristan. That cleft chin. That straight Roman nose. That's Tristan as a baby.

That's Tristan and Carly's baby.

My legs start to shake. The acid in my stomach churns.

Carly and the baby have disappeared to some other part of their house, this Hampstead house in this neighborhood that Tristan loathes. I'm still standing in their front yard like a stalker, still staring at them through their window, trying and failing to make sense of what the hell I've just seen.

This can't be happening. But it is. I'm standing here, watching it with my own eyes . . .

Tristan is with his ex—he has a baby with his ex.

Which means he's been cheating on me. He fathered a baby with someone else behind my back.

Just then Tristan turns his head, meeting my gaze. It takes a second for the recognition to appear in his expression, to register that I'm standing in front of this house, watching him and his ex and their baby.

His smile drops. There's a flash of panic in his eyes. A hard swallow moves down his throat before he darts for the front door.

I'm still standing in that same spot on the sidewalk, still paralyzed with disbelief as he walks up to me. He moves to touch my arm but seems to think better of it and keeps his hand at his side.

"Riley, you shouldn't be here."

I blink, my eyes burning with hot tears. They tumble down my cheeks. "Tristan. That's your ex . . . and your son . . ." My voice breaks.

I expect an explanation, a desperate apology for cheating on me, for him to grovel. What I don't expect is for him to frown and let out an exasperated sigh. Like he's annoyed with me.

"This again?" he mutters.

He rolls his eyes and looks behind him in the direction of the house. Then he grabs me by the arm and walks me down the block.

"I told you to meet me at the hotel. Not here, Riley. Never here. You should know that after everything that's happened."

I yank my arm out of his hold and stop walking. "What the fuck does that even mean?" I snap.

Tristan's worried gaze darts around us. He aims a placating smile to an elderly couple walking by before frowning at me. "What are you talking about? Riley, why did you even come to see me at my pub if you were going to do this? If you were going to get all huffy and upset like you always do?"

My jaw drops. He can't be serious. He's been cheating on me with his ex—he got her freaking pregnant behind my back, and he's upset with *me*?

"You fucking cheated on me, Tristan. With your ex. You had a baby with your ex behind my back."

I wipe my tear- and snot-soaked face with the sleeve of my shirt. The whole time Tristan looks annoyed at me. No, "pissed" is a better word. Anger overtakes the pain coursing through me. The fucking nerve of him to be mad and irritated at me right now, in this moment, when I discover that he's betrayed my trust in the worst, most heartbreaking way.

Closing his eyes, he pinches the bridge of his nose and is quiet for a few seconds. He looks at me. "Riley, I don't know what kind of sick game you're playing at here. Maybe you think it's funny to run me through the wringer like this again, but I don't. Not after what went down a year ago. I don't have time for this anymore."

A year ago.

My mouth hangs open. I'm so confused.

"What game?" I sputter.

"Is this your idea of a sick joke? We had this exact same conversation a year ago," he mutters, his tone tired and annoyed.

"A year ago? A year ago we got married . . ."

He stares at me, the look in his gaze cold. He huffs out an annoyed breath.

"Tristan, I had no idea about any of this until today," I say.

He lets out a bitter laugh. "Very funny, Riley. I think we both know exactly what happened last year."

A year ago . . . last year . . .

Tristan sounds like Milo now.

My brain feels like soup as I struggle to put this all together.

"What's with all this 'last year,' 'it was a year ago' bullshit?" I finally blurt, my tone a hair under a shout. "Last night, everything was fine between us. Last night, we had our first wedding anniversary, you surprised me with my car, you punched Milo at Last One Standing in front of all your family and . . ."

I trail off as I take in the expression on Tristan's face. He's looking at me like I've lost my mind.

He frowns, and then he shakes his head and takes a step back. "You know, when you showed up at my pub this morning, I thought it was a sign. You were over what went down between the two of us last year. And the way you were so happy to see me . . . the way you hugged me . . . I thought maybe, just maybe, you wanted to get together again for old times' sake."

He shakes his head at me, like he's disappointed.

"Whatever this is? I don't have time for it." He glares at me. "And if you're suddenly having trouble remembering what exactly happened between us last year, go ask Milo."

I'm off-balance, dizzy, barely able to stay upright as Tristan turns around and walks back into the house. This can't be happening . . .

But I saw it happen. I saw Tristan with his ex. I saw him kiss her. I saw him happily greet her and their child like it was the most natural thing in the world.

He thinks Milo and I are together . . .

But how? How the fuck is any of this happening? How did I fall asleep last night and wake up to my entire world flipped upside down . . . ?

A couple of teenage girls in school uniforms walk by me, chattering quickly in pitchy voices.

"So glad the Northern line is finally running again."

"Ugh, I know! I was so sick of taking the bus."

My brain sticks on the mention of the Northern line. I spin around and stop them as they walk past.

"Excuse me, I'm sorry, but did you say the Northern line is up and running again?" For the millionth time today, I'm confused. That tube line was down for repairs starting this winter. It's not meant to be up and running until next year.

They look at me, clearly surprised that I stopped them.

One of them glances at me and says, "Uh, yeah, miss. It's running."

"But that's not supposed to be up and running until 2025 . . ."

The two of them exchange a look that's something between confused and freaked out. "Um, it's 2025, miss," the other girl says. She holds up her phone and shows me the date. There it is, clear as crystal. Again.

February 14, 2025.

They walk off. And that's when the realization starts to set in, when the dread embeds like a needle in the pit of my stomach.

The date on my phone isn't wrong. It can't be if that girl's phone has the same date too.

Which means this life I'm currently living isn't some elaborate prank that Milo has pulled off. Somehow, someway, this nightmare is real.

Chapter 8

It doesn't matter how long I sit here in my parked car and look at the date on my phone. It doesn't matter how many times I call random businesses to ask them what day and year it is. I've called a restaurant, a hospital, a school, a retail store, a bakery, and a petrol station. I've gotten the same answer every single time.

February 14, 2025.

It doesn't make sense, though. How did an entire year pass by in a single night?

I let out a shaky breath as I toss my phone in the passenger seat next to me. And then I close my eyes and press my fingers to my temples, hoping that will ease the tension that's been building in my skull the whole day.

It doesn't.

I give up and open my eyes. And then I see them.

I see Tristan, Carly, and their baby trot from their front door to their car. I watch as Tristan holds Carly's hand and cradles their son in his other arm. I watch as he opens the back door of his car and gets him settled in his car seat. I watch him make a funny face at his baby before shutting the door and rounding the car to the driver's-side door. I watch him drive off, a cloud of numbness, confusion, and pain washing over me.

If this time jump is real, if I've missed an entire year, then that means we were married for just a year before I found out about his affair.

I start doing the math in my head, over and over, just to be sure. I get the same number every time.

Six. Six months.

If this is real, then that's how long Tristan and I had been married when he likely got Carly pregnant.

I don't know their son's exact age and birth date. But judging by his appearance, he's got to be around nine months old, which means he must have been born in May or June of 2024.

And if he's that old now on February 14, 2025, then that means he was conceived around August of 2023.

We were in full-on newlywed bliss then. Or so I thought.

I think back to all the spontaneous date nights, the times he surprised me with champagne, the sleepy and slow middle-of-the-night sex we'd indulge in whenever he'd work so late I fell asleep before he came home. Acid burns my throat and chest.

I think of the long weekend away in the Cotswolds that Tristan surprised me with in October of 2023 after an especially busy few weeks of work for him. Carly was pregnant then.

My stomach churns like I've downed a bottle of acid. Hot bile creeps its way up my throat.

I gag before throwing open my car door and spewing chunks onto the road.

Footsteps sound around me. "Darling, are you all right?" a voice above me asks.

I nod, even though I'm still spitting up. I've never been a quiet vomiter. I'm loud as hell, retching and choking as though I'm exorcising a demon deep inside me. Spit dribbles from my lips, and my eyes are so watery that I can't even make out the concrete below. All I see is a blurry pale-orange mass on top of a blurry gray mass.

"Fine," I groan. "I'm fine."

"Oh, my dear. Are you sure?"

I wipe at my eyes and mouth, then look up to see an elderly lady gazing down at me, her brow furrowed, a million worry lines etched all over her face.

"Yes. Just a bout of food poisoning," I lie through my trembling lips.

"Oh goodness. Here." She pulls a ginger candy from the pocket of the long sweater she's wearing. "To settle your poor stomach."

That single gesture breaks me. I sob as I scoop the candy from her tiny palm. The simplicity, the purity of it, is what hits the hardest. She's a total stranger—she doesn't even know me. And here she is showing me such kindness and generosity, while my husband was fucking his ex behind my back for who knows how long.

"Dear, you sure you can get home all right by yourself?"

I sniffle and nod. "Yes. Thank you for being so sweet."

She nods, too, then steps back to give me enough room to shut my door, but her concerned look remains trained on me. As I pull away and head down the street, I see her reflection in my rearview mirror. She stays standing there, gazing at me until I turn the corner and lose sight of her.

~

I don't know how long I drive or where I'm going.

I never knew being cheated on could be so disorienting. Sickening, sure. Infuriating, of course. But to have it flip your entire sense of time and place upside down is something I never anticipated.

I drive until the city skyline of London disappears in my rearview mirror. It's just roadway and rolling emerald-green hills ahead. The sky turns from the gray-blue of daytime to sunset orange to indigo. I pull off to the side of the road when it gets so dark that the signs become too difficult to read through my swollen, tired eyes. I pull my phone out of my bag and see multiple missed calls, all from Milo, along with a half

67

dozen texts. I must have set my phone on silent by accident, because I didn't hear it at all.

Hey. Are you okay?

Do you think you'll be back soon?

I get that you need space today, but will you just let me know that you're safe?

I called your store, but they said you didn't stop by. I'm worried, Riley.

Please let me know you're okay. I'm going nuts here.

I read the messages over and over again, unable to shake just how disorienting it feels to hear him sound so concerned about me. Even over text message it's clear he's worried sick. I've never seen him like this. This isn't the same Milo who gives me shit every time he sees me, who joked behind my back that I'd never be anything more than a trophy wife.

Guilt lands like a rock in my gut. I don't know what is going on, how I got here, how I went to sleep on Valentine's Day last night and woke up a year later, my entire life in shambles. I don't know how Milo and I got to this point, where he's being so kind and affectionate toward me. I don't know if today is some unexplainable blip in the universe, a time warp, or if that one time I dropped acid at a music festival with Poppy years ago is now resurfacing as a disorienting and nightmarish trip.

Whatever the reason, Milo is genuinely worried about me, and I should let him know I'm okay.

Hey. I'm safe and okay. I just need some time by myself.

He replies instantly.

Milo: I get it. Thank you for letting me know.

Milo: If you need me for anything, at any time, just call or text me. I mean it. I'm here for you in whatever way you want me, Riley.

I gaze at the words on my phone screen, taking them in over and over. In this parallel universe or bad acid trip, Milo and I are friends. It's the weirdest feeling ever . . . but it's also the biggest comfort, even if I don't know what exactly is happening or what to do about anything.

Me: Thank you.

I tuck my phone back in my bag, lock the car, and crawl in the back seat. There's no way I have the strength to make it back home after I've depleted every last bit of my energy today. I need to sleep. And maybe tomorrow when I wake up I'll have the faintest idea of where to go from here or what the hell to do.

I curl onto my side, my eyelids growing heavier and heavier each time I blink. It doesn't take long before I'm out cold.

Chapter 9

Something soft is wrapped around me. A blanket? Eyes closed, I begin to stir. I take in the sensations around me. Something plush underneath me, something soft over my skin. Something firm and warm across my stomach.

It feels like an arm . . . but not my arm.

My eyes fly open. I'm at home in my bed. How the hell . . .

"Good morning, Sleeping Beauty," a deep voice groggy with sleep says from behind me.

I freeze before glancing down at the massive toned arm that's wrapped around my bare midsection. That tan skin, those dark hairs dotted along the muscled flesh . . .

That's Milo's arm around me.

I jump out of bed like I'm on fire. Over and over I smooth my hands over my sleeping shirt, grateful to feel fabric against my skin.

"Whoa. What's the rush?" He starts to sit up, rubbing his eyes with his fists. My heart has rocketed to my throat, and my chest is heaving as I process this impossible moment.

I'm in bed. With my husband's cousin.

He aims a sleepy smile at me before running a hand through his mussed hair. "Bad dream?"

I gasp for air. "Something like that."

He starts to open his mouth to speak, but I hold up a hand. A million questions dance on my tongue. What in god's name are we doing in bed together? How did I even get here? I fell asleep in my car on the roadway hours from London . . . Did he come and get me and bring me back here?

Wait . . . are we a couple?

"I know what'll help," Milo says before I can get a word out.

He groans softly as he slides out of bed, scratching his bare, toned chest. I let out a breath when I see that he's wearing boxers. Thank Christ he's not naked. That would make this a million times more awkward.

"I'll put the kettle on." He swipes a T-shirt from the floor and pulls it over his head.

For a second I'm unnerved at how . . . good looking he is so early in the morning. He looks like an underwear model.

"Tea?"

"Don't worry, I know the special way you take it. The only way you take it."

He winks at me, and my stomach does something strange, something traitorous. It flips, like I'm happy and excited to see him do something so playful, so flirty.

It's a strange clash of sensations taking place inside me right now. Right now, my brain is scrambling to figure out how I woke up in bed with my husband's cousin. But my body seems to be enjoying it.

I rest my hand on my chest and try to steady my breathing. I watch him walk out of the bedroom and down the hallway toward the kitchen. My phone buzzes on my nightstand. When I see it's Poppy calling me, I answer immediately.

"Morning, Ri. Sorry for the early call, but just wanted to give you an update on the store before I head out on holiday with Desmond."

"Oh, um, great." I scurry to the primary bathroom and shut the door behind me. What holiday? She never told me she was planning to go on vacation.

She talks about some shipment due to be delivered to the boutique next week while she's gone, but I stop her. "Never mind that right now, Poppy. Did you get my voicemail yesterday?"

"What? No."

"Are you sure? I called you in the morning and left a message."

"Positive, Ri. I was at the store all day with my phone on me."

"Oh."

I go quiet, confused as hell.

"You sure you're okay, Ri? You sound a bit freaked out."

"Um, no. I'm actually very not okay."

She lets out a heavy sigh. "I figured this would happen. Just pretend like tomorrow isn't Valentine's Day."

An invisible record skids in my brain. "What do you mean 'tomorrow'? Valentine's Day was yesterday."

"Christ, if only. Whatever you need to tell yourself to get through that dumpster fire of an anniversary, you do it, Ri. We can pretend Valentine's Day doesn't exist from this day on if you'd like. You know I'd do it for you."

I stammer, confused to hell for the millionth time.

"Hang on," I tell her before swiping at the calendar app on my phone. It's February 13, 2025.

I stare at the date for what feels like a solid minute before pulling up my internet browser and checking the date on a dozen websites. They all say the same thing: today is February 13, 2025.

I plop on the toilet seat, suddenly so disoriented that I'm dizzy.

Because if this is real, then I've lost my grip on reality. If this is real, we're moving backward in time, and I'm the only one who seems to notice it.

"Ri? Ri, you all right?" Poppy's worried tone blasting from my phone speaker jerks me back to the moment.

"Not even close," I mumble.

"Oh, Ri. I knew I should have canceled this trip. Look, I can still do that. Desmond will understand; he adores you and wants you to be okay."

I press my eyes shut, shaking my head. "No, don't. Please don't do that." Whatever warped shit I'm currently going through, I don't want to drag my best friend into it. "Sorry, I'm just feeling a bit off today. I'll be fine, though. Go on your trip. Seriously."

A heavy sigh rockets from her end of the line. "You sure? Where we're going in Malta is so remote the cell service is going to be awful."

That explains why I couldn't get a hold of her yesterday . . . or technically tomorrow. Jesus, this is such a mind-fuck.

"Really. It's okay. *I'll* be okay, I promise."

"Milo's with you, right?"

"Um, yeah. He is."

I blink and think back to just minutes ago, when he was standing right here, bare chested in my bedroom, flashing that charming smile and winking at me. He's so comfortable being here, like he's done this a million times before.

"Good," Poppy says. "You shouldn't be alone right now. He'll take good care of you, I know it. He's a gem, that guy. Had him pegged all wrong this whole time."

I almost scoff. Poppy likes Milo now? I'm about to ask her to explain what he did to change her opinion of him, but the sound of Desmond's voice pulls her attention away.

She groans. "Desmond is insisting we leave for Heathrow now so we can be three hours early."

"It's an international flight," Desmond says in the background. "That's the recommended time nowadays."

A yippy bark follows. Desmond coos at Gus.

"Give him extra treats, will you? The expensive-as-fuck organic ones that are made of dehydrated chicken," Poppy says.

"Too many treats is bad for him. It's crucial that he maintains a balanced diet at his age."

"Oh Christ, Desmond. I've been feeding him table scraps ever since he was a puppy. He's fine. Besides, treats are the best way to get him to calm down so he isn't a ball of nerves for the dogsitter." There's a pause, then a muffled kissing sound.

"I suppose you're right," Desmond says.

"Can you believe I fell in love with such a rule follower?" Poppy says to me before chuckling. Another kissing sound. Despite the confusing-as-hell shit show that my life currently is, it's a comfort to know that Poppy and Desmond are still solid, still as in love as ever.

"Have the best time, you two," I say.

"See you in two weeks!"

We hang up. I stand at the sink, splash cold water on my face, and try to figure out what exactly is going on.

Yesterday I woke up exactly one year into the future. Today I woke up the day before that. I seem to be living life backward, one day at a time, while no one else notices—they're living their own lives unbothered.

What. The. Fuck. Is. Happening.

I don't know how long I stand there, but the skin on my face and hands has turned to ice. I shut off the water and dry myself. Clearly I'm not going to solve anything by attempting to give myself hypothermia in my bathroom.

I'll just have to figure this out as I go, one day at a time.

I pee, wash up, pad to the kitchen, and see Milo standing at the marble island, reading something on his phone, a mug of tea in his other hand.

I breathe in the familiar smell. Dank and faintly citrus with wet-dirt undertones. Only unlike before, I don't make a face. My stomach doesn't curdle. I inhale again. This time the smell is warm and soothing.

He looks up at me and sets his phone down. The corner of his mouth hooks up. "Hey. I made you your favorite."

I glance at the steaming mug on my end of the island. "I like tea now."

75

It sounds like a question, the way my voice hitches at the end.

The low rumble of Milo's chuckle echoes in the kitchen. "I'm still surprised about it too. And I still can't believe you let me convince you to try it all those months ago."

I almost say, "I did?" but catch myself. I should try to learn as much as I can about every moment and memory I've missed.

"Tell me again."

He smiles before taking a sip and glancing off to the side. His gaze cuts to me. My stomach flips again for the second time this morning.

"I texted you 'Happy Easter.' You texted back that there was nothing happy about the way you were annihilating that package of marshmallow Peeps. I texted that they'd go down easier with some tea. You sent back a string of vomiting emojis."

I let out a chuckle.

"I claimed that I could make you love tea," he says. "You said there was no way in hell that would happen; you've always thought it was gross. I said that if you tried it one more time and hated it, I'd sign over my flat to you. You said 'game on.' So I took you to that tea shop in my neighborhood. I ordered a half–Earl Grey, half-hazelnut blend. I figured hazelnut tea would be a good bet because—"

"Because I like hazelnut coffee."

He grins. "Right. And when I ordered it from the guy at the counter . . ." Milo shakes his head, chuckling, reminding me of what he told me while driving my car yesterday morning—tomorrow morning, technically. God, this is going to take some getting used to.

"He was pissed. He's always pissed every time we order it," I add.

Milo grins. "Yup. But he made it anyway. And when you sipped it, your eyes went wide. You smiled like you couldn't believe it."

"I liked it."

He nods once, a half smile tugging at his lips. "You liked it."

I pick up the cup, blow, and take a small, slow sip. The warm liquid coats my tongue. The flavor hits differently than the times I've tried it before. It tastes exactly how it smells—earthy, faintly citrus, like wet dirt, but in a good way. The hazelnut adds a richness that makes it heartier, fuller, more comforting.

I make an "mmm" sound. I like this. A lot.

"Good?" Milo asks.

None of this makes sense. Not me suddenly liking tea after a lifetime of loathing it. Not me waking up one year into the future. Not me living life backward while time moves forward for everyone else around me. Not Milo and I living like a couple in what used to be my home with Tristan.

But something about this feels comfortable. And in this confusion and chaos, in this impossible space of time, in the aftermath of finding out Tristan cheated on me, after finding out the life I loved so much was a lie, I'll take this feeling. It's the one thing that feels good. And I need that right now.

I sip again. "It's really good."

Chapter 10

February 13, 2025

I drain the rest of the tea in my mug. Milo brews me another cup before downing the rest of his.

He lets out a satisfied "ahh" noise that sends goose bumps flying across my skin. It's so guttural, so low. Has he ever made that noise around me before? I don't remember him doing that. It's so . . . pleasant sounding. He rinses the mug and places it in the dishwasher. A bell sounds from the living room. I twist around and see Coco the cat hop down from her perch on the back of the sofa and trot over to me.

"Someone wants their morning cuddles," Milo says.

I smile down at her before scooping her up and giving her chin a scratch. She purrs instantly. Amid all the chaos of this impossible time flip that's turned my reality upside down, being able to cuddle a cat is a nice surprise.

Milo walks over to me and gently pats the top of her head. When he dusts a kiss on my cheek, I freeze. I lean back and out of his touch. It happens like a reflex. Something about this—about us, about Milo being physically intimate with me—feels . . . not wrong. But different. Jarring.

When I look up at him, I take in his slightly raised brow. How he looks shocked.

I clear my throat. "Sorry, I just . . . it's just that it feels a little . . ."

As I stammer, I notice the look in Milo's eyes shifts from shocked to shy, then to hurt. A pang of guilt flashes through me.

"You're not comfortable with me kissing you," he says, his tone soft and resigned.

I shake my head. "I'm sorry. I know we're . . . together, but . . ."

Just saying that feels wrong. I know that's the reality of the situation—in this timeline, in this universe, Milo and I are together.

Just silently admitting that to myself has my nerves going haywire. Is this my life now? Will this ever end? Will one day I wake up and start living life forward again? Or will I wake up on some random day in the future? Or god . . . will I be like Benjamin Button and live my entire life backward?

I start to feel lightheaded at the thought of the rest of my life being that random, that chaotic and disorienting . . .

I press my eyes shut for a second to ground myself. When I open my eyes, I look at Milo.

"I'm sorry to give such mixed signals," I say. "I guess I'm still getting used to this. To us. Sometimes it's hard for me to believe we ended up together."

I regret the words as soon as I say them. I sound so harsh. But to my surprise, Milo's expression softens. He still looks sad, but he looks like he understands how I feel too.

"You're right. It's definitely weird, the two of us ending up together. A lot of people think so."

I instantly think of Milo's family . . . who's also Tristan's family. God, they must fucking loathe me now.

I swallow back the fresh wave of nerves firing through me at that thought.

"You're probably feeling that way because of tomorrow," Milo says.

I frown. "What do you mean?"

He swallows, like he's unsure of what he's about to say. "Tomorrow's Valentine's Day. Yours and Tristan's anniversary. With that coming up, I can understand how you'd be feeling a bit hesitant about things."

"Oh. Right." Tomorrow . . . which already happened in my time-line. "Yeah, I guess I'm a bit hung up on that," I say quickly.

"We should head out of the city. Get away for the day, take your mind off things," he says.

And that explains why I woke up to Milo driving my car out of London on Valentine's Day.

It feels like one tiny bit of the confusion fog in my brain is clearing up.

"Okay. Yeah." I try to smile back. "That's a good idea."

He nods once and turns away. "I'm gonna jump in the shower."

I watch him pad down the hall and disappear into the bedroom. He crosses the open doorway a second later, wearing just his boxers. My gaze pauses at his toned, muscled form before I force myself to look away. I'm a scumbag to ogle him right after I've rejected him.

Coco slow-blinks as she gazes at him right along with me.

I glance down at her. "I know, right?"

Standing alone in the kitchen while cuddling Coco, I take mental stock of this situation. I'm divorced. I finally have the adorable and cuddly cat I always wanted. My personal life is a *Jerry Springer*–level trash fire given the fact that I'm now shacking up with my ex-husband's cousin.

Unease simmers inside me like a quiet current. I won't ever be able to fully relax into this new reality, not when there are still a million unanswered questions. I still have no idea how I got here. Or why I'm here. I could wake up tomorrow (yesterday) and face a completely new disaster I'm not prepared for since I'm essentially living my life backward.

The gears in my brain start to grind. For a second I contemplate doing something completely nuts to disrupt the timeline. Like rob a bank. Or set my car on fire. Would that be enough to throw everything off, maybe even reset this backward timeline?

But then I remember how I fell asleep in my car the previous night. I woke up in bed with Milo anyway—where I had likely fallen asleep the "day before." It doesn't seem to matter what I do throughout the day. The timeline jumps me backward.

A restless feeling courses through my body. The urge to do something, anything, to regain some semblance of control is hitting me hard. But I can't. Even if I did set my car on fire today, I'd wake up yesterday and have it be just fine. I have to just let this timeline run itself back. But back to where?

A weird wave of grief washes over me. It's jarring, but the longer I think about it, the more it makes sense. My sense of comfort and security, my joy, my old life, my sense of control . . . I've lost it all. Even though it was all a lie, even though I don't want to be married to Tristan anymore after finding out what a cheating scumbag he is, I can't help the sadness I feel. I thought I was so happy. I thought my life was perfect. It wasn't even close.

I close my eyes for a long sec, my brain aching at what a mind-fuck this all is. I suddenly feel like I'm going through the stages of grief.

Now I guess I have to accept that this is all real.

When I open my eyes, I see Coco staring at me with adorable sleepy eyes. Her cuteness is a needed buffer in the midst of this madness.

I give Coco another chin scratch and a kiss on the top of her impossibly soft head, set her back on the couch, and open one of the kitchen drawers. I'm weirdly relieved when I see the notepad I stored there ages ago. And comforted. It's one familiar thing in this place where so much is different.

To help me make sense of it all, I stand at the island and write out everything I've learned since I've experienced this weird-as-hell time warp.

Things I know for certain:

- I fell asleep February 14, 2024.
- I woke up on February 14, 2025, one year into the future from when I fell asleep.

- Tristan and I split up because he cheated on me. He's with his ex-girlfriend Carly now. They have a kid together.
- Milo is my boyfriend. We live together.
- I got to keep Tristan's house on Dorset Street.
- I'm living my life backward in time.

Things I need to find out:

- How did I find out Tristan was cheating on me?
- When did I find out about Tristan's affair and Carly's pregnancy?
- How long had their affair been going on?
- Has he cheated on me before?
- How did I end up with the house?
- How did Milo and I become close?
- When did things between Milo and me turn romantic?

I scan the dizzying list of questions, feeling the slightest bit intimidated. This is a hell of a to-do list. Where do I even start?

I walk slowly around the apartment, hoping that something will jump out at me and magically answer any of my questions.

When my gaze lands on the desk in my bedroom, I zip over and start yanking out the drawers. A glossy blue folder in the top middle drawer nabs my attention. There's a law firm logo embossed on the front of it—I've never heard of it before. I pull the folder out and quickly flip through the stack until I see the text on top of one of the pages.

Dissolution of marriage

There are my name and information along with Tristan's. And a date that the paperwork was initially filed.

February 24, 2024.

Jesus. That was less than two weeks after our first-year wedding anniversary . . . which means I must have found out about Tristan's affair soon after we celebrated one year together.

I stare at the date until my eyes burn, unable to move or blink. When I finally do move, I tear up but press on. There's a morbid curiosity taking hold of me at the moment. I know I'm not going to like what I find out, but I'm too curious. So I keep reading.

I see that I selected "adultery" as the reason for the divorce.

I swallow, my throat aching.

I see the name Lara Chan. She was my attorney.

"Hey."

I look up to see Milo standing in the open doorway of the bathroom, clad in just a towel, his bare chest dotted with water droplets, gazing down at me with concern in his deep-brown gaze.

"What are you doing reading that?"

I stammer as I look between the pile of legal documents that I've set on my lap and him. "I don't know," I finally say.

He walks the few steps over to where I'm sitting and kneels down next to me. He takes the pile of papers from me and sets them on top of the desk.

"You haven't looked at these in a while," he says softly.

I shake my head. "I just can't believe it's real. That this actually happened."

He runs a hand through his damp hair, nodding.

"I guess I'm still trying to process everything."

Milo hesitates for a few seconds. "Of course."

He stands up and starts to turn toward the bathroom, but I catch his wrist and turn him back to me. "What did you think when it happened?"

He frowns slightly. "When what happened? When you got divorced or when I found out what Tristan did?"

I swallow. "Both."

"You really want to talk about this again?"

I nod. I need answers to my questions. I need to know what exactly happened.

I let go of his wrist, and he moves to sit on the foot of the bed. I twist in my desk chair to face him.

"When I found out that Tristan was cheating on you, I was beyond pissed. But I, uh . . . I wasn't exactly surprised."

I frown. "What do you mean by that?"

He hesitates, glancing away for a second. The clouds have dissipated, and a sunbeam now filters through the nearby window. It illuminates Milo like a spotlight on a stage. His skin glows tan-gold. The drops on his chest dazzle like tiny diamonds.

"I never told you this," he murmurs while rubbing the back of his neck.

"Tell me now. Please."

He looks at me again. "Tristan has cheated on every woman he's ever been with. That I know of, at least."

I don't know why hearing that guts me so much. It takes a moment for me to catch my breath. I shouldn't be surprised. If one of my friends told me that their partner was having a long-term affair with his ex and got her pregnant, I'd assume that's not the first time he's strayed. It comes off like textbook serial-cheater behavior.

Milo reaches over and grabs my hand. "I'm sorry, Riley. I should have told you sooner."

I shake my head. "No, it's . . . it's not your fault Tristan is a serial cheater."

"No, but maybe I could have warned you about him."

"I probably wouldn't have listened to you. I didn't really like you for the longest time."

"Fair point. So, yeah, I was pissed when I found out what happened. And I mean, you know the rest."

"Yeah, but I want to hear it again."

His thick eyebrows furrow slightly. "Why, though?"

I scramble, trying to think of a way to explain this without out-right saying, "Because for some impossible, unexplainable reason, in one night's sleep I lived an entire year, a lot of fucked-up shit went down, and I don't remember any of it, so now I'm trying to figure out what I missed without everyone around me thinking I've lost my mind."

I study Milo's concerned gaze. "Because I know now so much of my relationship with Tristan was a lie. I was so happy with him, but that was because he was hiding everything from me. I want to remind myself of the truth of what happened, even if it makes me sad and angry. At least those feelings are honest and genuine."

I can tell by Milo's hesitant expression that he's not totally on board with this.

"Tell me, Milo. I already know what happened, but I need to hear it again."

He scrubs a hand over the dark stubble covering his face. "A few days before your one-year anniversary, I was in Soho for a work meeting and I saw Tristan with Carly. They were leaving one of his restaurants. They were laughing. He had his arm around her. And I saw . . . I saw her stomach. She was pregnant. And then Tristan patted her stomach, and I just knew. That baby had to be his. As she moved to leave, he pulled her back into him and kissed her. And then she walked off."

The sensation that hits me feels a lot like someone's fist just wrapped around my stomach. I swallow and silently command every muscle in my face to remain neutral, like I've heard all this before.

"When she left, he saw me staring at him from the sidewalk," Milo says.

"Tell me what happened next."

"We just stood there looking at each other. Like some sort of messed-up staring contest. After a few seconds, he walked up to me and started to say something, but I told him to shut up. I told him that I knew he was cheating—I knew he got Carly pregnant—and that he needed to come clean to you."

"Right." My throat feels like I'm trying to swallow a tennis ball.

"But when I came to Gran and Grandad's anniversary party and saw you there and how happy you looked with him, I knew he hadn't told you. About his affair. Or that he got Carly pregnant."

I nod and think back to that night. How Milo was immediately hostile to Tristan, why he made those comments about my anniversary gift, why he taunted Tristan about being such a decent and thoughtful guy.

"That's why you were such a dick that night," I say. "You were angry with him and couldn't think of any other way to deal with it than make sarcastic comments about his character." I swallow. "And you got punched for it."

Milo shrugs. "And again when I came to your house the following day to tell you about Tristan's affair."

My eyes go wide for a split second, but I blink and rein it in. Coco pads into the room and hops on the bed to sit next to him. He scratches under her chin. "You had just gotten this fluffy little diva."

My mouth falls open slightly as my brain scrambles to take in everything Milo's saying.

His face twists slightly, and his expression turns pained. "Seeing that look on your face when I told you, you were so confused. Especially when Tristan denied it at first. But I swore I was telling the truth. And that's when I think it started to set in for you. I could tell by the shocked expression on your face. You believed me. And then when it sank in what he did, you looked so broken. I hated being the one to make you feel that way."

I don't say anything in response. All my energy is being channeled into keeping my face as neutral as possible while my brain scrambles to process everything he's telling me.

"You're not the one at fault," I finally say a few seconds later, when I'm sure my voice will be steady. "This is all on Tristan."

"But I was the messenger. I was the one delivering the news that broke your heart—the news that ruined your life."

I grip the back of the chair just to have something to steady me. I take a long, slow, silent breath. And then I look at Milo.

"You're upset," he says softly.

"Yeah. But that's the way I should feel reliving the moment when I found out my husband was a lying, cheating bastard."

Milo nods, his expression turning regretful as he looks off to the side.

I grab his hand. "I needed to hear this again. Thank you."

He shakes his head, and that sad smile pulls at his lips. "Don't thank me, Riley. I'm the one who should be thanking you."

"For what?"

He leans forward, the broad spread of his shoulders closing the space between us. When he cups my cheek, my skin tingles. I tense under his touch. A second later he seems to notice, and he pulls his hand away. He presses his eyes shut and shakes his head. "Sorry, I shouldn't have touched you like that when you already said you're feeling mixed-up about things."

"It's okay," I say quickly.

"It's not." Milo clears his throat and scoots away, widening the space between us. "I just meant that I'm grateful for the way you were. The way you are. For giving your husband's cousin a chance when you had every reason to tell me to fuck off. For not totally writing me off as a pathetic loser when I confessed that I'd been carrying a torch for you ever since the night I met you."

I can't blink or move. All the skin on my body is on fire.

He flashes a soft smile at me before standing up and walking back into the bathroom while I sit here and attempt to work out the bomb he just unwittingly dropped on me.

Chapter 11

Instead of driving to work, I opt to walk. I need to be outside in the cold, wet London winter, moving my body while I untangle the thoughts crashing together in my brain.

Milo just admitted to me an hour ago that he has had feelings for me ever since he met me—for the entirety of my relationship with Tristan. I had no clue, not even the slightest inkling.

But why would I have? As soon as I overheard him make that trophy wife comment, I wrote him off as a douchebag and was curt and snippy with him whenever we interacted. He was teasing and biting in return, and we settled into that dynamic easily over the years.

But now everything has changed. We're a couple.

Milo is the opposite of what I thought he was. He's sweet and kind and doting and caring. And he's got an impressive moral code, considering he burned bridges with Tristan, his own cousin, to defend me.

I know how I should feel for Milo. I should be swooning. I should melt under his touch. I should have kissed him this morning instead of quickly getting ready and sneaking out while he was still getting dressed in the bathroom.

But I can't. I still feel completely off, completely disoriented. And it's because I'm missing that entire chunk of time that everyone else except me seems to have lived.

That tidal wave of nervous energy levels me once more as I think yet again about the prospect of living life in this backward timeline . . . in a relationship with a man I loathe.

The thought feels off even as it formulates in my brain.

That's not true. Not anymore.

The truth is I don't hate Milo, not in this warped backward timeline. In this timeline I . . .

My head spins as I struggle to search for the right words to describe how I feel about him. Unsettled . . . but not in a bad way. Heartened at his kindness. Surprised by how attractive I find him.

That unsettled feeling takes hold, like a hook digging into my side. Will I hate him again tomorrow/yesterday? That doesn't seem to be the case.

I reach the storefront of Luscious. Before I can even unlock the door, my phone rings. When I see it's my little brother, Jordan, I'm shocked. He hardly ever calls me. Especially not when it's the middle of the night in his time zone. He's a teacher and wakes up early in the mornings.

"Hey, Riley. Just wanted to say hi."

"Oh. Um, why?" I almost laugh. I love my little brother to death, but he's not the kind of sibling to call out of the blue. We mostly communicate via text and by sending each other funny memes.

"Can't a guy call his big sister just to chat?" His tone is light and playful, like it often is when we talk, but it almost sounds forced right now.

"Come on, Jordan. What's really going on?"

He huffs out a breath. "I just wanted to make sure you're okay. Valentine's Day is tomorrow, and I just . . . look, I know I've never been the most emotionally sensitive sibling. I can be pretty oblivious. And awkward."

I think back to how uncomfortable my brother gets whenever he sees our mom or one of our aunties cry. Instant "deer in the headlights" face. If he's feeling brave, he'll offer a stiff hug before making an excuse so he can run away from all the heavy feels.

"I know I'm bad at this stuff, Riley," he says. "But you're my sister. I want to be there for you. Especially after what Tristan did to you."

I instantly soften. "That means a lot, Jordan. Thank you. I'm okay, though."

"You sure?" There's a firmness in his voice that I'm not accustomed to hearing. I'm used to my kid brother acting like a goofy teenager despite the fact that he's in his late twenties.

But he's not just silly and goofy. I see that now. He can be caring and observant when it counts—when it comes to me. And it means so much.

"I'm sure, Jordan. Thanks."

"Milo's taking good care of you then?"

I stammer at his question. It's weird to hear my brother ask about Milo. But obviously he'd know about him at this point in this timeline.

"Yeah. He is."

"Glad to hear that. He's a good one, Riley. I know that probably doesn't mean a whole lot coming from me, given my history with Tristan, but I really do mean it. I like Milo."

I'm speechless. Jordan's never liked any of the guys I've dated. He hated Tristan from the moment he met him.

I think back to the very first time the two of them met, at least in my original memory. Jordan was visiting London for a month during his summer off from teaching, and I insisted that he meet my new boyfriend. We met up at Last One Standing, because we did almost everything at Tristan's restaurants.

I think back to the firm handshake they exchanged, the polite smile on Jordan's face, how it didn't reach his eyes, how he was cordial and pleasant. I could tell he couldn't stand Tristan.

When Tristan left early to go to a business meeting, I remember the incredulous stare my brother leveled at me. The way his eyebrow quirked up, the tilt of his head.

"This guy, Riley? Seriously?"

The defensiveness I felt was instant. And funny in a sad way, looking back now, given that if it had been Tristan's relative who insulted me, Tristan wouldn't have addressed it at all.

"Yes! I'm serious. We're serious," I said to Jordan.

He shook his head, glancing off to the side. It was such a dismissive gesture. And for the first time in my life, I felt insignificant in my younger brother's eyes. I wasn't used to it. Not after a lifetime of looking after him, of helping him get dressed when he was a toddler, of babysitting him, of walking him to school, of telling him what to do even when I knew he wasn't going to listen. But he still respected me. I was his older sister, and he looked up to me always.

Except the day he met Tristan. Something in the way he looked at me that afternoon read disappointed. I felt it deep. I've carried that feeling with me ever since. It has sprouted up every time they've been together, pretending to be polite, pretending to get along.

"You could do a lot better than Mr. Money Bags, Riley," Jordan said that day.

"Of course you'd say that. You've never liked anyone I've dated."

When he shrugged, that only spurred me on.

"Can you drop the protective-little-brother act? I'm an adult, Jordan. I don't need you to vet my partners. I never have."

"I never said you did, Riley. Just something about this guy rubs me the wrong way. I just . . . he's not good enough for you, okay?"

"I don't care. I love him and I want to be with him."

Something flashed in my brother's eyes as he looked at me. Something more than disappointment. More than worry, more than sadness.

"Really, Riley?"

"Yes. I'm very serious about Tristan. I think he might be the one."

He scoffed, then laughed.

"Fuck you, Jordan." I shot up from my chair and turned to leave, but he reached up and grabbed my hand.

"Hey. I'm sorry, okay? Please don't leave."

"I'm not asking you to be best friends, okay? Just please don't hate my boyfriend."

His expression shifted from panicked to tender. Resolute. He nodded once. "Okay."

And that was it. Jordan was polite to Tristan every time he was around him, despite the undercurrent of dislike that remained. I felt it always. Even on my wedding day, when I was all smiles and giddy with excitement and joy, even when Jordan hugged me and said how happy he was for me. It was there, like an invisible cloud wedged between us, always.

So to hear Jordan say that he likes Milo, that he thinks he's a good guy, that he's happy I'm with him, is as unbelievable as it is shocking. I need an extra moment to process it.

That uncertainty I felt when thinking about my relationship with Milo wanes, replaced by a surge of something warm. I start to feel dizzy, I'm so overwhelmed.

"I won't keep you any longer," Jordan says. "I know you're about to start work. Just wanted to let you know I'm thinking of you."

"Thanks, Jordan. Love you."

"Love you too."

We hang up and I try to push aside the whirlwind of emotions so I can focus on work. When I unlock the front door and flip on the lights at Luscious, I'm comforted instantly. Being here feels like home. I do a scan of the racks of lingerie and the displays of makeup. Poppy and I must have rearranged the setup sometime in the past year. I take in the blouses and dresses near the front door. I smile, happy to see that we're selling even more clothing now. We've expanded, which means business is doing well. That's one change I'm ecstatic to see.

The display near the front of the store catches my eye. I spot the familiar kelly-green blouses with the lace-trim neckline—the blouse I wore the night of my first wedding anniversary with Tristan. There's a small sign next to it.

The "make your in-laws blush" blouse. Bestseller!

I pause, unsure how I should feel. Did I seriously come up with that name? Or did Poppy?

I decide I don't have the energy to figure that out right now.

The morning passes in a blur as customers filter in. I'm ringing up an order when the front door swings open and in walks Nesta holding her daughter, Molly, who looks to be just over a year old.

I'm too stunned to move. Just seeing Molly at this stage is beyond jarring, a reminder of how real this time jump is—she was a tiny baby the last time I saw her, just days ago.

I beam so wide, my cheeks ache. As soon as I finish helping the customer, I walk over to Nesta. I'm about to pull her into a hug when I notice the hesitant look in her gold-brown eyes. She fixes her gaze on the floor, like she's scared to look at me for too long.

I stop short of her. "Hi."

"Hey." She opens her mouth like she's going to say more, but clamps it shut and shakes her head. She tugs at her messy bun of copper curls. "I don't know why I thought I could come here. I should have called you first. It's been so long . . ."

A nervous laugh falls from her mouth, and it rattles me. Nesta's never acted this shaken up around me before.

"Why wouldn't you come here? Nesta, you're always welcome here."

Her expression turns pained. "Really? After letting all this time pass without checking in on you? After what my cousin did to you?"

As I observe the hesitant look on her face, I can tell that whatever went down between us, it's taken a toll on her. I can spot it in the worried look in her eyes, how she speaks like she's scared I'm going to kick her out of my store.

I don't care what happened. I'm just happy she's here.

I pull Nesta into a hug, careful not to squeeze too hard around Molly.

"Nesta. I love you. I'm so glad you came."

I hear her sniffle. When I let her go, I glance at Molly, who's smiling and drooling. I grab a tissue from my trouser pocket and dab at her plump face.

"My lord." I grab hold of her chunky thigh.

"She's huge, isn't she?" Nesta lets out a watery chuckle. "You want to hug her? She missed her auntie Riley."

Without even saying yes, I scoop little Molly up into my arms. Her brown eyes go wide at first, like she's unsure about me holding her. But then I shift slightly so she can see her mom, and she relaxes in my hold.

Nesta whips out her phone and snaps some photos.

"You wanna shop a bit while I hold Molly?"

She looks like she's going to burst into tears of joy. She yanks me into a hug. "God, I missed you, Riley. I'm sorry I let months pass before coming to see you. I just . . . I was so busy with this little fireball of energy, and then we went away for a while, and when we got back I wanted to come see you like I said I would, but then Molly got sick and I was so busy with her and work." She hesitates for a second. "Everything was so chaotic, and I guess I just lost my nerve after not seeing you for so long." Her eyes go misty, the look in them tender and regretful all at once. "I know we had that conversation after things went down between you and my nobhead cousin, I know I said I was on your side and that I'd be there for you no matter what, and now I just feel like the worst friend in the world to wait so long to reach out."

When her voice starts to tremble, I give her a squeeze with my free arm. "Nesta. It's really okay. It was a complicated situation. To say the least. He's your family. I didn't expect you to disown him or something like—"

She pulls away, shaking her head as she wipes her nose with the back of her wrist. "That tosser is my cousin in name only. I can't stand to be around him. Especially after what happened at the . . . well, you know. I don't want to bring it up again."

I bite my tongue to keep from saying that yes, actually, it would be quite helpful for her to rehash a memory that clearly has her distraught, because I'm missing that patch of time.

Instead, I flash what I assume is a sad-looking smile.

"But still, it's no excuse for not reaching out to you. I'm sorry, Riley. That's why I came today. I wanted to see you and tell you how sorry I am in person. And to check on you since tomorrow is . . . erm."

Valentine's Day. Our anniversary.

I nod once. "Of course. You're so kind to do that. Swear I'm all right, though."

She smooths back a few fiery curls that have come loose from her bun. "I assume Milo is looking after you well? If not, I'll have his balls."

I chuckle and gesture for her to check out the clothing racks. I follow her as she browses, Molly cradled against my side.

"Yes, he is."

She smiles at me. "Good."

I ask about Roland, and she tells me he's been promoted at the law firm. I ask how the rest of her family is doing. Again she hesitates before playing with one of the wooden hangers on the rack we're standing next to.

"Everything is pretty much back to normal since the incident. People no longer bring it up at family gatherings, not at the ones I've been to, at least. I don't go as much anymore with how busy this one keeps me. Plus I can't stand seeing you-know-who and having to bite my tongue so I don't walk up to him and tell him yet again what a massive piece of shit I think he is. Apparently saying all of that would be impolite, according to my mum."

She reaches up to adjust Molly's pacifier.

"The incident?" I ask, confused.

Nesta bites her lip. "Oh hell, I'm sorry, Riley. I shouldn't have brought it up."

Well, now I have to know what in the world she's talking about.

I try to play it cool. "Nesta. It's okay. I'm over it."

She scoff-chuckles. "I bet. You know, some of the family think that somehow you started the kitchen fire even though you were out in the pub with us the whole time. Can you believe that?"

I'm jolted back to when I saw the Last One Standing burned to a crisp. Shit. Did I start the fire as a way to get back at him for cheating? I would never do something so psychotic . . . at least I don't think I would. But maybe in this weird and messed-up reverse timeline things are different. I ended up with Milo, after all.

I'm in the middle of trying to figure out a way to ask Nesta this without giving away that I'm utterly clueless when I notice her expression darkens slightly.

"Tristan's mum was just in the hospital. Not sure if anyone told you."

"Oh. Um, no. That's horrible. Is she all right?"

"Yeah. It's her own fault, really. She got so drunk one night after fighting with Tristan's dad that she tried to drive away in her car."

"Oh my god."

Nesta nods while examining a flowy maxi dress.

"Thankfully she immediately crashed into a streetlight down the road from their house. It's a miracle she didn't hit anyone. But she ended up with a broken leg, a couple of bruised ribs, and a sprained neck. Serves her right for potentially endangering the lives of strangers by driving in such a state."

"Wow."

I'm quiet for a long stretch while Nesta checks out the jewelry. Molly starts to fuss, so I hand her to Nesta, who pulls a snack out of the diaper bag that she set by the register. While Molly sits on the floor and chows down on some cheese crackers, Nesta turns back to me.

"Sorry to bore you with all this. That was probably the one plus of breaking up with Tristan—not having to deal with or hear about his mum anymore. And here I am talking your ear off about her."

"No, that's . . . I appreciate you talking to me like it's old times. Truly. I don't miss the lies and deceit, but I do miss seeing you regularly."

Nesta gives my hand a squeeze. "Well, if it's all right with you, I'd like to see you more regularly too."

"I'd love that."

She brings her haul up to the register, and I start to check her out. I glance at her. "Can I ask you a question?"

"Of course."

"What does your family think of me being with Milo now?"

I'm certain I know the answer, but when a knowing smile tugs at Nesta's lips, I'm thrown.

"Like you don't already know," she says.

"Ha. I guess I do. I'm sure they think I'm a tramp working my way from Tristan to his cousin, soiling the pristine Chase family name."

Nesta rolls her eyes good-naturedly. "Tristan's mum thinks that, but that's no surprise. They're insufferable. But everyone else understands, Riley. Really."

I pack her purchase into a brown paper shopping bag. "I'm sure his grandparents feel the same way."

When Nesta doesn't say anything, I glance up.

"Of course they don't," she says. "Not since Milo gave them a talking-to. Surely you remember that."

I stammer. Milo defended me to his grandparents?

I attempt to play off my misstep. "Right, but I mean, no matter what they say, deep down they must think awful things about me."

Nesta shakes her head. "No way. Milo is their beloved grandchild— their favorite grandchild. Believe me, I'd know—I teased him about it all the time as kids, about how wild it was that two of the most stereotypical British grandparents favored their American grandchild out of all of us. But he was always so excited to see them. He loved spending time with them and always remembered to call them on their birthdays. He was the only grandchild who'd remember to write them thank-you notes for the birthday and Christmas gifts they'd send him. And he brings Gran flowers every time he visits her. Of course they loved him the most. But when they stepped out of line, he made it clear that he'd drop out of their lives completely if they weren't polite and welcoming to you."

"Oh."

I'm stunned. At how easily that seems to have gone down. At how it sounds like it was a nonissue for Milo to stand up to his own family for my sake.

And then, like some perfectly timed flashback, I think back to the times that Tristan's parents and grandparents were low-key and/or outright rude to me, and Tristan either ignored it or didn't even notice.

My chest squeezes. Another sensation appears behind it. Warmth. Actually, "heat" is a better word. It feels like a small flame simmering in my chest at the thought of Milo standing up to his grandparents and defending me. I have no idea what he said, of course . . . but just the fact that he said anything, that he put his relationship with his grandparents on the line because of his feelings for me, leaves me dizzy in the best way. And something else. Some other disorienting feeling that I can't quite put a name to.

"So. Does my cousin have any more romantic surprises up his sleeve for you?" Nesta's question pulls me back to our conversation. "I heard from my mum about the trip to Portugal he surprised you with."

"Oh." Again I'm stammering, struggling to keep pace in this conversation where I don't know half of what she's talking about, but I have to pretend like I do. "Not that I know of. But I guess that's why it's called a surprise."

She chuckles. "Christ, he's got it bad for you. I've never seen him like this with anyone."

Her comment sets off the singular question in my brain. "Nesta, did you know that Milo liked me? That he had feelings for me ever since . . ."

I trail off when I see the regretful look on her face. "Yeah. I did. Honestly, it was obvious as hell. I thought you knew."

I shake my head. "I didn't. Until he told me."

"I suppose I should have told you."

"I honestly don't even know what I would have done if you did. I was totally in love with Tristan. I didn't even like Milo."

Nesta chuckles as she picks up Molly. "Oh, I remember."

"Did he ever talk to you about me?"

She shakes her head. "Even when I tried to bring it up with him, he always refused. I get it. I mean, no one likes to be vulnerable, especially not to admit that they've got it bad for their cousin's wife. Milo can be a smug bastard at times, but he didn't want to come off like a slimeball."

"I guess I had him pegged all wrong for a really long time."

"Well, it looks like you two have got it all figured out now." She winks at me. "That's all that matters."

I hug her and Molly goodbye before they leave, the whole time thinking, "God, Nesta, if only you knew. I haven't got any of this figured out, not even close."

But that's not the main thought on my mind anymore as I get through the rest of the workday. All I can think about is Milo defending me, standing up for me.

When I walk through the door of the Marylebone house, Milo is standing in the kitchen, frowning at a label on a box of pasta. When he looks up at me and smiles, that flame in my chest burns hotter.

"Hey. How was your day?" he asks.

I don't answer him. I shed my trench coat and drop it on the couch as I make my way over to him, my heart racing, that heat in my chest burning hotter and hotter by the second. I stop in front of him and look at him. I wait for the nerves, the uncertainty that burst through my chest and stomach this morning when he touched me. They're nowhere to be found. That fire in my chest must have burned them away.

I reach up and cup my hand to his stubbled cheek. I hold my breath, waiting to see if that hesitation resurfaces, if those nerves reappear. They don't. All that's left is heat as I stand here and touch Milo. Milo, who defended me without hesitation.

I swallow as I work up the nerve to test this new feeling blooming inside me. I lean up and press a quick kiss to his lips. It's a chaste kiss—lips only and lasting just a couple of seconds. But it's exactly what I need.

That touch of my mouth to his causes the heat in my chest to intensify for a split second before warmth takes over. It spreads through my chest and all over my body. All of me relaxes now that I'm near him.

Warmth. Comfort.

There's still so much I don't know about what happened in that year I lost. There's still so much I don't know about Milo, about our relationship.

But what I do know is that it turns me on to know that he defended me. And I know that tonight is when I start to feel something for him.

I step back and soak in the surprised smile he gives me.

And then I finally answer his question. "It was a good day."

Chapter 12

"Are you excited?" Milo glances at me from over the rim of his tea mug.

"For what?" I glance out the kitchen window, mystified by the fluffy snowflakes falling from the sky. It's wild to see snow when my body and brain think it's March. I'm expecting rain every time I step outside. But since time is moving backward, it's now January, so a little bit of snow is to be expected. I still can't wrap my head around it, though.

"Date night with Poppy and Desmond."

I thumb through the stack of mail on the kitchen island and down the rest of the tea in my cup.

I smile up at him. "Yeah. I'm pumped."

I think about yesterday (tomorrow, actually), how Poppy chatted at work about what a great time we all had. I only wish she'd given me specifics.

Milo grins back at me before turning to open the fridge door and peering at the contents inside. "I think I'll make my famous homemade bolognese. Poppy's favorite recipe of mine. You know she demands I make it every time we have them over." I still for a moment, soaking in what he's said. I can't seem to wrap my head around the idea that my best friend, who used to despise Milo, likes him and sees him often enough that she has a favorite dish he cooks for her.

"I think I'll make it with white wine this time." He pulls a half-full bottle of pinot grigio from the fridge. "Think she'll like that?"

"She'll love it."

He smiles, and that familiar warmth courses through me. The two weeks since I kissed Milo have been a blur. Work has been busy for the both of us. And he's been out of town a handful of times for work trips. By the time Milo made it home at night, it was so late I was already in bed. And most of the mornings when I woke up, he was already gone for work.

It's done the strangest thing . . . it's made me miss him.

"It's good that we're making time to get together with them," Milo says as he gathers ingredients and sets them on the counter. "I'll be swamped with work these next couple of weeks."

I remind myself that he's moving forward in time; he hasn't already lived these days like I have.

"Yeah. You're right," I say as I stand in the kitchen and watch him. This is the first night we'll go to bed together.

That feeling in my chest intensifies.

He rubs the back of his neck, his burnt-sienna stare flitting to the ground before meeting my gaze once more. "Sometimes I think about how she hated me. Before she got to know me."

"She was kind of like me in that way," I say.

The corner of his mouth yanks up in a half smile as a quiet chuckle falls from his lips. He steps over to me, pulling me close against him. I don't freeze. I don't tense. I sink into the sensation. I like this, the way he touches me. I like feeling his body against mine.

"I won you both over eventually," he says before winking at me. His phone rings. He sighs. "Work again. I'll cook when I get home later."

He answers and chats while putting away the ingredients, then gathers his wallet and keys. He walks over to the coat closet, grabs his coat, and heads out to work.

I watch him, finally able to put a name to that feeling inside me.

Anticipation.

I'm eager and curious to see how things end up between us tonight.

⁓

"Swear to bloody fucking god, I'm done with red wine in bolognese. White wine is a thousand times better. Well done, Milo." Poppy raises her wineglass, which makes Milo, who's sitting across from her at the tall, pub-style wooden dining table in the kitchen, laugh.

"I mean it," she says after taking another bite of pasta. "I never knew it was this much better with white wine than red wine."

"My mom's recipe," Milo says. "She'll be thrilled to know she's converted another bolognese lover to the white wine side."

Milo offers both Poppy and Desmond another helping of his pasta, which they both say yes to.

"Can you teach Desmond this recipe?"

"You don't want to learn?" Milo asks her.

Desmond chuckles. "Mate, she doesn't cook, remember? That's my job in this marriage. Keep her well fed."

"And well fucked," Poppy murmurs before sipping her wine.

Milo and I burst out laughing the same moment Desmond turns beet red.

He lets out a huffy stammer. "Christ, Poppy. Must you be so crass?"

She rolls her eyes before bumping him affectionately with her shoulder. "Babe, we're amongst friends. They know what I'm like."

I pat Desmond's hand. "It would be weird if she didn't have a filthy mouth."

His pinched expression eases slightly. "I suppose you're right."

Poppy leans closer to him. Her face is so close to his that if he turned to look at her, they'd bump noses. "Admit it. You love my filthy fucking mouth."

Despite his cheeks being on fire, he starts to smile. "I love your filthy mouth," he mumbles to his plate of pasta.

She tilts her head at him. "Say it."

Desmond sighs and shakes his head. The corner of his mouth quirks up slightly, indicating he's secretly into all this teasing. "I love your filthy fucking mouth, Poppy."

Milo claps. "Aww, man, you did it. You said something dirty. In front of other people. This is huge."

I fall back in my chair, I'm laughing so hard.

"But the real question is . . ." Milo takes a breath, suddenly serious. "Does Gus like the sauce?"

We all laugh as Poppy lowers a tiny spoonful of beef to Gus, who's been napping at her feet. He sniffs it before devouring it.

"It's a winner," Poppy announces.

Just then Coco trots out from the bedroom. She takes one look at Gus and hisses at him.

"Coco, be nice," Milo says.

She completely ignores him and hisses once more before darting back to the bedroom. Gus gives a weak yip before scurrying back to Poppy's feet.

"Aww, so brave," she teases.

"Someday they'll get along," Milo says.

"Fat chance," Poppy says.

I almost tell Poppy that she's right, but I catch myself. I already know that Gus and Coco won't warm up to each other.

Milo stands up from his chair, heads to the fridge, opens it, and pulls out a chilled bottle of sparkling white wine. "I'd say Desmond's dirty-talk moment calls for a toast."

He fetches four champagne flutes from the cupboard. As he pops the bottle and pours, I take in the scene. Milo, Desmond, and Poppy chatting, getting along as though they're old friends. Which I suppose they sort of are, given that it sounds like we've all been friends for the better part of the past year. I suppose I'll find out more as I go back in time. *If* I continue to go backward.

Still, though, I'm stunned as I sit quietly and take it all in. Never in a million years did I ever think things would turn out this way. But there's something about this dynamic—it's so easy and fun and natural. It feels different from when I was with Tristan and we'd hang out with Poppy and Desmond. Yeah, we had fun, but not like this—not bellyache-inducing laughs or hilarious inappropriate conversations. I've never seen buttoned-up Desmond so relaxed and jokey before.

Even as I observe them chat and laugh, something about this feels so surreal, like it's a dream.

And then I think about what will happen if I keep going backward in time . . . eventually I'll hit the moment when Tristan and I were still together, still married . . .

What will I do then? Will I have to live that nightmare over and over, waking up every day to a husband who I know is cheating on me? Will we fight and argue every morning when I wake up and confront him? That sounds like hell . . . I don't want to live like that . . .

My stomach folds into itself, threatening all the yummy food I just ate. I take a slow, quiet breath and try my best to shove the thought from my mind. I can't worry about that. I need to just focus on the moment and enjoy the time now.

Milo hands me a glass of sparkling wine and sits back down next to me at the table. "A toast to my boy Desmond for waving his freak flag." He tilts his glass to Desmond. "Congrats, man. I always knew you had it in you."

"Hear, hear!" Poppy cheers.

The four of us clink glasses and down our drinks. We finish up, and Desmond offers to clear the table.

When Milo starts to work on the dishes, Poppy makes a face. "Oi, leave it. That can wait till later."

Milo chuckles and joins the rest of us on the sectional in the living room.

"You know, you two are the only people I know in all of London— no, England—that have a couch this massive," Poppy says, topping off her glass.

"It's a sectional," Milo says.

Poppy frowns. "A what?"

Milo explains what a sectional is.

Poppy shakes her head. "So bloody American."

"I guess it makes sense seeing as we're both American." I gently elbow Poppy.

Milo flips on the TV so he and Desmond can catch the end of some football game. Milo offers Desmond the last of the champagne.

"No more?" Poppy asks.

Milo shakes his head. "All we've got left is hard alcohol."

"Oh!" Poppy claps her hands. "How about a drinking game?"

Desmond groans. "What are we, sixteen?"

"Oh, don't be a killjoy, Des. It's been ages since we've done a proper drinking game."

"And for good reason. We're not teenagers."

Poppy gives Desmond a playful kick with her bare foot. She turns to me. "Please, Ri? One drinking game?"

I release a dramatic sigh. "Okay."

She lets out a squeal. Milo stands up and grabs a bottle of bourbon from the drink cart that rests along the kitchen wall. Coco saunters out from the bedroom and hops on the arm of the couch next to me, all the while eyeing Gus, who's snoozing next to Poppy's purse across the room.

"What should we play?" Milo asks as he pours shots in our empty flutes.

"Truth or dare."

Desmond groans at Poppy's suggestion. "I'm not doing dares. That's childish."

"Fine. How about we just play the truth part; then if you don't want to answer the question, you drink a shot?"

A light bulb in my head goes off. This game could be a way to get more info on the year that I missed.

I flash a thumbs-up at Poppy's modification. Milo and Desmond say yes.

"Okay! Desmond, you're first: If you could shag anyone in the world other than me, who would it be?"

Desmond's cheeks go crimson for the tenth time this evening. He stammers, then pulls off his glasses, opens his mouth, and immediately shuts it. He downs the whiskey in his glass.

"Aww, Des. Come on," Poppy coos.

Milo chuckles. "You're gonna give the poor guy a stroke."

She stands up to switch places with Milo and snuggles into Desmond after she sits back down. "Come on." She slinks her arms around his neck. "I'm dying to know."

"Well, if you must . . ." Desmond huffs out a breath. "Priyanka Chopra."

Poppy beams and pats his back. "Good choice. She's stunning. I'd shag her too."

Desmond shakes his head. "Okay, I suppose I get to go next?"

We all say yes.

"Milo, what is your death row meal?"

Poppy rolls her eyes. "Christ. That's not a fun question at all."

"Yeah, come on, Desmond," Milo says good-naturedly. "Gimme a tough one."

"Oh. Well." I smile at how Desmond rolls his shoulders back and frowns slightly in concentration. He pulls out his phone.

"What are you doing?" Poppy asks.

"Looking up the most common truth-or-dare questions."

"Of course you are," she says before downing a shot.

"Oh, I've got a good one! If you could run over anyone with your car without consequence, who would it be?"

Poppy gives Desmond a nod of approval.

Milo chuckles. "Easy. Kim Jong Un. Or Vladimir Putin. Or Craig at the office, who always shirks out of buying a round during office get-togethers."

"You can only pick one."

"Vladimir Putin."

Milo turns to Poppy. "Okay, you. What's your favorite sex position?"

Poppy raises an eyebrow as she takes Desmond's bearded chin in her hand. "Doggy."

She plants a kiss on him, and he makes a muffled noise. I burst out laughing. Desmond shakes his head, looking both amused and flustered.

"Okay, Ri! Your turn. What do you prefer: cut or uncut?"

It takes me a second to understand what she means. When I do, I nearly spit out my shot. It's been so long since we've played a drinking game, I forgot just how wild my best friend gets.

"Um, well . . ."

My gaze flits to Milo, who sports an amused smirk. Here's the problem: I haven't the slightest clue what Milo's dick looks like, and I don't want to hurt his feelings based on the answer I give.

"I like both," I say quickly.

Poppy rolls her eyes.

"I'm serious," I say, my tone strong with the conviction I feel. "I honestly like the way both look. Because, well, you know, when a dick gets hard, cut or uncut, they look pretty similar."

Milo laughs. Desmond makes a choking noise before staring at the TV screen.

"That's an epic nonanswer," Poppy mutters.

I shrug. "It's the truth. Ugh, fine." I down a shot of bourbon. "Okay, my turn to ask a question: Poppy, when did you start to like Milo?"

The slight rise of her brow indicates that she's surprised at what I've asked.

"Hmm. Bold question there, Ri. You should already know the answer to that." She frowns at me, but I can tell she's more amused than annoyed. She turns to look at Milo. "The night of the pub fire."

I think about when I saw Nesta at Luscious, how she mentioned that night and what Milo did, how he stood up for me. That must be what Poppy is talking about.

"Same," Desmond adds.

I'm about to ask another question, eager to find out more, but then
I look at Poppy. I go quiet at her expression, how it borders on tender
as she focuses on Milo. Desmond has a similar look on his face. Less
tender, though, more like he respects the hell out of Milo for what he
did that night.

Milo looks between them, a soft, shy smile on his face. "Glad I
could finally change your minds about me." He lets out a weak laugh.
I can tell he's half joking, but there's a rawness in his tone and his
expression. It means a lot to him to hear Desmond and Poppy say that.

Poppy reaches over and pats Milo's arm. Desmond nods once at
him. I suddenly feel like an outsider intruding on this moment between
the three of them as they quietly acknowledge a significant moment in
their friendship.

In their timeline, I know what happened. But in mine, I don't. If I
keep moving backward in time, though, I'll find out eventually.

The air in the room has shifted now. Like an emotional quiet has
fallen over us. And now I feel like a jerk for trying to turn what should
be a lighthearted game into a fact-finding mission.

Maybe I shouldn't be so focused on digging up information. Maybe
I need to just accept the timeline I'm currently in, no matter how strange
and disorienting it is. Things will unfold the way they're supposed to.

I clear my throat. "Sorry, I didn't mean to throw off the vibe like
that."

Poppy knocks back a shot. "It's all right. Next question!"

We play two more rounds, with Poppy sticking to sex-themed questions and Desmond getting huffy each time.

"Looks like it's up to me to restore some degree of sensibility to this
game," he says before consulting his phone once more. "Ah! This is a
good one: Milo, what was the last lie you told?"

It's not till I'm downing the last of my drink that I notice that Milo
has gone quiet. His stubbled cheeks turn rosy, and he can't seem to meet
the eyes of anyone in the room.

His jaw muscle bulges as he bites down. I think he's going to say something, but his lips stay pursed until he knocks back his entire glass of whiskey.

I exchange a look with Poppy, who presses on with the game, offering another ridiculous question that lightens the mood. The rest of the night, though, I wonder what in the world that look on Milo's face was about.

Chapter 13

"You're wondering what I lied about, aren't you?"

Milo's whispered question while we're in bed together catches me off guard. It shouldn't. It's exactly what I was thinking about as I lay down, eyes closed, trying to force myself to go to sleep.

But I'm wide awake, and the reason why is exactly what he's said.

I shift and roll over so I'm facing him. Even though it's dark, I can still make out the shape of his body, the expression on his face. His eyebrows are knitted together, like he's worried about what I'm thinking—about what I'll say.

"Yeah, I am," I say after a moment.

He nods and glances at some spot over my shoulder. "It was nothing bad."

"I know." I don't know why I know this. I just do. Just like I know the sky is blue and grass is green. "You don't have to tell me," I say after a quiet moment. "I'm just curious. I don't have a right to pry."

"Riley, if I were you, I'd be curious too." He pauses. "It was nothing, really. Just something so silly, so insignificant, I don't even know why I . . ." He tugs a hand through his hair. I can just barely make out the movement as my eyes adjust to the darkness.

I rest my hand on his arm. He relaxes immediately. I can feel his muscles under my palm loosening the longer I touch him.

"It was this evening on my way home from work," he says. "I passed by a street vendor selling tulips. He said to me, 'Why don't you take some home and surprise the wife? Make her day with some lovely tulips.' And I dropped a few bills into his jar and said, 'My wife prefers peonies.'"

He sighs, his hot breath sheeting across my neck and chest. Goose bumps fly across my skin. For a long moment I'm quiet. I'm stunned. I wasn't expecting him to say that.

Wife.

"It was strange," he says. "The words just rolled off my tongue. I wasn't even thinking about it in the moment as I said them. It wasn't until I got a few steps down that I realized what I said."

More silence. Another heavy sigh.

"I'm sorry, Riley. I . . . I know I had no right to lie about you like that. I swear it was harmless, but I know that doesn't take away from how wrong it was. Or how weird it was. I swear, I'm not engaging in some creepy fantasy about you as my wife."

He laces his fingers with mine. His skin is warm and dry despite the flat's chilly temperature. He gives my hand a squeeze, then another. Something about that double squeeze is so comforting. It's playful but at the same time heartening.

I lie there and take in the significance of this moment, what all this means.

It means that at this point in our relationship, Milo has developed some serious feelings for me.

His admission should freak me out. I should be running for the hills.

But I don't feel panicked or freaked out. I'm surprised, for sure, but also intrigued. I feel even more drawn to him, more comforted, more content. He starts to speak, but I press my fingers to his mouth, shushing him.

"Don't say another word," I whisper. I've scooted so close to him that I can see the gleam in his eyes, how he's confused and intrigued all at once.

I take my hand away, replacing it with my lips. It's a soft kiss I press on Milo's mouth. It lasts only a few seconds before I pull away, but I don't miss the dazed look in his eyes.

By now I can see Milo almost perfectly in the darkness. I can make out all the features on his face—that thick, dark stubble, those deep walnut-hued eyes, the hard angle of his jaw, the fullness of his lips, the slight furrow of his brow, the wave of his black-brown hair.

I slide my palm to the front of his chest, the steady thrum of his heart a soft drumbeat against my hand. I close my eyes and savor his warmth, the firmness of his body, the even rhythm of his breath.

My muscles relax as my entire body sinks deeper into that comforted feeling.

I move even closer to him, pressing my body against his until all I can feel is heat.

He pulls away slightly. "Riley, wait."

I open my eyes. His hands cup gently around my face. His gaze is cloudy and searching.

"What I said really didn't bother you?" he asks, his chest rising and falling when he breathes.

"It didn't bother me. I like that you called me your wife."

He blinks, staring at me for a few seconds, like he's thinking about what I've said. Like he's trying to make sure he heard me right.

I can tell he's still unsure. But instead of trying to think of more things to say to convince him, I stay quiet and cuddle back into him. I slide my arms around his chest and hold tight, hoping this is enough to show him exactly how I feel about him. A beat later, his body relaxes against mine. He strokes my hair, his hand so gentle as he threads it through the strands, emotion surges up my throat. I take a second to breathe, to swallow.

"So we're good then? You're not upset?" he asks, his voice soft.

"Not upset at all. We're good."

I feel his body relax around mine, like the stress and tension he carried in anticipation of this conversation are melting away.

I know there's still so much I don't understand; there's still so much I don't know.

But what I do know is that I like Milo. I like how much he cares about me. I like that his feelings for me have deepened.

And in this moment—in this world, in this timeline—he's the only one I want.

Chapter 14

When I wake up, I'm naked.

"What the . . . ?" I mutter to myself right as the sleep fog dissipates. And that's when I notice Milo isn't in bed.

I start to sit up and blink furiously in the dimness of early morning. I frown when I spot the white Christmas tree lights hanging around the bed. A second later, as I wake up even more, I spot the Christmas decorations I set out every year in the bedroom: a cute Santa figurine on the nightstand and a mini fake Christmas tree in the windowsill.

As the sleep fog dissipates, I remember that it's the first week in January. I always leave the Christmas tree decorations out until this week.

But that doesn't explain why I'm naked this morning.

Just then I hear soft clanking through the bedroom door. Milo must be doing something in the kitchen.

My bladder is aching, so I crawl out of bed and spot my pajama top, which is in a pile on the floor in front of the bed. I throw it on and scurry to the bathroom, pee, wash my hands, then step back into the bedroom right as Milo opens the bedroom door, mug of tea in hand.

He stops when he sees me, a hesitant look on his face. "Hey."

His voice is soft and low and gravelly like it always is this early in the morning. But his expression is off. His mahogany eyes are shy. He's hesitating.

"Bedside tea service?" I joke.

The corner of his mouth hooks up in a crooked smile. "Yeah. Figured it would be a good way to make amends."

"Make amends?" I almost say, "For what?" but I catch myself. There's no rational way to explain that I'm living life backward, and I have no idea what went down between the two of us.

He shrugs. "I know you said last night that everything is good between us, but I had to do something. I was kind of a jerk."

Oh. We must have had an argument.

I think about the days that I've already lived—the days that technically come after today. Nothing felt off. Whatever we went through, we must resolve the last of it today.

He steps toward me, closing the space between us. He sets the steaming tea mug on the nightstand, grabs me gently by the waist, and pulls me into him. He presses his lips to my forehead.

"I'm sorry, Riley."

For a moment I'm tense. It's hard not to be when I don't really know what's going on. But a beat later, it's like my body knows exactly what to do. I feel my muscles relax. I start to sink into Milo's embrace.

It's like my body is able to gauge what's going on before my brain can process it.

My body is saying this hug, this embrace from Milo, is safe. It's all okay.

"It's okay," I say out loud.

His body relaxes under my embrace.

He pulls away before flashing a tender smile down at me.

"Breakfast?" he asks.

I nod. "That sounds nice."

I grab my tea mug and follow him into the kitchen. As I lean on the island and sip my tea, Milo cooks for the two of us. I watch him as he moves effortlessly through the kitchen. The expression on his face is relaxed and easy.

I think of the night when he admitted he called me his wife to a stranger and felt guilty about it, how we resolved it before falling asleep. I think about how we seem to work out whatever problems we have quickly. I think about how Milo is direct yet kind when he's bothered by something. He doesn't push his feelings aside and instead comes to me to try to work out whatever we're going through.

It's so different from what I was used to with Tristan. Because Tristan and I hardly ever fought or disagreed. But now I realize that wasn't a good thing. We never fought because he hid all the awful things he did to me. And because I pushed aside my hurt feelings whenever his mom or grandparents insulted me.

I think of my own parents—how much they fought about everything while they were married. In most of my memories of them, they were arguing, over bills, money, spending time with us, chores, visiting relatives, how to raise my brother and me. I told myself I'd never marry someone if we argued all the time.

That's probably why I thought Tristan and I were so solid. We never fought. I thought no fighting and arguing automatically meant a healthy relationship. But it doesn't, not always. Not when you're hiding things from your partner. I sip my tea as I think over what I'm about to wake up to in the morning. Milo looks up from the stove and flashes an easy smile. I smile at him in return, feeling calm. Whatever it is, we work through it. It's all okay.

Chapter 15

January 6, 2025

"We should go for a walk," Milo says as he peers out the kitchen window.

I look up from my phone at him. "It's snowing."

He aims a teasing smile at me. "And?"

"And it's cold. It'll be a slushy nightmare out there."

"So?" he says, that teasing smile still in place. He shakes out his hands at his sides. "Come on, we've been cooped up indoors this past week because of the crummy weather. Maybe we should just embrace it and trudge out there."

I groan, not at all in the mood to head out in this wintry mess.

Milo sticks out his bottom lip. "Please? Just, like, a half hour of walking around. Then we'll stop someplace warm for a drink."

I chuckle. "Okay. I'm in."

He fist-pumps the air. I head to the closet and grab my coat. As I'm slipping on my boots, I wonder if the weather is what we end up fighting about.

It can't be. That would be too cute. Like something out of a Hallmark movie.

It's a slushy trudge through the neighborhood.

"See? Told you this would be an absolute blast." Milo laughs and tugs at his beanie, which is covered in fat snowflakes. "Better than a walk on the beach, right?"

I laugh. We make it to a pub, and Milo rushes ahead to grab the door for me. When I peer around the dimly lit space, I'm surprised it's so crowded on a day when the weather is so bad.

"Guess we weren't the only ones aching to get out for a bit," Milo says.

We find an empty booth near the back. He heads to the bar and returns with a pint for himself and a mug of something steaming for me.

"Hot toddy," he says when he sets it in front of me.

I thank him and take a long sip, humming at the rich and satisfying taste. Just then I'm jolted by a shriek-laugh noise in the booth behind us. I frown while Milo winces.

"Damn. They sound like they're having a good time," Milo says.

I chuckle and start to say something, but I trail off when I hear what they're talking about.

"I just feel so guilty, how we started out," a gentle voice says. "I mean, by all accounts it was cheating. Plain and simple. I was the other woman for months and months. Until I . . . well, you know."

"Oh, hon, don't beat yourself up about it. You weren't the other woman. You were the right woman. Tristan just took a while to figure it out."

That sip of hot toddy settles like acid in my belly. When I look at Milo, his cheery expression melts from his face. He goes pale.

"I chalk it up to first-marriage syndrome," a woman with an Australian accent says. "Some men just need to get that first one out of their systems, hey. His ex was a lingerie model, right? Not many red-blooded men can resist a pretty tart, as sad as that is."

A chorus of murmured agreeing noises follows.

"The important part is who he ended up with. And that's you, Carly. Maybe it wasn't the neat-and-tidy fairy-tale love story, but it ended up that way. Now you've got a boyfriend and a baby and your dream house in Hampstead. You came out on top, hon."

It feels like a million tiny, invisible needles are stabbing into my skin. A second ago I was chilly, but now the heat of shame has consumed me as I sit here and listen to Carly and her friends talk shit about me, unaware that I'm sitting right behind them and can hear every word they spew.

When I glance up at Milo, he's clenching his jaw, death-glaring his pint glass. I notice he's gripping it so hard, his knuckles are white.

When he looks at me, raw pity paints his gaze and his expression.

Carly's crew lets out another shriek-laugh. Milo's eyebrows crash together. "Enough of this," he mutters.

He bolts up from our table. "Milo, don't," I say. But he clears the few steps to their booth in a second.

I twist around and see him standing at their booth. He smiles at them, and for a second I'm jolted. That's the same smile he used to give Tristan and me. That taunting, insincere smirk.

"Ladies. I couldn't help but overhear your lively chat."

A few of them chuckle, clearly dazzled by Milo's handsome sudden appearance.

"Milo? What are you doing here?" I hear Carly say.

"I just had to stop by and say that your friends are some of the most classless assholes I've had the displeasure of sitting next to."

My jaw plummets to the floor at what Milo has just said. I hear some of them gasp.

"Milo, how dare you speak to my friends like that," Carly bites.

He lets out a bitter laugh. "Carly, I've always been cordial to you. And if I happen to see you after this at some family event or with your baby, I'll be cordial again. But I'm sure as hell not going to be cordial while you and your friends loudly shit-talk Riley within earshot of us."

Silence follows. It's then that I realize just how fast my heart is beating. And the fact that almost the entire pub has gone quiet as they watch Milo go off on Carly's table of friends. All of them peer over at me, and that "needle in my skin" feeling intensifies. We're a sideshow. Great.

Anxiety sweat seeps through my pores.

"Riley hasn't uttered a single negative word about you this whole time. Did you realize that?" Milo says.

There's no response, only silence. I hold my breath as I wait to see if Carly or any of her friends attempt to reply. But as the seconds crawl by, still nothing.

Milo shakes his head. "Pathetic."

He starts to leave but stops and turns back around to Carly. "You should probably start getting regular STI checks now that you're with Tristan. He's not the most faithful guy on the planet. What a lucky lady you are to land a catch like him."

Someone sitting in their booth gasps. Milo walks back to me, grabs his pint glass, and downs half of it. He grabs his coat, clearly a silent proclamation for us to get the hell out of here. My stomach is so knotted, I don't even bother to drink any more of my hot toddy. I grab my coat and yank it on. My face burns as I walk toward the entrance, feeling every stare from Carly and her crew like laser beams searing my skin.

I shove through the door and walk as fast as I can along the slushy sidewalk.

"Riley, wait!" Milo calls behind me.

I don't bother to stop, though. I can't. I'm too upset, too humiliated.

I don't slow down until I feel a gentle hand on my shoulder. "Riley, would you hold on?"

I spin around and look up at Milo. His cheeks are flushed as he catches his breath.

"What's wrong?" He scans my face, like he's worried about me.

I shake my head, the frustration bubbling in my chest like lava. "Why did you cause such a scene?"

He stands there, his mouth agape, like he can't fathom why in the world I would be upset.

"Wait, are you mad at me?"

I let out an exasperated laugh. "Yeah, Milo. I'm pissed. That was fucking humiliating."

He holds up his gloved hands like he's surrendering. "Whoa, whoa, hang on a second. You think *I* am the one who humiliated you? Not Carly and her friends?"

I press my eyes shut and tug a hand through my hair, which is covered in snowflakes.

"Carly and her friends were assholes. But god, Milo. You made it worse. Everyone in the pub was staring at us like we were a *Jerry Springer* segment."

"So?" Milo says without missing a beat.

I let out another laugh of pure disbelief. "Do you really not understand why I'm upset?"

He exhales. "I really don't, Riley. I thought I was doing the right thing, sticking up for you."

"Milo, this is a fucked-up situation. You're in a relationship with your cousin's ex-wife. You think getting into a public fight is going to make family gatherings and holiday dinners easier? It's going to be a million times more awkward now. Sometimes it's better to just ignore the crap and keep the peace."

Milo blinks like he doesn't understand a word I'm saying. A beat passes. His frown eases as he gazes at me. He takes a step toward me, the look on his face sad, bordering on pitying.

"Riley. If you want a guy who just stands on the sidelines when you're being insulted, you're with the wrong one." He pauses to swallow. "I know Tristan didn't stand up for you around his family—*our* family. And when it happened, I stood by and bit my tongue, too, because it wasn't my business. But now that we're together, it *is* my business. I don't care who it is. I don't care how awkward it makes family dinners or gatherings or holidays or whatever. I'll always defend you."

He walks off in the direction of the flat, leaving me stunned on the sidewalk as I realize just how wrong I was to get upset at him.

～

I spend an hour walking around the neighborhood, going over everything that happened tonight. By the time I make it home, Milo is in bed. I shed my soaking-wet coat and hang it up by the fireplace to dry. As quietly as I can, I walk into the darkened hallway to the primary bathroom.

As hot water rains around me, I think about everything Milo said, and everything I said when we argued outside the pub.

He was right.

The moment he walked away, I knew he was right.

I think about how, in the three years we were together, Tristan hardly ever defended me when his mom or grandparents would lob some insult or underhanded comment at me. Or ignore me.

I think about how badly it stung that first time . . . and how I pushed aside my feelings, my urge to confront Tristan, just to keep the peace. Just to fit in with a family that didn't want me in the first place.

That shame from earlier roasts me from the inside out again. Only this time I'm embarrassed at myself. At how long I put up with that. At how it warped my sense of right and wrong. At how my first instinct was to lash out at Milo when he defended me instead of feeling happy to be with someone who would stand up for me without a second thought.

I think of what Nesta said, how Milo stood up for me to his grandparents. Was he as angry and bold with them as he was with Carly and her friends?

If he was, I'm blown away. He's incredible not to let who he's standing up to affect how he reacts.

I close my eyes, savoring the hot water as it pummels my body. When I finish washing up and rinsing, I turn off the water. I dry off and get ready for bed.

I slip on my pajamas and crawl into bed beside Milo, my heart racing. His back is facing me. I slide my arms around him and hug him from behind. I feel him stiffen underneath my embrace. His breathing changes from the steady rhythm of sleep to a long inhale. He's awake.

I kiss his bare shoulder and whisper, "I'm sorry."

"I'm sorry too," he murmurs, his voice soft and low and thick with sleep. "I shouldn't have gotten so upset. If you really want me to back off when—"

"I don't want that," I say, cutting him off. I hug him tight. "I'm not used to having my partner defend me. It threw me off. I realize now how messed up that is. And I don't want to be like that anymore. I liked that you stood up for me, Milo. It meant everything. Thank you."

He lets out a slow hiss of breath before turning over to face me. By now my eyes have adjusted to the darkness, and I can make out Milo's open expression, the tender look in his eyes.

I cup his face in my hands and pull his mouth to mine. I press a soft kiss to his lips. I don't pull away; I let my mouth linger. I savor the soft feel of his lips, the warmth of his skin, the soft hum he makes. It feels good. Really, really good.

I probably shouldn't be doing this. But I don't care. For a long time I did everything I was supposed to do. I was a loving and supportive wife who never questioned my husband, who trusted him implicitly. For a long time I loathed his cousin and gave him the cold shoulder. And look how well that all turned out.

For a long time I had the wrong idea about Tristan *and* Milo.

From now on I'll do what I like—what feels right.

With my lips still pressed against his, I run my tongue along his bottom lip. When he moans softly, I shiver. His hand grips my hip as I part his lips with my tongue. He's letting me lead this, letting me set the rhythm, letting me deepen the kiss.

I moan, my skin flushed and hot. I run my fingers through his hair, tugging lightly. We're pressed together now, just the thin fabric of my shirt separating us, since he sleeps shirtless.

I lean back, breaking the kiss. I reach down, palming the hardness between his legs, never once breaking eye contact. His eyes flutter slightly as I work him in my hand. Between my legs, I'm aching and soaked.

I lean in to give Milo a soft kiss. With my hands on his chest, I push him to lie on his back and straddle him.

I pull up my sleeping shirt and push at the waistband of his boxers. Those mahogany-brown eyes widen slightly. Then the corner of his mouth hooks up. He licks his lips. He rests his hands on my hips and groans slightly as I press against the hardness between his legs.

I'm on fire. Inside, outside, everywhere. There's heat at my core—it's spreading up my chest to my neck, down to my lower abdomen. I'm panting as I work against him, that spot between my legs aching.

There's so much that I can't control in this timeline. But this? My pleasure, Milo's pleasure, our pleasure together . . . that I can control.

"I want you, Milo." My voice is a breathy whine.

He nods, moving me slightly farther up his body. "I want you too." He reaches for the drawer of the bedside table next to him, pulls out a foil square, and rips it open with his teeth. I swipe it from him and twist my torso slightly so I can roll the condom on him.

When I get a look at him down there, I pause. I can't help but think of the game of truth or dare when Poppy asked if I preferred cut or uncut. When I told her both, I was being honest. And now that I get a look at what Milo has, I can confirm to myself that it still holds true. He's uncut and it's hot as hell. But I'd like him just as much if the opposite were the case.

When I slide onto him, we let out dual curses.

Our language gets even filthier when I start to ride him. He leans up, taking my nipple in his mouth. My eyes roll back at the jolt of pleasure, at the shivers that ghost across my skin, the pleasure that builds within me at just the swirl of his tongue.

His hands are everywhere. My back, my hips, my ass, my hair. He ends with his thumb on my clit, circling gently, confidently. My jaw plummets to the floor, and I know I'm about to break. He tells me how beautiful I am, how hot this is, how good I feel. It's a pleasure cocktail, a turn-on to the nth degree. Sex with Milo feels physically amazing, but to hear him shower me in praise takes the pleasure to stratospheric levels.

It's not long before I'm shouting and writhing around him. I collapse on his chest, hugging his sweat-soaked skin.

"Wow," I mutter.

I feel the rumble of his throaty chuckle vibrate against me. "You always say that."

I bite my tongue just before I say, "Do I?" If that's what it's like every time with Milo, of course I'd say "Wow."

He rips off the used condom and tosses it to the floor. When he rests his hands on my waist, I think he's about to move me off him so he can run to the restroom, but he pulls me up his body until I'm straddling his face.

I glance down, my heart thudding in giddy anticipation of what he's about to do.

He licks his lips before kissing the inside of my thigh. "Riley."

My name is a whispered request on his tongue. I nod at him, ready for everything Milo is about to give me.

When his tongue makes contact with the most sensitive spot on my entire body, I'm trembling with pleasure.

Screw everything around us. Screw what anyone thinks. This is right. This is what I want. This is what *we* want. That's all that matters.

Chapter 16

November 20, 2024

I don't know why I let myself get comfortable, to expect that things would stay this way indefinitely. I'm living life backward. Each morning I wake up, I have no idea what's in store for me. I should expect the unexpected. But December was an exquisite month. Like, truly exquisite. Mornings filled with sleepy cuddles and kisses in bed, busy days at work, quiet evenings at home eating dinner on the couch together. Christmas was perfectly low-key. Instead of a grand gift exchange, Milo and I spent the day lounging around the flat, drinking hot cocoa and watching our favorite holiday movies. A few times we hung out with Desmond and Poppy. I've gotten used to this new routine of our life.

For that reason, I yelp when I walk out to the living room this morning and see my younger brother, Jordan, passed out on our sectional. There he is, his six-four frame sprawled over the plush white couch cushions, his socked feet dangling off the arm. From under the fuzzy beige blanket, he snores. Coco is curled in a fluffy white circle on top of him.

"He sounds like a freight train," Milo mumbles from the kitchen.

"Um, how did he . . . when did he . . . ?" I catch myself as I drift off.

Milo's chuckle is a low rumble in his deepened morning voice. He takes a long sip from his coffee mug. "Glad I'm not the only one who's lost track of time during his impromptu visit. Two weeks is more than long enough with your brother. Especially all the late nights. Don't get me wrong. I love the guy."

Milo groans softly as he rubs the back of his neck. "Your little brother lives like a tornado."

I nod, taking in the state of the living room. Jordan's open suitcase rests in the corner, looking like a bomb exploded out of it. Wrinkled clothes and shoes lay scattered in and around it. His coat sits in a rumpled pile on the floor. On the coffee table are his phone, a half dozen empty coffee mugs, and three plates.

"I guess he couldn't even make it to the guest room last night." Milo sighs.

"I'll take care of it," I say to him. "Sorry about all this. And sorry we were out late on a work night."

He smiles and reaches to tuck a chunk of my hair behind my ear. "Don't be. He's your family. This is your place. And he doesn't get to visit often, so I'm happy to stay up and hang out with him when he's here." He glances at his phone. "His flight's at noon. You still good to take him to the airport?"

I nod, feeling a pinch in my chest that my little brother, who I haven't seen in more than a year, is leaving. But then I remember that I'll have two whole weeks to spend with him, just backward.

Milo's phone buzzes. He smiles at the screen. "It's my mom. Get ready, she's gonna wanna talk to you."

"Oh . . ." I'm nervous. I have no idea if that's a good or bad thing.

Milo takes my hand gently in his and walks us back to the bedroom as he answers. "*Mãe.* How are you?"

My stomach ties itself in knots as I listen to Milo chat happily to his mom. Tristan never handed the phone to me to talk with his mom, and for good reason, since she couldn't stand me. But I'm guessing by the way Milo was smiling when he said his mom will want to talk with me, she likes me.

I hope she does. At the very least I hope she doesn't hate me.

After a minute of Milo chatting in Portuguese and English, he chuckles.

"Sure, she's right here." He smiles and hands me the phone before stepping away and into the bathroom, closing the door behind him.

"H-hi . . ." I realize that I have no idea what her name is.

"Riley! *Querida!* How are you?"

I'm quiet for a second, stunned at how genuinely happy she sounds to hear from me. Actually, "giddy" is a better word.

My shoulders begin to loosen. I register that she's used a Portuguese word that I remember hearing growing up in the Bay Area. I think it means "dear."

My insides go warm. "Dear" is such a common word of endearment that exists in so many languages, but that doesn't matter. She sounds like she means it when she calls me that.

"I'm good, thanks," I say. "How are you?"

"Oh, you know how it is. Work, work, work. But! I took today off to go shopping with my sister. Actually . . . what's the word Milo uses . . . 'hooky'? I'm playing hooky."

She lets out a melodic laugh that reminds me of the way Milo laughs. His is lower and deeper than her sweet tone, but the rhythm is the same. Boisterous and full and bright.

"Good for you," I say, feeling even more at ease. "You deserve to have a little fun when you've been working so much."

Another sweet chuckle. "I knew you'd understand. So tell me! How's your shop?"

I tell her how busy the store has been while I silently try to figure out just how well we know each other. Based on how comfortable she is when she speaks to me, it seems like we've met and talked to each other before. And we seem to get along pretty well.

"That's lovely to hear, *querida*. You work so hard, be sure to take some time for yourself too, okay?"

I can't help but smile at how sweet she's being.

"And how's my Milo treating you? He'd better be good to you."

I'm taken aback by what she's said. Not the way that she's phrased it. Her tone is sweet and light, not accusing at all. It's more that I'm surprised that his own mom would care so much about me, my well-being. It's so . . . genuinely kind of her to care about me like this.

Portia never seemed to care how Tristan treated me.

"He's amazing," I say. "You have nothing to worry about."

"That's good, *querida*." I can tell she's smiling. "But if he slacks off, you just tell me, okay? I'll get him back in line."

She lets out another sweet chuckle. I know she's teasing, but I can also tell she's serious at the same time. And that does something to me. Emotion bubbles in my chest at just how kind she is toward me. How she seems to genuinely care about me. How good it feels. How I never felt it with Portia.

I clear my throat and tell her I will. We say a quick goodbye right as Milo walks back into the bedroom. I hand the phone back to him, and he converses in Portuguese for a moment before hanging up and tossing his phone onto the bed.

He grins at me. "She adores you."

"You think so?"

"Absolutely." Milo reaches both arms up and stretches. "Shower time," he groans. "Good luck with waking up your brother."

He kisses my cheek before heading back into the bathroom. I step to my nightstand, grab my phone, and look up the word "querida" just to be sure. This backward timeline has scrambled my memory a bit.

"Dear."

I take a moment to let that joy settle deep inside me. After having a mother-in-law who hated my guts, that one little word means everything.

I walk over to Jordan, my phone in hand. I carefully scoop up Coco before giving her a kiss on the top of the head and setting her on the nearby armchair. I pull up the Rage Against the Machine playlist on my phone, turn it to full volume, hold it next to Jordan's ear, and blast it. His eyelids fly open, revealing bloodshot eyes, and he shoots up to a sitting position.

"Wh-what the fuck, Riley?" He rubs his eyes with his fists. His floppy ink-black hair sticks out in every direction. "God, turn it off!"

I bite back a giggle and jump-hug him after pausing the music. He makes an "oof" sound but wraps his massive arms around me.

"God. You haven't done that since we were teenagers," Jordan mutters when I release him from the hug and sit next to him on the couch.

"Well, you're pretty much reenacting your teenage days. It seemed fitting." I glance around the living room draped in his dirty laundry and dishes.

"Okay, yeah, you've got a point," he mumbles and inhales. "Coffee?"

"Made by Milo. You need to tell him 'thank you.'"

"I've told him 'thank you' every morning for the coffee."

"Not just that, Jordan. For crashing here."

"I know, I know."

I hold up my hand to block his bottom half, which is adorned only in snug boxer briefs. "Ugh, seriously?"

"What?" He flashes his trademark confused frown and scratches his mop top. "It's uncomfortable to sleep in my jeans."

I groan and roll my eyes. "Can you maybe invest in a pair of pajama pants? Good god."

He leans down to give Coco a scratch under her chin. "Hey now. I make a lowly teacher's salary. Pajama pants are for rich people." He swipes his jeans from under the coffee table and yanks them on over his legs. "I gotta piss."

"Thanks for sharing."

He starts walking toward the hallway bathroom, then stops before turning back to me. "Admit it. You missed me."

He flashes that smug smile I remember from childhood. It conjures a familiar mix of irritation and nostalgia. My little brother drives me nuts. He always has, and I have no doubt he always will. But I love him. This is our dynamic. Giving each other shit and bickering in that good-natured sibling tone between bouts of pulling pranks on each other. We'll be a hundred years old living in the same nursing home doing exactly that all over again.

I smile. "Of course I missed you. Now hurry up and get ready so we can grab breakfast before I take you to the airport."

~

Half an hour later we end up at a café across the street. Jordan wolfs down the biggest full English I've ever seen. I take in his puffy eyes, how his baby face is stubbly. There's a bluish tinge under his eyes. He must be hungover. I glance down and notice that the knuckles of his right hand are swollen. I wonder what he got up to last night.

I scrunch my face at him in mock disgust. "Jesus, Jordan. I'm not gonna take your food from you."

"Ha," he says around a mouthful of toast and black pudding.

The server stops by to refill our coffees. She aims her unblinking stare at Jordan as he does his best impression of a competitive eater.

"Good lad. Quite the appetite."

He smiles up at her, his mouth full. She chuckles and pats his shoulder, her brown eyes lingering on him. I roll my eyes. My little brother is the textbook definition of tall, dark, and handsome, with his leanly muscled build, wavy dark hair, and equally dark eyes. Women go gaga over him everywhere he goes. Drives me mad.

She asks if we need anything else, and I tell her "no, thank you" before taking a few bites of my massive blueberry pancake. "Have I ever told you just how annoying it is that you can charm everyone around you even when you're being absolutely disgusting?"

He chugs his coffee and lets out a satisfied "ahh" sound. "All the time."

"It's because you're a pretty boy, you know," I tease, cutting through my pancake. "No one would put up with you if you looked like an ogre."

He flashes an incredulous look at me. "I know. I'm just flaunting what I've got. Sue me."

I chuckle and roll my eyes.

"So." Jordan pushes his empty plate away from him. "You ready for what I have to say?"

"Um . . . I guess?"

"Come on. I'm leaving in three hours. We put this off long enough. I need to say this."

"What are you talking about?"

"I know you probably don't want to talk about it." He opens his mouth, hesitating. "But I know I have a lot to answer for."

I'm quiet as I process the serious look on my little brother's face. My goofball little brother who often acts more like the teenagers he teaches geography to than the twenty-eight-year-old man he actually is.

"Then say it," I tell him.

He cups his hands around his mug, his dark-brown eyebrows furrowing slightly. I can't remember the last time he looked so serious.

He breathes in, his shoulders rising. "I'm sorry for how I acted last night."

"Okay . . ." What the hell happened?

"I had a lot to drink, but that's not an excuse. And, yeah, I shouldn't have let what Tristan said get to me, but . . ."

As Jordan goes quiet, trying to think of his next words, my brain screeches to a halt, like a record scratch. Jordan got into it with Tristan last night? When? How?

I zero in on his swollen right hand. He winces as he shakes it out. Shit, did Tristan and Jordan fight?

"I never liked the guy. That's no secret." His shoulders slump, and his gaze falls to the tabletop before he looks at me again, his expression somber.

The waitress returns with a plate of spotted dick and sets it in front of him. "Dessert for you, love?"

137

"Always. Thanks, gorgeous." He winks up at her, and she turns five shades of red before walking off.

He devours half of the pudding in a single bite before turning back to me. "Look, if I could take back what I said and did last night, I would. I'm sorry for that. But in the moment, I meant what I said and what I did. You're my sister, Riley. You're my only sibling. Tristan hurt you, and that was bad enough, but the worst part is that he doesn't even seem sorry. And I'll always hate him for that."

I'm quiet for a moment as I take in what he's said. "I probably should have listened to you all those years ago when you met him and said you didn't like him."

He shrugs. "You were in love with him. I wouldn't have listened to you, either, if you had trashed someone I loved."

He finishes the rest of his pudding before sighing and looking at me. "So about Milo." He sighs, his deep-umber eyes softening. "I was wrong about him. He's a good guy. Like, truly. I like him. A lot. You two are good together."

"Seriously?"

He nods and his gaze turns thoughtful. "I can tell you're happy, Riley. It's nice to see after what you went through."

I nod, in quiet awe that my little brother actually likes Milo.

"Thanks, Jordan."

He nods once and taps his palms on the table. He digs out a wad of cash from his wallet and drops it on the table along with a hefty tip. "We'd better head back so I can pack. Don't wanna miss my flight and have to stay with you guys even longer. I know I've worn out my welcome."

We stand up, and I ruffle his hair. "Not quite yet."

A few hours later I drive him to the airport, and we hug goodbye. That night, as I get ready for bed, my body stiffens. When I wake up, I'll get to find out what exactly went down between Tristan and Jordan.

Chapter 17

"Shots! Shots! Shots! We're doing shots, everyone! Woo!"

Jordan carries a tray of tequila shots from the bar and sets it at the standing table where Milo, Desmond, Poppy, and I are.

Desmond pulls a sour face. I touch his arm. "You don't have to drink that."

He flashes a grateful smile and sips his lager, wincing when the beat of an EDM song drops. "I feel about ten years too old to be in here," he says, glancing around at the circular space.

"You and me both." I down the tequila shot and chase it with a gulp of Poppy's cocktail.

Around us a million early twentysomethings dance and writhe. Onstage at the far end of this club, a DJ with spiky fuchsia hair grooves and bobs his head along to the frenetic beat. A rainbow of laser beam lights illuminates the room. A second later, confetti falls from the ceiling for no apparent reason. Everyone on the dance floor cheers.

"This is the last time you get to pick where we go out," I say to Jordan.

"Duh, it's my last night here."

"I mean forever. We're never going out with you again, ever."

"Oh, come on. This is a blast!" He spins around to dance with a group of people nearby. They playfully toss confetti at one another.

I shake my head as I watch him, in disbelief at his energy. This morning he woke me up at the crack of dawn, excited to go sightseeing. I forgot how little sleep he needs.

"Fucking twentysomethings," Poppy mutters before sucking on a lime wedge.

"You were like this once, too, you know." I elbow her.

"I was, wasn't I?" She lets out a "Woo!" that gets swallowed up in the music and cheers. Jordan winks at her and shimmies over to dance alongside her.

"Imagine if we had gone to uni together!" she shouts.

"Oh, we'd have destroyed the city. For sure." Jordan bumps his hip into Poppy's, making her cackle.

A beat later, Poppy glides up to Desmond and slinks her arms around his neck. The corners of his mouth quirk up as he fights a smile.

"This is what you were like in uni?" he teases.

"Aren't you glad you didn't know me then?" She bumps her nose gently against his before kissing it.

"So glad." He raises an eyebrow, and Poppy playfully shoves his shoulder.

"Probably best that we didn't meet until years later," she says through a sly smile. "You would have pulled all the muscles in your face frowning at all the trouble I got up to."

Desmond grins. "Maybe. But I still would have gone along with you. I would have been in awe of 'uni party girl' Poppy." He kisses her forehead. She closes her eyes, her teasing smile turning tender.

I let out an "aww," seeing my best friend and her husband share this sweet moment, watching them connect over something they didn't even experience together. And then I think about how it reminds me of what I'm experiencing. In a way, I'm not really connected to the life I'm living, since I'm living it backward . . . but in a weird way I feel more connected than before. Because at least I'm not being lied to and cheated on, and that's made this life more honest and true.

I glance around, searching the crowd, like I have the past couple of hours we've been here. We haven't run into Tristan yet, which is no surprise. This place isn't the kind of spot he'd ever want to go to. But this is the night we're meant to see him and Jordan throw down.

I gulp ice water instead of taking another shot. Milo slides his half-full glass to me as soon as I set my empty one on the table.

"Thanks. And thanks for being a good sport about all this," I say to him.

"Don't worry about it. It's fun."

I quirk an eyebrow at him. "Fun?"

He shrugs before flashing that killer half smile that has every woman in the vicinity checking him out. "Maybe 'interesting' is a better word."

There's another whooping noise from Jordan, who's dancing it up with yet another random group of nearby people. Forty-five minutes later Jordan and Poppy whine that they're famished, so we make our way out of the club and down a few blocks to a hole-in-the-wall curry joint. Everyone takes their place at the end of the line, which snakes out the door. I opt to stay outside since I'm not hungry.

I yawn, stepping off to the side, and pull my phone out of my jacket pocket.

"You sure you don't want anything?" Milo asks before pressing a kiss to my forehead.

I blink, my eyelids heavy from staying out hours past my bedtime. Even in this backward timeline, I've kept to my nighttime routine. I'm usually in bed by eleven thirty most nights, not partying into the wee hours of the morning. "I'm sure. Thanks, though."

He heads into the shop, and I stay outside and read the news on my phone. Heavy footfalls echo behind me, followed by a muttered curse about how long the line is.

"Sorry, you in line?" a female voice asks.

I glance up and immediately freeze at the sight of the blue-eyed blonde and the man beside her.

Carly and Tristan.

Their eyes go wide at the same time. Mine do too, actually. For a silent few seconds, the three of us just stand there and gape at each other.

"Oh, um . . ." Carly frowns, as her wide-eyed gaze darts between Tristan and me.

I wait for the surge of disbelief, then anger, then pain to hit, just like it did when I saw them at their Hampstead house playing with their son. But it doesn't. Instead, the only familiar emotion I feel is shock.

Tristan looks at me, his eyebrows furrowed the slightest bit, his lips pursed. Shock fades, leaving behind the crackle of my nerves. They simmer under my skin, like hot oil warming on a stove.

The longer I stare at him, the less familiar he is. Like I'm gazing at a stranger who looks like someone I used to know. Like all the features are similar but not quite a match. Those are his blue eyes I've gazed into a thousand times, but the look of affection is gone. That's the mouth that I used to kiss, that I used to crave. But now it's just a thick pink line I wouldn't look twice at. The delicate waves of his strawberry-blond hair are gone. It's shorter, neater now. The thought of running my fingers through it seems so awkward. So wrong.

Carly moves to grab Tristan by the hand. "Let's go," she says curtly.

She pulls him to walk past me right as I hear Milo's voice.

"Sleeping Beauty," he singsongs. "Do you have cash on you? Their card reader's down . . ."

When he looks up and sees Tristan, they both stop in their tracks.

"What the . . ." Milo straightens up, his easy expression now a frown.

Tristan returns a frown of his own as he looks at his cousin, except his is etched deeper. *That* frown. I know that frown. I remember it from the night of our wedding anniversary, right before he punched Milo.

"Sleeping Beauty, huh?" A bitter laugh falls from his lips as his gaze bounces between Milo and me before he rolls his eyes.

"Tristan. We're going. Now." Carly tugs on his arm, but he doesn't budge.

"Listen to your girlfriend," Milo says, his tone on the edge of a bite. I take in his stance. It's the same one from that night too: tall, solid, refusing to back away. The only thing that's different is that he's not taunting or joking. Right now Milo is dead fucking serious.

Tristan steps into his cousin's space and points his finger an inch from Milo's face. Milo doesn't even blink.

"You don't fucking say a word to me," Tristan growls. "Not after stealing my fucking wife."

"Tristan!" Carly hisses. She yanks harder, this time managing to budge him slightly back.

Milo's stare goes hard. I'm not used to seeing his face like this, like he's on the verge of a roar, like he's tasting acid. Even I can feel the anger radiating off him from feet away.

"Steal? Are you fucking kidding with that shit?"

"Sis, I need money! Cash money money mo—"

Jordan's shout cuts off the minute he's outside the curry shop and sees Milo and Tristan in a standoff. My stomach churns, and I start to move toward Jordan.

"What the hell are you doing here?" Jordan barely slurs. That drunken haze is gone from his eyes. He looks alert now, like he's had a B12 shot instead of a gallon of hard liquor. His gaze darts to Carly.

"Is this her?" he asks.

I nod, my face hot.

"You two are a class act. You fucking deserve each other."

"Jordan. Don't."

He bites his lips at my scolding. As much as I dislike Carly and Tristan for how they cheated, I don't want this to escalate. I don't want to make a scene . . . or a bigger scene than the one we're already making. People step around us on the sidewalk, some stopping to gawk at the standoff we're having at midnight in front of a curry joint.

"You're such a piece of shit, Tristan," Jordan spits. "A selfish, narcissistic, phony piece of shit. I'm so fucking relieved my sister is finally done with you."

Tristan's frown turns incredulous the longer he looks at Jordan. He chuckles like he's going to spit poison from his mouth. "You think I give a shit what you think of me? I never liked you, Jordan. Such trash."

I open my mouth to yell at Tristan, but Milo barks at him before I can utter a sound.

"Shut your mouth, Tristan. You're one to talk."

Tristan turns back to face his cousin. "Am I? Because if I'm trash, so are you. You're worse actually. You stole your cousin's ex-wife. You swooped in for my sloppy seconds, you shameless twat."

Jordan's fist connects with the side of Tristan's face, causing a crunching sound. Everyone around us gasps or makes an "oooh!" noise.

Tristan hunches over, cradling his nose with his hand. Carly yelps before running over to him and reaching for his face.

I look on, unable to blink, my jaw on the concrete. Barely three seconds have passed, but it feels like slow motion.

Jordan shakes out his right hand as he heaves a breath. Milo gawks at him. He looks like he's in as much disbelief as I am. I rush over to the two of them, now standing side by side.

"We've gotta get out of here," I say to them.

Jordan nods at me, his expression pained, probably because his hand is throbbing. Milo sticks his head in the shop and yells for Desmond and Poppy to come out now. They appear with two giant paper bags of takeaway in their hands.

"No worries, lads. We got the takeaway. You owe us, tho—" Poppy's eyes bulge out of her head as she takes in the visual of Tristan hunched over just a few feet away. "Fucking hell, is that—"

"Yup." I grab her arm and start to lead her away.

"And is she—"

"Yes. We gotta go now. I'll explain later."

The five of us jog down the road. Desmond hails the first black cab that comes into view.

"Good call, Des." Milo pats him on the back, and we all jump in.

"To Dorset Street in Marylebone," Milo says to the driver.

Poppy, Desmond, and I take one side. Milo and Jordan take the other. As we ride, I give Poppy and Desmond a quick rundown of what happened.

"Goodness me," Desmond says, looking positively dazed. "Glad I missed that."

"I'm not. That would have been a perfect fucking ending to the night, seeing that bellend get his comeuppance. From your little brother, of all people," Poppy says.

Jordan shrugs, still rubbing the knuckles of his right hand. "He deserved it. He had no right to say that about my sister. Or you."

He juts his chin at Milo, who responds with a slight smile. I watch as he reaches his fist to Jordan's uninjured hand. Jordan bumps him in return.

It's a small gesture. But seeing it—seeing my brother and my boyfriend getting along—sends a strange and wonderful feeling through me.

Poppy hands Jordan a takeaway box of chips in curry sauce. "For tonight's MVBP. Most valuable bellend puncher."

Jordan accepts the box with a chuckle. "What can I say? No one fucks with my family."

I catch the look of surprise that dances across Milo's expression, taking in what Jordan's just said and just how much it means.

Chapter 18

I wake up on an airplane. My heart jumps in my chest at the shock of opening my eyes and finding myself in the air.

For a few seconds, I take in my surroundings. It's dark in the cabin. This must be a late-night flight. Yawning, I blink until my eyes adjust to the dimness. That's when I notice I don't have anyone sitting on either side of me. I'm sitting in what looks like a roomy private capsule. Oh damn. I'm flying in first class.

Beside me, I hear a low groan that I recognize immediately. I slide back the partition and see Milo leaning forward in his seat-capsule thing as he stretches. The white T-shirt he wears rides up his torso, blessing me with a peek of his hard, tan stomach.

"Good morning, Sleeping Beauty," he says through a sleepy half smile. He squints at the window near my seat. "Or maybe I should say, 'Good middle of the night.'"

The pilot makes an announcement—first in English, then in Portuguese—about the possibility of some minor turbulence over the next leg of the flight.

"Should be cleared up by the time we cruise over France, then smooth skies all the way to Heathrow."

Milo reaches over to tuck a chunk of my hair behind my ear. "Thanks again for being such a good sport about this. I know leaving for two weeks on such short notice was a colossal ask. My mom was so excited to finally meet you in person, though."

I put it all together: we're traveling back from Portugal, where Milo's family lives, after an impromptu visit.

I think of the phone conversation we had a few months ago, how she sounded like she genuinely liked me, how heartened I was. Since then, she's said hello to me in text-message conversations with Milo. She's always so sweet and attentive, making sure to ask how I'm doing and telling Milo to take care of me.

As good and comforting as that felt, a sliver of doubt lingered at the back of my mind. Milo's mom sounded lovely on the phone and over text, but would she be like that in person? Or would she dislike me if she actually met me?

I hate how pessimistic and negative it is for me to think that. But my experience with Portia Chase left me skittish about significant others' mothers and how they truly feel about me.

But when I focus on Milo's gaze, I spot a warmth in his eyes and in his smile that tells me this visit must have gone well. And even though I don't yet know his mother and can't recall any part of this trip, there's a swell in my chest.

"She loves you. She couldn't get over how good you were with my grandma. With how bad her dementia is getting, she has a hard time with new people. But you were so patient with her, and that meant a lot to my mom."

There's a warmth to his expression that I don't think I've seen before. But I recognize it. He's feeling something deep, something joyful. Like what I felt when I saw him and Jordan getting along. It's a feeling that everyone hopes for, that their family will like their significant other.

He reaches over, scoops my hand in his, and smiles. "You two got on like a house on fire."

"Did we?"

"Yeah. Like old friends. I was kinda shocked, honestly."

"Good shocked?"

He cups my cheek with his hand. "Very good shocked. Daniela Costa-Chase is officially your biggest fan."

I can't help the relief and joy that swells inside me. Maybe it's because I know just how shitty it feels when your significant other's mother hates you.

"Well, that's good," I say. "Because I'm her biggest fan too."

Chapter 19

September 17, 2024

Waking up in Milo's childhood bedroom is a weird type of déjà vu. I've never been here before, of course, but something about it feels so familiar. I take in the buttery-yellow hue of the walls, the wooden desk, the *Star Wars* poster near the armoire, the worn hardwood floors, the tiny window shrouded in white linen curtains that are so light and threadbare, they're practically see-through.

Maybe I've seen a room like this in a photo of a similar vacation rental. Maybe he showed me a photo of it once.

Or maybe it's because I'm living life backward—technically that means I've been in this room already, even if I don't remember it.

I shake my head at myself right as Milo starts to stir next to me. I glance over my shoulder and see him blink awake before yawning. He scratches his hand across his bare chest.

"Still not weirded out staying in the bedroom I grew up in?" he asks, his voice low and gravelly.

I roll over to face him. "Not at all."

I press a kiss to his mouth. Before long things are getting heated and handsy. I wonder how in the hell I ever let something like the fear of bad breath stop me from experiencing the hottest way to wake up in the morning.

When I start to slide my hand down his boxers, he stops me with a hand on my wrist. "We probably shouldn't." He groans like he doesn't want to stop, even though he's the one choosing this. "My mom is an early riser and . . ."

On the other side of the bedroom door, I hear the sound of footsteps, then dishes clanking.

I make a face. "Okay, yeah, I definitely can't fool around with your mom just a few feet away. That's just . . ." I make a quiet gagging noise before shoving a pillow over my face.

Milo chuckles before ripping away the pillow. "Come on. You know she's dying to cook us breakfast."

We hop out of bed, get dressed, and slip to the bathroom next door to Milo's room. When we emerge from the hallway into the kitchen, my eyes nearly pop out of my head. Milo's mom is a stone-cold stunner. She could be the stand-in for Monica Bellucci. She's all height, long limbs, and curves. And Christ, how old was she when she had him? A teenager?

I try my best to rein it in and follow Milo's lead. He pads to the kitchen and presses a kiss to her cheek before taking the basket of berries from her hand and washing them in the sink. She beams widely at me and pulls me into a hug.

She looks at me and smiles. "*Querida*, how'd you sleep? Good?"

I need a second to process the fact that she's talking to me. There's a fluttering sensation in my stomach at how natural that term of endearment sounds when she speaks. Like she's said it a million times. It feels just as amazing as the first time she called me that when we spoke on the phone.

I nod and try not to gawk at her. "Yes, thank you. Um, can I help with—"

She frowns and shakes her head, her cascade of long, thick ebony hair swooshing with movement. "No need. My Milo's got it. I've trained him well, no?"

He winks at us before dumping the berries in a bowl and putting on the coffeepot and teakettle. Daniela motions for me to take a seat at the small table in their kitchen while she fetches some cheese and cured meats from the fridge.

"Good to see all our years in America didn't spoil you," she says.

"What's that supposed to mean?" Milo says through a chuckle while pulling down a couple of mugs from the cabinet.

"I was always afraid you'd become one of those lazy, entitled American kids. You know, the ones who sleep in and play video games all day. But no. You were always so good about helping me and your dad. All those summers spent here in Portugal with our family served you well."

She reaches up to pat his cheek with her hand. "My helpful boy."

I watch as mother and son work side by side in the small space, quietly scooting aside when one needs room to prep or the other needs to reach a cabinet or drawer. It's like a well-rehearsed choreographed dance. They don't even bump into each other.

The memory of Tristan and his mother tumbles to the front of my brain. I think back on how many times I saw them together. It was never like this, like it is between Milo and Daniela. Tristan and Portia were never this smiley; they never laughed this much with each other; there was never this ease or comfort between them when they chatted. Their interactions were always so rigid. They hugged sometimes, but they always looked so stiff when they did it. I saw Tristan give his mom a kiss on the cheek a couple of times, but her expression was always so pinched, like she didn't even enjoy it.

All I remember from their conversations were strained tones and awkward pauses. Almost like they were going through the motions, talking because they thought that's what families should do, not because they actually wanted to. They chatted about their lives, about work, about their upcoming plans, like everyone does. But there was no warmth, no joy, no ease. It felt like I was watching two strangers acting like mother and son.

Sadness flashes through me. I may not like Tristan or Portia, but I still feel bad for them. What a depressing kind of relationship to have with your family.

Milo and his mom move around in the kitchen, pulling me back to the moment. When I see Milo mix two tea bags—one Earl Grey, one hazelnut—I smile. The nutty-floral aroma mingles well with the bitter-earth scent of the brewing coffee.

He sets a steamy mug in front of me. "Your favorite."

I tell him thanks and take a careful sip, humming quietly to myself at how good it tastes, even still.

"So. What should we do on our last day in Porto?" Milo asks when the three of us are sitting together at the kitchen table.

"I was thinking Riley and I could have a girls' afternoon of pampering while you help your dad once he gets back. He's gone fishing. Again."

Daniela rolls her eyes, and Milo chuckles.

"Of all the retirement hobbies your dad could have picked, he chose the most dangerous one."

"*Mãe*, fishing is hardly dangerous."

She scoffs behind the mug of her coffee. "It's the way your father does it, without wearing a life jacket. He can't even swim."

She mutters something in Portuguese that has Milo chuckling once more.

"Can you just please meet him at the docks when he's due back in a couple of hours and take him to do something safe on land? Take him to a bar, order him a beer. He's English, after all."

"No problem."

She squeezes his hand and flashes an adoring smile at him. "Thank you, *querido*."

She turns to me. "How does a girls' day sound?"

"Fantastic."

Two hours later we're walking down the hilly cobblestone streets of Porto. We zip into a nearby salon, where Daniela treats me to a manicure and pedicure, despite my protests to pay for it.

She rips my credit card out of my hand when I try to hand it to the nail technician and tsks at me. "When I say my treat, my treat."

I tell her that I'm getting lunch, which she agrees to. We end up in the Cais da Ribeira neighborhood, meandering along the hilly roads. Older multistory houses line the blocks in every color of the rainbow, all of them topped with adobe tile roofs in burnt orange. It's like an artist painted the horizon. They look a lot like the medieval-style town house that Milo's parents live in.

We meander for a while before settling on a small café. We sit at one of the dozen wrought iron tables in the outdoor seating area, under a massive canvas umbrella. After placing our order, I quietly take in how perfect this day has been. I'm getting along with my boyfriend's mother. She actually likes me—she's treating me like an old friend rather than a succubus who's stealing away her beloved baby boy.

"So, Riley," Daniela says as she adjusts her sun hat. "It is too presumptuous to assume that you'll come visit again? Hopefully sometime soon?"

I take in the hopeful look in her eyes and smile down at my glass of sparkling water before looking at her. "Not presumptuous at all. I'd love to visit you and Milo's dad again. You've been so welcoming to me, and I've had the best time. Thank you for that."

She frowns slightly, like she's confused. "You don't have to thank me. That's what parents should do—welcome new loved ones into the family."

"Of course. I guess I'm just not used to this kind of welcome."

I pull my lips into my mouth, feeling the slightest bit sheepish and unsure if I should say more. In the time that I was with Tristan, I met Milo's dad twice, but I never met Daniela. She was never at any of the family gatherings in London, since she and Milo's dad live in Portugal. I remember years ago Milo saying that his mom was born and raised in Portugal, moved to the US for college, and that's where she met his dad. He had moved there to open the American office of his international real estate company, which Milo now has taken over since his dad retired. They raised Milo in the US but traveled to Portugal and England often to visit their families.

Now that I think about it, it does seem strange that Daniela didn't come along when Milo's dad traveled to London.

"I know what you mean," she says in a soft voice.

I don't miss the knowing look in her burnt-sienna eyes—the exact same shade as Milo's. "Do you?"

She nods. "I'm well aware of how Portia treats outsiders. Our husbands are brothers, which means we're sisters-in-law. But she never treated me like family. I remember how cold she was the first time I met her, the way she looked at me, like I didn't belong in their family."

She pauses to take a sip of her water. Her expression twists the tiniest bit, like she's hurt thinking about the way Portia has treated her.

"I'm sorry she made you feel that way, Daniela," I say, sad that she's experienced the wrath of Portia too.

But Daniela waves a hand like it's no big deal. "It's okay."

"It's not, though," I say.

She offers a warm smile. "I tried for a long time to get her to like me. I was nice to her, I invited her to spend time with me, I sent her gifts. But nothing worked. She was always cold and dismissive. Probably because I'm twelve years younger than Hugh. A lot of stuck-up people like her don't approve of anything outside of the social norm, like age gaps, despite the fact that we're consenting adults. That and the fact that I was too different. Too Portuguese, too American."

I touch my hand to her arm, hoping it offers her comfort. But judging by the easy expression on her face, she doesn't need my comfort. She's okay.

"But I finally realized there was nothing I could do to change her opinion of me. And I realized, too, that I didn't want or need Portia's acceptance," Daniela says. "I have my husband, my son, and my family. They love me and defend me, always. And Hugh's other relatives are good to me. That's all I need."

Daniela gives my hand a gentle squeeze. "I can only imagine what you went through with her," she says. "I know how . . . territorial Portia is over her son. Plus, she's a bit of a bitch on top of that."

I choke on my sip of water. One of the waiters stops and asks if I'm all right, and I nod while wiping my mouth with my napkin.

"Sorry. I shouldn't be so crass." Daniela aims a sympathetic look at me and pats my hand. "I can imagine the hell it must have been being her daughter-in-law. If anything, she owes you an apology."

"It wasn't fun, that's for sure. I don't think she liked me, either, because of my background."

"Oh, Riley. I'm sorry."

"Honestly, I could have dealt with it okay had Tristan defended me. I mean, I thought he did at first. But now I realize what he was actually doing was keeping the peace by placating her. Whenever she'd say something snide, he'd pull me aside and tell me to ignore her, but he would never outright tell her it was wrong. He never defended me when she'd make some thinly veiled comment about my ethnicity or the way I looked. I didn't notice just how awful that was at the time. But I do now."

Daniela's expression turns pained.

"And the whole time he was cheating on me," I say quietly.

I'm surprised as the words come out. I've never been this open, this honest, with a significant other's parents before. But Daniela is different. Being around her makes me feel comfortable. There's a genuineness about her that I felt the moment I met her. I feel it when I'm with Milo too.

I clear my throat. "Love really does blind you to someone's flaws," I say, almost to myself.

In the quiet moment that follows, I take stock of how I feel. Not angry or bitter. More just reflecting on the things that happened to me in a relationship that feels like it took place a hundred years ago.

I glance up at Daniela and take in her thoughtful expression as she looks at me. Suddenly my cheeks are on fire. As comfortable as I feel around her, it's impolite for me to go on and on like this. I really shouldn't treat lunch with my boyfriend's mom like a confessional.

"I shouldn't have unloaded all that on you . . ."

She takes my hand in hers. The warmth and softness are instant comfort.

"*Querida*. If there's one thing I want you to leave this place knowing, it's this: you can always be open and honest with me. About anything and everything. I won't judge you. Ever."

I squeeze her hand in thanks. Something about the way she speaks, the honesty and sincerity, rattles me. It's almost unnerving, and I have no idea why until it hits me: I'm used to dishonesty. When I found out that Tristan was cheating on me, I realized that our years-long relationship had been rooted in lies. I had no idea what was true and what was a lie. And that's warped my sense of reality.

I take in Daniela's expression as she looks at me. Concern. Focus. Care. For me.

"Thank you," I say in a quiet voice.

The waiter drops off our food. We spend a quiet few minutes eating and people watching before Daniela speaks.

"I'm so sorry for what you went through. Being cheated on . . . it's one of the most painful things someone can do to you," Daniela says. "But I hope you know you're better off without Tristan."

I flash a small smile. "I do know that."

"Good," she says with a nod. "I know he's technically my nephew, and for that reason I'll always care for him and wish him the best, but I won't stand by a cheater, family or not."

If we weren't on a crowded outdoor dining patio, I'd leap over this table and hug her. This woman is legendary. Honest, loyal, fair, and not unwaveringly supportive of someone just because they're family.

"I don't know where things went wrong with Tristan," she says. "He was such a sweet little boy. He and Milo actually played so well together when they were little."

She turns her head to gaze at something in the distance, a faraway look in her eye. "It seemed like one day they just started hating each other. And now all they do is argue and fight. And to think that Tristan is a liar and a cheater. I just . . ."

"Some people are very good at hiding who they truly are." I'm surprised at how unbothered I sound when I say it.

"You're right. *A mentira tem perna curta.*"

"What was that?"

"'The lie has short legs.' It's a thing my grandmother used to say to me and my siblings when she'd catch us lying. I'd say it to Milo when he was little and I caught him in a lie to help teach him the importance of honesty. You can lie, but the truth will come out. Always. Maybe Tristan's parents never taught him that, and that's why he ended up the way he is."

"Or maybe they did and he didn't listen."

Daniela makes a face, as if to say, "Good point."

"Thank you for teaching Milo to be honest. It's one of the things I love most about him. He's such a good person."

Her eyes turn misty. "The greatest compliment I could ever hope for is to hear that my child has integrity. Thank you."

We eat our meals in companionable silence, and for a moment I think this is actually perfect. My boyfriend's mother and I just navigated a personal conversation about complicated family dynamics, shitty relatives, and cheating exes, ending on a hopeful and heartfelt note.

But then I look up, and the momentary joy is shattered. Because there's Portia Chase, with the most lethal scowl I've ever seen her make, staring right at me.

Chapter 20

For several seconds, all I can do is blink and gawk. This can't be real, right? My ex-mother-in-law isn't actually standing in a crowded plaza in Portugal a dozen feet away from me. She lives more than a thousand miles from here, and she's never, not once, mentioned ever traveling to Portugal in the time that I've known her.

Maybe in this timeline she lives in Portugal now?

I shake my head as I look at her. Or maybe I'm mistaken. Maybe that's someone else who looks like her.

I look away for a few seconds to let my vision reset. When I turn my gaze back on her, there's no mistake. Those are her blue-gray eyes, reminiscent of storm clouds. That's the same murderous, unmistakable scowl that she's trained on me a million times before.

I almost laugh. The universe has got to be fucking with me.

The waiter stops by to clear our empty plates, and I try to refocus on my lunch with Daniela.

The waiter asks her something in Portuguese, and she looks at me. "Should we order dessert?"

I smile and nod, hoping that I don't look as shocked as I feel. Given how we're sitting, Daniela's back is to Portia, so she can't currently see her. We've had such a nice time so far, I don't want to ruin it by mentioning that my former mother-in-law—who is also Daniela's sister-in-law and who has treated her cruelly—is somehow standing just a dozen feet away from us, looking like she wants to murder me.

"You choose," I tell Daniela. "I like anything with sugar."

She chuckles and skims the small paper menu the waiter hands her. "I won't let you down."

I gulp my water and use the lull in conversation to look back over at Portia. It's too late to ignore her, to pretend that I didn't see her. We're both fully aware that the other is right there. Now I just need to figure out what the hell to do. Do we leave this as a silent standoff? Do I go over there and tell her exactly what I think of her, something I've been dying to do for the past three years?

"Riley, is something wrong?"

I look at Daniela and shake my head. "Um, no. Sorry, just got distracted for a second by some people that walked by."

She chuckles. "That's why I love dining outdoors. People watching is always so fun."

Her phone buzzes with a text. "Pardon me for a moment," she says before typing furiously on her screen.

"Of course, take your time."

"Actually, I should just call them back. It's work. Sorry, one second."

I tell her no problem. She gets up to talk on the phone.

When I glance back up at Portia, I notice she watches as Daniela walks off. Portia frowns, like she's worried Daniela will see her. As soon as Daniela disappears inside the restaurant, the expression on Portia's face eases. When she turns back to me, she's frowning once more. A strange sort of calm washes over me. We can definitely leave this nonverbal interaction at that. Or I can be bold and actually walk over to her. And talk to her. I have plenty to say.

Before I have the time to talk myself out of it, I'm standing in front of Portia. To my surprise, her scowl has morphed into shock, like she can't believe I actually did that.

"Hi, Portia."

Her eyes widen the slightest bit, like she's shocked I'm even speaking.

She clears her throat. "Hello, Riley."

"What are you doing here?"

She leans back slightly, clearly put off by the straightforwardness of my question, how I've skipped any and all niceties. It's so unlike how I used to speak to her when I was with her son. Our conversations were loaded with meaningless comments about the weather and traffic and other things that neither one of us gave a shit about; we just didn't like each other and couldn't think of anything else to say.

"I could ask you the same thing," Portia says curtly. "You're having lunch with Daniela. My sister-in-law."

There's a small pause before she says "sister-in-law." Like she's not sure she has the right to say it. It makes sense. Based on everything I know about Portia and what Daniela has told me, they're not close at all. They don't even like each other. They're relatives in name only.

"Things with you and Milo must be going quite well." Her tone is clipped. It makes me flinch.

Clearly Portia is pissed to see me with Daniela, probably because it means my relationship after splitting up with Tristan is good. It shouldn't surprise me that she wouldn't like to see me happy after divorcing her son.

A familiar defensiveness courses through me. The muscles in my neck and shoulders go rigid with the urge to defend myself and Milo. But I stop myself before I can say anything. She's not part of my life anymore. I don't owe her anything, not even an explanation.

"What are you doing here, Portia?" I ask again.

Her eyes widen slightly at the bluntness of my tone. And the fact that I so blatantly ignored her dig about my relationship with Milo.

She clears her throat and crosses her arms. "That's really none of your business, Riley."

When I chuckle, she frowns once more.

"You're right. It's not." What was I thinking, coming over to talk to Portia? That we'd have a pleasant conversation? There's no use in me sticking around for more.

Sarah Echavarre

I'm about to turn away and walk off when a handsome fortysome-
thing man walks up to us. He turns to Portia and scoops her hand in
his. Her gaze turns horrified as she focuses on their joined hands.

"*Meu amor.* Who's your lovely friend?"

My eyes go wide as I take in the sight of them. Holy shit. Is this
Portia's boyfriend? Is she . . . cheating on Tristan's dad?

The man presses a kiss to her lips, which earns him a wide-eyed
stare from Portia. She quickly pulls away, breaking their kiss.

He chuckles. "What's the problem, *meu amor*? You don't want to
hold my hand or kiss me? You did a minute ago." He slinks his tan arm
around her waist and nuzzles the side of her neck. "You're sick of me
already?"

Portia closes her eyes and inhales, like she's digging into her inner
well of patience. "Alejandro, can you, um, give us a moment? There's
something I need to speak to my friend about."

"Of course, *meu amor.*"

He leaves her with a kiss before extending his hand to me. It takes
me a second before I register what he's doing. I'm too shocked at the
scene of this PDA-obsessed charmer all over frigid Portia Chase.

"I'm Riley," I say as I go to shake his hand, but he pulls my hand
to his mouth and presses a kiss to my knuckles.

"Delighted to meet you, lovely Riley."

My cheeks burn, and I can't tell if it's from the shock of such a
romantic gesture from a stranger, or if it's because I can feel Portia's
death glare on me for capturing her lover's interest for a fleeting second.

When he walks off, I check out her ring finger. Her diamond wedding band is still there.

I look at her. "Are you cheating? Or did you and Tristan's dad split
up and you just haven't removed the hardware yet?"

Portia Chase does something she's never done in the years that I've
known her. She hesitates. When she opens her mouth, she makes a
stammering noise. Her eyebrows crash together, creating a pained look
on her face. I've never seen her make that expression before.

"I'm cheating," she finally says. I can tell it takes a lot out of her to say those two words. She looks like she's in actual physical pain.

I don't say anything at first. I just nod and say "okay" as casually as if someone has just told me that it's going to be chilly this evening, so I should wear a jacket.

Her jaw goes tight as she crosses her arms over her chest. She glances down at her shiny black kitten heels. A transformation is occurring. Her shoulders slump forward. So does her head. Her posture sinks from its usual "straight as an arrow" stance. It's like she's trying to hide inside herself. Like she's ashamed and embarrassed at what she just admitted to me.

"Weston cheats on me all the time. He always has," she finally says. She looks up at me, and I take in the misty look in her eyes. She's sad. She's heartbroken. She's ashamed.

For the first time ever, I feel something other than annoyance and anger at Portia. I feel pity.

"I didn't know that," I say softly. "I'm sorry."

She blinks like she can't believe what I've just said. She glances off in the distance, where Alejandro is standing, smoking a cigarette in front of some building that boasts ornate stone carvings and an exterior that looks like swirled marble. He catches eyes with Portia and grins, then hooks his thumb at the nearby entrance. Two cherubs flank either side of the carved-wood double doors. He laughs, then makes a kissing face at her, and she chuckles softly. I almost stumble back. That's the most genuine, joyful noise I've ever heard her make.

"I suppose years of watching my husband go behind my back finally took its toll. So I decided some months ago, why not let myself have something on the side," she says quietly when she turns back to me. "I was away on holiday in Majorca, and a handsome man chatted me up in a bar one night. I figured it would be okay if I flirted back a bit. But we really got on. More than I thought we would."

A million questions swirl in my head. How long has Portia known that her husband has been cheating on her? Why don't they get divorced?

Will she leave her husband for Alejandro? Is this why Tristan cheated on me, because he saw his dad do it to her?

That last one stings, even just to think about. But I swallow back those questions. Because like Portia said, it's none of my business.

"I bet you find this quite satisfying," she says. The comment catches me off guard.

"Excuse me?"

She purses her lips and crosses her arms, as if to prepare a defense against me. "Having this to hold against me," she says. "Especially after how I treated you. This must feel rather good, to know that you could use this against me if you wanted to."

She glances at Alejandro. I catch a glimpse of worry in her stare. When she looks back at me, it's gone. "It would be so easy for you to ruin me, Riley, now that you've seen me—seen *us*. You could tell Daniela. It wouldn't take long for the news to work its way through the family."

I wait for satisfaction to hit, but it doesn't. The thought of ruining Portia or telling Daniela or anyone about her affair doesn't thrill me. I feel uncomfortable at even entertaining the thought. It feels petty. And vengeful. And I don't want to be like that, even to Portia.

I look at her. "Yeah. I guess I could. But I'm not going to."

Her pink-shellacked lips part, like she's waiting for the catch.

"I'm glad you found someone who makes you happy," I say instead of whatever cruel thing she expects me to say.

Portia scoffs and shakes her head.

When she opens her mouth, I brace myself for a thinly veiled insult or a dismissive remark.

"I never liked you, Riley. That's no secret."

I almost laugh at how perfectly I predicted that.

"I know you didn't like me either," she says.

"You're right. I didn't. It was hard to like you when you made underhanded comments about my ethnicity and my job and how I was never good enough for your son or your family."

166

Her brow raises the slightest bit, like she wasn't expecting me to lay it all out like that.

"Right." She clears her throat. "That's why it's quite surprising that you'd choose to be so kind to me in this moment. Especially after that disastrous dinner at Tristan's pub."

It takes a second before I register what she's talking about. She means *that dinner*—the incident that Nesta mentioned.

The fire.

I want to ask her what happened, to tell me everything. But I don't. I'll find out soon enough.

I refocus. "It's easy to choose kindness when you're happy." I sound like a fortune cookie. "It's easier now that I don't have to see you or deal with you anymore."

If I had run into Portia right after seeing Tristan with Carly for the first time, I would have definitely yelled at her and told her to fuck off. And if I had seen her with her paramour, I'd have been tempted to snap photos of them and forward them to everyone in my contacts list out of sheer vengeance.

But I don't have the urge or the energy to do any of that. The truth is I don't care about Portia enough to do anything to her, good or bad.

She nods at what I've said. "That makes sense."

A quiet moment passes where we stand there and say nothing. Around us people walk and eat and chatter and laugh and take photos.

"You can keep the flat."

It takes me a second to understand what she means. But then it registers: she means the flat I currently live in, the flat that used to be Tristan's—the flat that she and her husband gave him all those years ago. The flat that's now devoid of any of Tristan's remnants and possessions. The flat that I now share with Milo, that's filled with a mix of cute and tacky knickknacks that I've grown to love in reverse.

The flat that I couldn't for the life of me figure out how I ended up with since it was never mine to begin with.

"I won't go after it—go after *you*—anymore." She speaks quietly, like she doesn't want anyone around us hearing that she's conceding a piece of her family's prized property to her harlot ex-daughter-in-law.

The missing puzzle pieces in my mind slowly come together. Portia was likely pissed that I kept the flat when Tristan and I broke up, and probably urged him to fight like hell to get it back. But now that I've discovered her dirty little secret—her affair—she's giving up on fighting me for it.

I stare at her, taking in how different she looks. She's no longer the unflappable ice queen I knew when I was with her son. I see the pain and shame in her eyes. I see the worry in her frown, in the lines that flank her pursed lips.

For the first time ever, she's not looking down on me, despising me, loathing me.

For the first time ever, she's the one seeking approval from me.

"I can't say this feels like a win, Portia. Or that it even feels good."

She frowns. "What do you mean? You're getting a very nice home out of this . . . situation."

"All I ever wanted was for you to like me."

I'm surprised that the words come out of my mouth. And the lump that suddenly forms in my throat. Portia looks shocked. But it can't be all that surprising, can it? That's all anyone wants when they're in a relationship—to be liked by their partner's family.

She opens her mouth, but nothing comes out. She gazes off to the side and shakes her head—like she's giving up, like she can't think of another word to say. And that's when I know: I'll never get an apology from Portia Chase. I'll never get any of the things I needed from her. Acceptance, warmth, respect. She doesn't even have those for herself. Why would I expect her to have them for me?

A flat in Marylebone is the best I'll ever get out of my former mother-in-law. I should take it.

"Thanks for the flat." My tone is borderline sarcastic; I don't owe her thanks for anything.

She nods anyway.

"Bye, Portia."

She looks the slightest bit jolted when I say it. But I don't have to stand here any longer—I don't have to be around Portia anymore.

"Bye, Riley."

She walks off, and I head back to the table. There's a small bowl of what looks like rice pudding and a trio of flaky pastries with what looks like burned custard in the centers.

I dig my spoon into the rice pudding right as Daniela returns.

"I'm so sorry about that. Work call." She makes an annoyed sound.

"Everything okay?"

"No, but it's not my problem. I took the day off. How's the *arroz doce*?" she asks.

"So yummy. Like a cinnamony rice pudding."

We dig in together. She tells me the trio of flaky pastries with custard centers are called *pastéis de nata*.

"It's probably too much, isn't it? Four desserts?"

I see Portia and Alejandro walk off in the distance hand in hand. None of those old feelings—annoyance, anger, hurt—are anywhere to be found. It's like I'm watching a stranger. I feel nothing.

I look back at Daniela, at her warm expression, at how she smiles when she looks at me. Inside I feel a surge of emotion. I'm happy. And grateful.

"Not at all. This is perfect."

Chapter 21

September 13, 2024

"Are you ready for today?" Milo asks when he steps out of his bed and pulls his T-shirt over his head.

"What's today?"

That low, throaty chuckle—his morning laugh—hits my ears. "You forgot already?"

My brain claws through the fog of being half-asleep. I roll over to face him. "Refresh my memory," I say in a playful tone. You'd think that living life backward over the past five months would have trained me to be more careful about what I ask, but no. Especially when I'm groggy from sleep.

Milo sits on the edge of the bed and brushes a chunk of hair from my face. "Costa family pool party. Annual tradition. Every September. The whole reason we came here," he says with a half smile.

"Right."

"Thanks again for being a good sport about it. I know taking off work at the last minute to fly to Portugal for a pool party isn't really a reasonable request."

I shake my head and clasp my hand around his, which is now cupping my face. This. His touch, his gaze, his morning voice, being in his bed in the home where he grew up—it all feels so right, like I'm meant to be doing this.

"I want to be here with you, Milo."

That half smile morphs into a full one before a sad sheen glistens in his eyes. "It means a lot that you're here, Riley. I want my grandma to meet you. I know with her dementia worsening, she probably won't remember anything, but we still want to do it. For her. When she was healthy, she loved the family pool party. It was her favorite day . . ."

He clears his throat at the same moment that I notice the gleam in his eyes. I sit up and cup his face in my hands. "Whatever you need me to do to make this the best damn pool party for your grandma, just say so. You say 'jump,' and my response will be 'How high?'"

Milo grins before kissing me. "You're the best, you know that?"

We get dressed together.

"Just remember what I said before," he says. "The Costa side of my family gets wild. There's gonna be lots of alcohol. And nudity. But it's all in good fun."

Milo winks and I chuckle. Not my standard reaction to hearing about the prospect of nudity at a family pool party. My old self—my pre–time warp self—would have been shocked. Now I'm just excited.

I smile at him. "I'm ready."

~

When we arrive at Milo's aunt's house, we're greeted with exactly what Milo promised: nudity and alcohol.

I let out a breath after I take in the adorable sight of a dozen little toddlers and babies swimming and playing naked. All the adults are fully clothed or wearing swimsuits.

"Mama, I don't want to wear my shorts!" announces a little blond boy who looks to be about three. He sheds his orange swim trunks and darts to the corner of the massive yard and pees into the grass.

Milo chuckles before turning to me and shrugging. "When you gotta go, you gotta go."

I laugh. We walk over to join the several dozens of his relatives milling around the huge pool. Half are lounging around in chairs; the other half are gathered around a long table that holds a feast along with at least two dozen alcohol bottles and mixers.

Milo offers a sympathetic look to an early-thirties woman who has the same shade of sandy-blonde hair as the little boy.

"Hang in there, Ana."

She shakes her head. "I always do." She beams at me. "And who is this?"

"Riley. My girlfriend."

Ana pulls me into a hug. "Oh, it's so lovely to meet you, Riley!"

When she releases me, she playfully smacks Milo on the arm. "It's about time you brought her around." She aims a conspiratorial look at me. "He's head over heels about you, you know. He's never brought someone home for our annual pool party."

Milo flashes a flustered smile. "Okay, thank you, Ana. We'll catch up later." He leads me away, his tan cheeks flushing pink.

"Is that true?" I ask him as I tug him gently by the hand to get him to stop.

He flashes a shy smile before nodding.

Something bursts at the center of my chest. I press a quick kiss to his lips before a group of his relatives crowd us, greeting us with hugs and demanding that Milo introduce me.

"*Tão linda!*"

"*Sim! Muito bonita!*"

"They're all raving about how beautiful you are," he says quietly to me.

This time I'm the one with flushed cheeks. "Oh gosh, thank you. And thank you for letting me come to your family gathering. I know it's so special."

Just then Daniela rushes up to us. She pulls me into a hug before hugging Milo. "About time you got here! Here, your cousin is trying to light the grill, but he's going to set the entire house on fire. Go help him."

Milo says he'll be right there. "You'll be okay while I'm gone?" he asks me.

I'm heartened that he thinks to check on me.

I kiss his cheek. "Yeah, I'll be good. I'll hang out with your mom."

Daniela scoops my hand in hers. "Absolutely. First, we need to get you some food to fuel up before you meet the rest of the Costa clan."

I follow her to the food table, which looks like a formal dining table that they brought outside. She piles a plate high for me. My mouth waters at the endless plates of grilled seafood and meat and veggies.

"Here. Sit. Eat."

I follow her instructions and sit at one of the handful of patio tables in the yard. I juggle eating and saying hello to all the relatives who come up and introduce themselves to me.

I'm quickly chewing so I can hug the tenth person who comes up to me when Daniela scolds them in Portuguese first and then in English.

"Goodness, stop swarming the poor girl. Her mouth is full."

I chuckle and tell her it's okay. My phone buzzes with a text, and I check it quickly.

Poppy: How's meeting the family going? Do you need me to call you with a fake emergency?

As I try to quickly type a response under the table, I hear Daniela. "You don't have to hide when you do that."

I look up to see her smiling at me. I grimace. "Sorry, I just didn't want to be rude and be on my phone in front of everyone."

She waves a hand. "Nonsense. They're all being rude by bothering you while you're trying to eat."

The handful of family sitting around us laughs in agreement.

"You go ahead and take that call," Daniela says.

I stand up and thank her, excusing myself as I walk off to the edge of the yard by the back of the house and call Poppy.

"Oh shit, that bad, huh?"

I laugh. "Not at all."

"Then why are you calling me?"

"Milo's mom saw me trying to text you back and insisted I just call."

"Wow. That's kind of sweet. So spill. How's it going?"

"Surprisingly well. All of his relatives are so warm and welcoming. I don't think I've hugged this many people since seeing my own family."

Poppy makes an "aww" sound I've rarely heard her make.

"Damn, did you just 'aww' at me, Poppy?"

"Fucking hell. I think I did."

I snort a laugh into the phone.

"Well. I think I've officially been proven wrong about Milo. He's not the twat I assumed he was." She lets out a heavy sigh. "Forgive me for being such a bitch to him when you two started hanging out."

I look down at my bare feet, curling my toes into the soft grass. "I forgive you, Poppy."

"Thanks, Ri. You know I'm not one to make excuses for shit behavior, but I swear I did it out of love for you. I just felt so protective of you after what you had been through with fuckface. I mean, Tristan. Just seemed a bit weird that Milo was there for you. Almost like he was waiting in the wings. I guess I read that wrong."

"It's okay, Poppy. I get it. Promise."

There's high-pitched barking in the background, followed by what sounds like Desmond shouting.

"Christ, Des. How many times do I have to tell you? Don't sneak up on Gus like that. It makes him nervous."

Desmond makes a huffy noise. "How is walking down the hall sneaking up on him?"

"Make your presence known. Talk. Sing. Whistle. Christ, perform a Gregorian chant, I don't care. Just don't quietly walk up to him; you know he hates that."

A few more seconds of bickering follow before I hear a muffled sound; then one of them goes "Mmm."

"It sounds like you two are kissing. I'm hanging up now."

"Bye, Riley," Desmond murmurs.

"Talk to you later, Ri. Glad it's all going well."

I hang up, laughing quietly to myself. When I turn around and head back toward the party, I spot an elderly woman standing next to a massive rosebush. She glances around, the look in her eyes confused, like she's seeing this place for the first time.

Then it dawns on me. This must be Milo's grandmother.

"Excuse me, Mrs. Costa?" I say gently as I walk up to her, trying to keep my distance. She's so small, just a hair above five feet. I take in her petite form, how the flowy, burnt-orange muumuu she's wearing hangs like a curtain on her tiny body.

She frowns at me. "How do you know my name?"

"I know your grandson Milo. He told me about you."

"Oh . . ."

The furrow in her brow deepens, and her lips purse. She tugs at the bun holding her gray-black hair back, save a few tendrils framing her face. I feel a slight pang in my chest. I've confused her even more.

"Here. Let's get you back to the party."

I offer her my arm, which she doesn't take right away. Instead, she stares at me, that same frown etched on her face, studying me like she's trying to memorize my face.

"Your children and grandchildren will be worried if you don't head back soon."

Eyes still on me, her expression starts to ease. And then, to my shock, she smiles. "Elena. Of course. Let's go."

She takes my arm, and together we walk back to the party. I spot Daniela looking around, then grinning wide when she sees us.

"*Mamãe*, there you are."

She takes her other side, and I let go. Daniela helps her back down into a patio chair, which is covered in plush cushions.

Milo walks over and crouches his tall, broad frame down to hug his grandmother. When he kisses her on the cheek, she smiles. "*Vovó*. I see you've met Riley."

He winks up at me. Daniela comes over and pulls me into a side hug. "Thank you for wrangling her," she says in a quiet voice. "She gets so confused now and sometimes will walk off when she gets overwhelmed. It's always so worrying."

I ache at seeing the pain in Daniela's eyes—the same eyes as her mother's. The same eyes as her son's.

"I'm glad I could help."

"Elena," Milo's grandmother repeats.

I smile down at her. I don't bother to correct her. I don't want to confuse or overwhelm her. If she wants to call me by some random name, that's fine by me.

But when I see the looks on Milo's and Daniela's faces, I pause. They look shocked and . . . worried? Milo seems about to say something but stops himself.

"Riley, *Mamãe*. Her name is Riley."

I smile. "It's okay, really."

One of Milo's uncles waves me back to the table, insisting that I finish my plate of food. I walk over and take my seat, chatting and eating with his family. Soon Milo walks over and moves to sit in the empty chair next to me right as one of his cousins stops by.

"Rafa, this is Riley, my girlfriend."

I stand up to shake his hand, taking in the amused look on Rafa's face. I smile politely and quietly wonder what that's about.

A beat later Rafa reins in his expression. He returns a cordial smile. "Pleasure to meet you, Riley."

"Dressing like a yacht d-bag today?" Milo says.

I'm caught off guard until Rafa laughs. "You know it." He runs a hand through his wavy, jet-black hair before elbowing Milo. They both chuckle. Clearly they're just joking. They walk off right as Milo's aunt insists that I try her rice pudding, so I sit back down and enjoy the most flavorful rice pudding I've ever had. I'm devouring the bowl, nodding along with the conversation at the table.

Behind me I hear Rafa.

"Really, Milo? Again? Is this a pattern with you?"

"Rafa. Stop."

The bite in Milo's tone is unmistakable, even though I can tell he's straining to keep his voice down. As much as I want to, I don't turn around to see what they're arguing about. No one else around us has seemed to pick up on whatever tension is between them, too busy laughing and talking.

"Look, man. I only ask because it's not a normal thing to do. To go after—"

"I didn't go after anyone."

Rafa scoffs at Milo's curt words. My ears perk up.

"You sure about that, Milo? Because even *Vovó* sees it. And she has dementia." Another scoff. "She called your girlfriend Elena, for Christ's sake."

"Rafa. Enough."

Milo is so loud that the people sitting around me look toward them. I do the same.

I take in their flushed cheeks and the startled looks on their faces.

"You two behaving yourselves?" someone asks, one of their cousins whose name I can't remember.

"Always." Rafa flashes a strained smile. Milo's mouth remains a straight line. He nods.

"Who's ready for the diving contest?" someone yells from the pool. Everyone cheers.

Several people ask if I'm up for participating, but I politely decline, saying I'm too busy enjoying the delicious food. Milo sits down next to me, and I can practically feel the tense energy buzzing off him, like an electrical current.

"You okay?" I ask.

He nods and finishes the rest of my rice pudding. "Yeah. Just hungry. Also, Rafa's a douche."

"I gathered that."

He offers a weak smile before turning to chat with his family. For the rest of the time that we're there, I laugh and chat and make sure that it looks like I'm having a great time. I am. But I can't help playing back what Rafa said over and over in the back of my mind.

She called your girlfriend Elena.

When we leave the party and head back to his parents' house, two questions dominate my mind: Who the hell is Elena? And why does Rafa think it's so awful that their grandmother called me that?

Chapter 22

"Can I ask you something?"

Milo looks up from the book he's reading while we're in bed. "Of course."

It's taken me all evening to work up the nerve to bring this up. I'm admittedly nervous to do it, and honestly, if I had the luxury of moving forward in time, I'd just leave it for the night and come back to it another day. But I don't. When we wake up, it'll be yesterday, and it'll be as if today never happened.

I need to ask Milo about Elena now.

"I heard something earlier at the pool party."

"That's not a question." He smirks.

I let out an uneasy chuckle. "I'm working up to it."

His gaze turns concerned. "What's wrong?"

"I overheard you and Rafa arguing about your grandma calling me Elena by mistake."

Milo's expression sobers. An uneasy feeling hits me.

"Why did it sound like Rafa thought it was a bad thing that your grandma called me Elena?"

Milo sits up against the headboard. I scoot up to join him, and he grabs his hand in mine. The muscles in my torso tighten like a girdle. This feels like it's gonna be bad.

"I just figured, given the way Elena and I got together, you'd be upset. You were upset when you first found out about it."

"Right . . ." Clearly we've worked through this in days I have yet to live through.

Milo lets out a heavy sigh, the look in his eyes hesitant as he gazes at me. "You're still bothered by what happened."

I'm quiet as I try to work out how to play this. I don't know who Elena is or what happened between Milo and her, or why I was so upset to find out about their relationship. And I don't know how to bring any of that up. In his timeline, we've already had this conversation; we've already worked through it since we're together now.

"It's not that . . . ," I finally say. I try to say more, but I've got nothing else. I have no idea what to say right now.

Milo's gaze falls to his lap, and he tugs a hand through his hair, like thinking about this, talking about this, still bothers him.

"I get it. I get why you'd still have an issue with what I did, even though it was years ago, when I was in uni. I'm still ashamed by it," he says. He blinks, and his eyes are shy, like he's embarrassed. "I'm not proud that Elena and I started hooking up when she was in another relationship."

Oh. *That's* why he's so uncomfortable, and why his cousin was giving him such a hard time at the family pool party. Elena was Milo's college girlfriend, and their relationship started as an affair.

I'm quiet once more as I reflect on the fact that Milo has been the other man in a past relationship. An unease settles in the pit of my gut, as sharp and unwelcome as a needle.

This is a hell of a pill to swallow. I hate knowing that Milo was capable of participating in cheating, even if it was years ago.

And I hate that it makes me think of Tristan.

Milo clears his throat and pauses, like he's working up the nerve to say more. "It was a horrible mistake. I hate myself for doing it. I would never do it again."

I'm quiet once more as I process everything he's said. Clearly Milo's sorry for what he did. And he's openly talking about it now. He's being honest with me; he's not hiding or being deceitful. That doesn't erase what he did. But his honesty in this moment counts for a lot in my book after what I went through with Tristan.

That sharpness in my gut eases the slightest bit. Milo's not that guy anymore. And if that's the only time Milo's ever done something like that, which was years ago, then it's not fair for me to hold it against him. He clearly seems to regret it.

I'd hate for someone to hold my mistakes from years ago against me now.

"I'll admit, I'm not, um, I wasn't thrilled at hearing you'd been the 'other guy' before," I finally say. "But I understand, too, that it was a long time ago. I mean, you were in your twenties."

"Barely twenty-one years old," he says in a quiet voice.

"Not that it makes it okay, but I get it. You were young and made mistakes. We all do."

There's a pleading look in his eyes as he grips my hand in both of his.

"I know we talked about this before, but Elena and I were together for less than a year. We weren't meant to be. I know that now." He huffs out a breath, like this is still weighing heavily on him. "When I told Rafa how Elena and I got together, he was pretty disgusted with me." He tugs a hand through his hair. "And when he found out about the two of us getting together, he wasn't thrilled either."

It all clicks in my head. "He assumed I was cheating with you?"

Milo nods. "Even though you and I didn't cheat. Even though neither of us did anything wrong. I swore up and down to him that there was no overlap, that you and I started up when you and Tristan were completely done. But he didn't believe me. He still doesn't. He just assumed I was the guy on the side again because I was before."

I take in the red hue painting Milo's cheeks, the color of the shame he feels admitting this to me. I take in his downcast stare, how he looked me in the eye when he spoke all this, then immediately dropped his gaze, as if the guilt he feels still weighs him down. As if he's carrying the weight of his cousin's judgment.

"Hey," I say. He looks up at me. "It's okay."

When I say it, I mean it. As unpleasant as this part of Milo's history is, I believe him when he says he regrets it and that he hasn't done it since. He's been up front and honest with me. That's all I've ever wanted out of a partner.

The corners of his mouth hook up the slightest bit, forming a sad smile.

"I don't care what you did when you were a lovestruck twenty-one-year-old, Milo. Uh, anymore. You're well into your thirties now. You said you'd never do that again. I believe you."

He blinks like he's stunned at what I've said. When he blinks again, there's a trace of that guilt, that shame, still clouding his burnt-umber gaze.

He raises my hand to his lips and kisses me. "No way could I ever be good enough for you, Sleeping Beauty."

We slide back into bed. Milo falls asleep quickly, but I'm awake for a while, feeling the slightest bit skittish after hearing Milo admit that he's participated in cheating.

And then I think about how Tristan cheated; how Portia cheated; how Weston, Tristan's dad, cheated. My head spins. The Chase family is something else.

I glance up at Milo, taking in his face's sharp angles, which are prominent even in the darkness of his bedroom. A small pang of guilt hits. I silently remind myself that what he and Tristan did were two completely different things. Tristan cheated on me for years and went out of his way to hide it from me. Milo was the other man in a short relationship more than ten years ago, before he even knew me. That was the only time he ever did something like that. It's not fair for me to lump him and Tristan together. They're not the same, at all. And it's not fair for me to focus on that one mistake when Milo's only ever been honest and open with me.

I relax into Milo's embrace and close my eyes. I make a silent promise that I won't let the past affect our future.

Chapter 23

"I have a question for you, Sleeping Beauty."

"What's that?"

I look up from the dining table in my flat and see shirtless Milo carrying Coco, who has a tiny note hanging from her collar.

I laugh. "What in the world . . ."

He sets Coco, who makes a disgruntled mewling noise, on my lap. I pet her as I read the note.

Come to Portugal with me? Pretty please?

"Oh . . ." I try my best to sound intrigued. I already know I'm going to say yes. "Um, when?"

Milo winces slightly. "In a week and a half."

He explains what I already know—that his grandma is suffering from dementia, that his family has a huge annual pool party every year in the summer that he hasn't missed, ever.

"My family wants to meet you. I've, uh, been talking about you. A lot."

He says it with such hopefulness in his eyes and voice that I'm smitten. Going through life backward has been disorienting as hell, but moments like this ground me. I know how this all turns out. We have a wonderful time with his family. They're sweet and welcoming and hug everyone for any reason. I discover that Milo cheated in a relationship in his early twenties. It rattles me, but we talk about it. He's open and honest and regretful about it. He doesn't get upset when I express my hesitation and reservations, and we work through it. I even run into Portia, and somehow that works out fine; I get this flat out of it.

It all somehow ends up wonderful. And because I know that, I can savor this moment, this moment when Milo is working up the nerve to ask me. It's sweeter. It hits harder. Because I already know how much I mean to him for him to have asked me in the first place.

"You told your family about me?" I ask, unable to rein in the wide smile that appears on my face.

He nods. "I can't help it. You're amazing."

I cup his cheek with my hand.

"I know it's last minute, but seems fitting, don't you think? Especially since I've already met your family."

I do my best to keep my smile in place and swallow back my surprise. "Good point. Of course I want to go to Portugal and meet your family."

He leans forward and presses a kiss to my forehead before petting Coco and standing up. "My mom's gonna flip. She's been dying to meet you. She's been asking to talk to you on the phone, but I don't wanna scare you off." He lets out a soft laugh like he's embarrassed.

"Why would I be scared off? It sounds like she's being so sweet."

"She is. She's just really affectionate. The entire Portuguese side of my family is. People can take it the wrong way, think it's over the top, or be turned off by it." He shrugs and flashes a flustered smile. It's cute. "I guess that's all my years living in England coming through. I don't wanna scare people off with all the emotional, touchy-feely stuff."

Even though I've already lived that part and I already know how well it all goes between Daniela and me, I'm still glowing at the feeling of meeting a significant other's mother who actually likes me.

"I would never be scared off by that," I say to Milo. "I love that your mom is so kind and welcoming to me already."

This time when he smiles, he looks relieved.

"It might be kind of nice to get away for a bit," Milo says. He swallows, like he's hesitating. "Especially after the disaster from earlier this summer."

"Good point." I do my best to gauge Milo's reaction so I can figure out what he's talking about, but he walks to the kitchen island to refill his coffee mug.

Milo shakes his head while looking down at his cup. "God, what a shit show. I still can't believe it. The nerve of Tristan. And Portia."

I brace myself. This must be the disastrous dinner everyone's been referencing. I can feel every muscle in my shoulders tense. I check the calendar in my phone. It's August now, which means this fiasco happens in either May, June, or July.

Sweat breaks out on the back of my neck. Something terrible is going to happen, *has* happened, and I have no idea how to prepare for it.

Chapter 24

June 2, 2024

When I walk into the living room Sunday morning, I see Poppy and Desmond passed out on the sectional.

"Morning, Sleeping Beauty."

I turn and see Milo standing in his usual spot by the kitchen island, brewing tea and coffee, dressed in boxers and a T-shirt. His voice is barely above a whisper.

As I walk over to him, I hear the sound of fabric rustling. I glance over to the couch and see Poppy stirring under the plushy fleece blanket shrouding her and Desmond. Gus pops his head out from under the covers, slow-blinks, then burrows back under.

"I think they're still pretty drained from last night after the craziness at Last One Standing," Milo whispers. He aims a shy stare at me. "We all are."

I nod, taking note that last night was *the night*.

The epic disaster at Last One Standing, where the pub ends up in flames.

"They didn't make it to the guest bedroom?"

Milo shakes his head. "I tried to tell them, but they pretty much passed out the moment they sat down."

He laughs quietly to himself before looking at me, his expression sober. "Hey. I'm sorry. For, uh, how brash I was when I walked into Tristan's pub last night."

"It's okay." I say it automatically. I know what's coming when I wake up tomorrow. For the past few days—days in the future, technically—I've heard Milo, Poppy, and Desmond make comments about how outrageous it all was. I've been trying to piece it all together since I can't admit to them that I didn't actually live through it with them.

But I won't have to wonder anymore. I'll get to experience it all soon.

Milo runs a hand through his hair, wincing slightly, before his arm falls back to his side.

He looks at me expectantly. "Did you mean it? What you said last night?"

Shit.

I take a second to swallow and breathe. I hate this part of living life backward. I hate not knowing what everyone else knows. I hate that I have to answer without knowing what happened, and that answer could mean that I hurt Milo's feelings without even meaning to.

"Of course I meant it." The words fall out as soon as I open my mouth, almost as if I've been programmed to say them. It's like I didn't even have to think; my mouth and my brain just knew what to do.

I hold my breath as Milo blinks. And then the smallest smile tugs at the corner of his lips. He looks relieved. So relieved. And happy.

He wraps his arms around me and pulls me into his chest. His skin is warm and soft, and it feels like coziness and heaven wrapped in one. I close my eyes and relax into his embrace. I breathe in his natural spicy scent and the aroma of the tea and coffee brewing next to us.

"Fucking hell. Ouch, Des. Off, will you?"

Desmond groans and yawns. "What's that?"

"Your leg. On top of my stomach. Christ, it's like you're made of lead."

"Oh. Sorry."

The sound of Poppy's hoarse morning voice makes both of us chuckle.

"Morning, you two," Milo says.

"Morning," Desmond says through a yawn. Poppy mutters a curse word.

She and Desmond sit up on the couch. She turns to me, peering at me through her smudged eye makeup. She aims a sheepish smile my way as she smooths a hand through her mussed blonde hair. "Sorry, Ri. Wasn't in my finest form last night."

"It's okay, Poppy," Milo says. "You said everything I wanted to say. And then some."

Poppy perks up. "And you, Milo, proved me wrong in the best way. You officially have my approval to shag my best friend."

"Poppy!" Desmond and I say in unison.

"Christ, your mouth," Desmond mutters.

Poppy gives him a cheeky look. He blushes, and the corner of his mouth quirks up. It's like their bickering is foreplay.

She turns to me, aiming a deadpan stare. "Don't pretend like that's not what you wanted this whole time, for me to like him."

I glance at Milo, who looks equal parts amused and relieved.

"Okay, yes. I'm very glad that you like Milo," I say.

Desmond stands up, puts on his glasses, then stretches toward the ceiling. Poppy smacks his ass. He lets out a grunt, his cheeks flaring red before he shuffles toward the bathroom in the hallway, scrubbing his hand along the chestnut scruff on his face. He stops suddenly, then steps back to me.

"Thank you for letting us stay here last night." He looks between Milo and me. "We were in no shape to attempt to go home."

191

Milo claps him on the back. "No worries, man. You're welcome here anytime. Both of you are. Especially after what you did. You can even sleep in the guest bedroom next time."

Desmond laughs before turning to me and patting my shoulder. "You've got a good one, Riley."

He looks at Milo before heading to the bathroom.

I catch Milo smiling right as Poppy stands up. "Please tell me you've got coffee brewing. I've got a bangin' headache."

Milo points to the full coffeepot. "All ready to go. And I've got breakfast coming." He holds up his phone. "Four full Englishes are on their way from the greasy spoon a few streets down."

"God love you, Milo."

Poppy walks over, pulling her leather jacket over the long dark maxi dress she's wearing. Milo hands her a full mug before turning around to the fridge. He pulls out a sleeve of crumpets and a jar of jam.

"Prebreakfast? It's all we've got, sadly."

She claps Milo gently on the cheek while sipping from her mug. "It's perfect," she says.

Desmond returns and joins us as we stand around the island and have impromptu prebreakfast together.

"I still can't believe what Tristan pulled last night," Desmond grumbles. Poppy elbows him. He winces before his expression turns sheepish. He darts his gaze to me. "Sorry, Riley."

"It's really okay, you guys. If you want to talk about last night so you can decompress, I completely understand . . . ," I say, hoping they do so I can piece together what exactly happened.

Poppy shakes her head. "Nope. We're not giving that tosser one more ounce of our energy. Or his bitch mum. Christ, I still can't believe them."

I stay quiet, eager for them to say more. I'm curious as hell to know what went down so I know what I'll be waking up to tomorrow. But save for a few grumbles, the three of them remain quiet as they chow down on their crumpets, still groggy from sleep.

Desmond quickly changes the subject, asking Milo about where he got the coffee beans they're drinking. For the rest of Sunday, as we hang out, eat, and go about our day, I feel the stress knots in my shoulders loosen. It's the eve of some disastrous event in my life, and I'm strangely calm. I probably shouldn't be, but I am. Maybe because unlike every other upsetting event I've ever experienced, I've had the chance to peek ahead, and this time I know it's all going to be okay.

Chapter 25

Riley. Don't ignore me. We need to sort out this flat issue.

I stare down at the text Tristan has just sent me.

I knew it was coming. But still. I'm pissed. And mystified. And unnerved for what is about to take place tonight.

Instead of texting back, I make myself take a long, slow breath when I sit up in bed. I close my eyes and do it again.

"Doing some yoga breathing to kick off the morning?"

When I open my eyes, the sight of shirtless Milo walking toward me with a steaming mug of tea in his hand eases me the slightest bit. The muscles in my shoulders loosen.

"Thanks," I say when he hands me the cup.

He sits on the edge of the bed, and I show him the text. The sleepy smile on his face morphs into a pissed-off frown.

"That fucking guy," he mutters.

"Yeah."

"I thought you had this all sorted out?" Milo rests his elbow on his knee. "It was stipulated in your divorce settlement. You got the flat and the car. He got to keep one hundred percent ownership of his restaurants and his retirement accounts. You split the savings accounts.

It's all settled. Lara made sure of all of it when I asked her to represent you. She said the settlement she got for you was ironclad."

I pause. The name Lara is familiar. It takes a second before I remember it from when I skimmed my divorce paperwork. She was my attorney. And a friend of Milo's too, I think. I soften at the thought that he went out of his way to make sure that I had a stellar lawyer to help me divorce Tristan.

But then I remind myself who I was married to—Tristan Chase, son of Portia Chase. This flat was his—it was his family's originally, which meant that it was his mother's too. And all this is happening before I ran into Portia in Portugal, before I saw her with her lover, before she displayed that fleeting moment of vulnerability, spoke to me candidly, and conceded the Chase family flat to me.

I'm guessing that Portia likely ignored our divorce settlement and pressed him to badger me into giving back the flat.

I sigh, my head spinning trying to keep it all straight.

"Tristan won't go down without a fight. You know that," I say to Milo. In the days before today, I pored over the divorce paperwork. It helped me feel calm about this evening, about what is about to go down.

Legally I'm protected. Legally there's nothing Tristan or his family can do to take this flat from me. That doesn't mean they won't try, though.

"But none of that matters," I say softly, staring down at the mug of tea. "I'm the American whore who stole their beloved family flat. They'll try everything in their power to take it back."

"Hey." Milo's hand lands gently on my arm. "Don't say that about yourself."

"I'm not." I shrug. "It's what they say about me behind closed doors."

Milo's brow furrows deeper.

"Come on, Milo. Don't pretend like you haven't heard them say it. Yeah, they never said it to my face, but I know deep down that's what Tristan's parents and grandparents think about me. I was never good enough for them. Because of how I look, because I'm mixed-race, because of what I do for a living."

"Riley." Milo closes his eyes, his hand still on my arm, his skin hot on mine. "Fuck them. Seriously."

I jolt back, my shoulder blades bumping the padded headboard. I'm used to him swearing in reference to Tristan. But not his grandparents.

"I know you don't like Tristan. And I know you've never been a fan of Portia or Weston," I say. "But you don't have to curse your grandparents just for my sake."

He shakes his head. "That's not why I said that." His toned chest heaves as he inhales. "Look, I love my grandparents, but it's no secret they're insufferable. They hold some pretty offensive views. They don't like foreigners. Or Americans."

"But they love you."

"Because my dad is their oldest son and I'm their grandson. Because I'm charming and funny and thoughtful. Because I always call them on their birthdays and anniversaries. Because I always remember that my gran loves roses and always make sure to bring her some whenever I visit her." He shakes his head, his brow furrowed, like he's conflicted by whatever he feels right now.

"That's okay, Milo. You don't have to feel guilty for your grandparents loving you. Even problematic people make exceptions for the people they care about. You're their grandson—of course they would accept you while disliking me. I'm not their blood."

"That doesn't make it okay."

He bites down, the muscles in his stubbled jaw bulging. "They love me because my dad's their white British son. They've warmed up to my mom over the years, but they didn't like her at first because she's Portuguese and American. I know it's some seriously hypocritical shit, and I've overlooked it because they're my family . . . but they don't get to treat you like shit anymore now that we're together."

He goes quiet, and I take in the look in his eyes as he gazes out the nearby window. Fiery and embattled, like he's fighting inside himself and not quite sure what he wants to say or do.

"This flat is yours, Riley. Tristan has no right to try to talk you into giving it to him."

I shrug. "You're right. He doesn't. But I know him. He's not going to give up until I meet him and tell him to his face to back off."

"I can come with you tonight. For moral support."

I smile at him, heartened at his offer. "I can handle it. Thanks, though."

Milo purses his lips like he's swallowing back the words he's aching to speak. But he stays quiet and just nods.

A few seconds later he stands up. The hard expression on his face eases. "Come on. You need breakfast."

"In a sec. Gotta pee first."

He walks off to the kitchen, and I pad to the bathroom. After I finish, I type out a reply to Tristan.

Me: Fine. Tell me where to meet you so we can talk.

Tristan: Last One Standing at 6. I assume you remember where that is or has my cousin manipulated you into forgetting that too?

What feels like a sting works its way across my skin. I don't expect warm and fuzzy and romantic Tristan, of course, but it still blows me away that this man I loved, this man who was my partner for more than three years, is capable of being so dismissive, so mean.

Me: Don't be a jerk. I remember.

I drop my phone on the bed and try not to think about tonight.

Chapter 26

"I can't fucking believe you're meeting your ex-husband at his restaurant to tell him what he already knows."

"I know, Poppy."

I weave my way through the crowded street to Last One Standing, clutching my trench coat tight with my free hand. It's June, so it's technically spring, but it's still chilly in the evenings. It's cool enough that I can see my breath in the air when I exhale.

God, it's trippy, watching summer shift backward into spring. I spot a cherry tree on the corner of the street I'm walking on. I slow my pace, shocked at the sight of the tight, pink buds dotting the branches. Just weeks ago I saw the cherry blossoms in London in full bloom. But to see them shrink back into their buds throws me off.

An unsettled feeling courses through me, like a silent undercurrent. No matter how much I think I'm getting used to this timeline, moments like this remind me just how wild it feels to live life backward . . . how I've done this for months and months . . . how I'm inching closer and closer to Valentine's Day 2024, the last day I lived normally until I woke up in this strange and backward timeline.

The unsettled feeling morphs into anxiety. My chest starts to go tight at the thought of what will happen when that day finally comes.

"Throw the fucking divorce settlement in his face, Ri. It's what he deserves." Poppy's sharp tone jolts me back to our conversation.

I can't get caught up in those thoughts right now. There's nothing I can do about the uncertainty of this timeline. I can't control it. All I can do is focus on living through each day, one at a time, like I've been doing so far.

"Christ, he cheats on you with his ex—he gets his ex fucking pregnant—and he has the nerve to demand you give him your home?"

Another muttered string of curses echoes from Poppy's end of the line. Hearing my best friend so heated on my behalf centers me. It helps ground me in this moment when everything from this timeline to my upcoming meeting with Tristan has me stressed and unsettled.

"You should have told me earlier," she says. "I could have come with you. I would have worn those pointy-toed boots and kicked that tosser right in the balls."

"Poppy, I appreciate the sentiment, but I've got this under control."

"You sure? It's been a while since I nailed someone in the family jewels. Not since the last time we went to Glastonbury and that T-shirt vendor tried to get handsy with me. I'd pay good money to give Tristan a solid kick between the legs. Really. Name your price and I'll pay it. One swift kick is all I want."

"As satisfying as that would be, I'll pass. I've got this under control. Seriously."

A heavy sigh rockets from her before I hear a metallic snapping noise. "Poppy, what is that?"

She pauses for a few seconds. "What do you mean?"

"That noise . . . wait, is that a lighter? Are you smoking?"

She huffs out a breath before I hear the unmistakable sound of a lighter flicking on and off. "Yes, Ri. I'm smoking. Sue me."

"But I thought you quit?"

"I did. Unless I'm stressed the fuck out. And when I'm stressed, I allow myself a single cigarette."

I bite my tongue and fight the urge to lecture her.

"Oh, don't give me that look," she groans.

"You don't know how my face looks right now."

"Oh yes I fucking do." She stops, and I hear the faint noise of her puffing on a cigarette.

I pass a glass storefront and catch my expression in the reflection: lips pursed and brow furrowed. Classic disappointed face.

"Okay, okay. I definitely have *that* look on my face. Wait, does Desmond know you're smoking again?"

"I told you, I have one when I'm stressed. And you, Ri, are stressing me the fuck out with your plans to meet your piece-of-shit ex-husband without me there to support you."

I feel guilty and heartened all at once. I'm touched that my best friend cares so much about what I'm going through, but I also feel terrible that I'm driving her back to such an unhealthy habit.

"And no, Desmond doesn't know. I'm currently in the bathroom with the window open, so he's blissfully unaware."

"Poppy, it's cold and rainy."

"I know. See what you do to me?"

I let out a breath right as she laughs.

"I'm sorry I'm stressing you out," I tell her.

"It's okay, Ri. I get it. You want to do this on your own. I would, too, if I were in your shoes. But you're my best friend, and that rat bastard ex put you through the wringer. He doesn't deserve one more second of your time."

"This is why I love you. Also, I don't ever, ever want to be on your bad side."

"No way that would ever happen."

Hearing the smile in her voice when she says that makes me start to smile.

"If you change your mind about wanting me there, just text me, okay?"

"I will."

There's a quiet moment before she speaks. "So. You're still shacking up with the cheating bastard's cousin?"

I almost trip on a cobblestone before quickly righting myself. I shouldn't be so thrown at the bitterness in Poppy's tone. It's June 1, which means I'm only three and a half months out from my split with Tristan in this backward timeline, and at this point Poppy doesn't like Milo.

She won't start to like him until this evening, when everything goes down at the restaurant.

"Yes, Poppy. Milo and I are together," I say.

"I know I've said it a million times, but bloody fucking hell, Riley. Why? Of all the men in London. Of all the men on the planet, why did you have to rebound with the bastard cousin of your bastard ex?"

I stop dead in my tracks and cause the person walking behind me to bump into me. After at least a few months of seeing Poppy and Milo chat and laugh and hang out, I've gotten used to them genuinely getting along. It feels like they've always liked each other. But they haven't. Poppy used to hate Milo because I hated him—and I'm back in that time right now. And even though it all changes in just a few hours, I can't help the surge of protectiveness that hits me.

I mutter a sorry to the person I bumped into before standing off to the side. "Poppy. I get that it must have been the shock of the century when Milo and I got together. But we did. It happened. You need to accept it."

"Riley, are you sure this isn't some strange third-life crisis you're having? I mean, I get it, that's a hell of a revenge move, to shag the cousin of your husband after he betrayed you in the worst way. A part of me respects you for it. I'd probably do it too. But Milo? After what a dick he was to you? After all those years of dismissing you and making snide remarks at you? After that awful trophy wife comment?"

The memory of overhearing Milo call me a trophy wife while he was on the phone all those years ago slingshots to the front of my mind. It stings, even now. But he's done more than enough to make up for it.

"Poppy, listen. I appreciate that you care about me and how you've always defended me, without question. But please don't disparage Milo like that. He's a good person—a truly good person I had pegged wrong all this time. You have too. It took time for me to see it, but I did. You'll see it. I promise you will."

Poppy makes a grumbling noise. "Fine, Ri."

A tense silence passes between us. I start walking again, turn the corner, and see the intact brick front of Last One Standing come into view.

"I have to go."

"Wait. I'm sorry, Ri." I soften at the pleading tone in Poppy's voice. She so rarely sounds like this—worried and vulnerable. "You're right. I shouldn't have said those things about Milo. If you like him and you say he's a good guy who treats you well, then that's all that matters."

I think of how quickly, in just a matter of hours, Poppy's opinion of Milo is about to change.

"Please don't hate me, Ri."

"I could never, Poppy. I'd die without you. You know that."

She laughs. The tension in my hands and shoulders eases.

"I know you're just looking out for me," I say. "Thank you. That means everything. Truly."

"Love you, Ri."

"Love you, Poppy."

"Keep me posted, yeah? And just say the words, and me and my nut-busting boots will be at your service."

I laugh. "I will."

We say goodbye. I hang up the phone and walk the remaining dozen steps to the entrance of Last One Standing. Before I reach for the door handle, I pause. I breathe. I steel myself.

I'm about to see my ex-husband. Yeah, it's going to suck, but I'll survive. I know what happens after all this—I get to keep my home. This is just a blip; it'll all be okay.

When I open the door and walk inside, I make my way through the darkened, short hallway to the main area of the pub. Tristan never said where exactly we were supposed to meet, and I never thought to ask. And it's too late now to clarify. As I walk in the main area and start to scan the dimly lit space, I freeze. There's Tristan's entire family sitting at a long table in the center of the pub, and they're all staring at me.

What the actual fuck?

Chapter 27

I don't know how long I stand there staring back at Tristan's relatives. Probably a while, given that I've had time to register almost everyone's face. There's Tristan's grandparents and Portia glaring at me. I see Nesta and her husband, Roland, aiming pitying glances at me. There are a dozen other relatives, whom I haven't seen since the infamous Valentine's Day anniversary party. Their expressions range from shocked to horrified at the sight of me.

Why the hell did Tristan insist that I come to his pub at the same time he's hosting a family dinner?

I shake my head out of frustration; then I catch sight of Carly. Her blue eyes are wide, like she wasn't expecting to see me either. She rests a hand on her massive belly. My stomach dives to my feet, and I quickly count backward in my head.

She's about to give birth to her and Tristan's baby, probably in just a few days.

She blinks, revealing a sheen of sadness I can see even standing ten feet away in this dim pub lighting. She blinks again and she's composed. She glances down at her stomach before looking up at me once more. I catch a flash of guilt in her eyes before she quickly glances back down.

"What are you doing here?"

I turn around at the sound of Tristan's impatient question and bite my tongue so I don't yell at him. For a moment all I do is study the look on his face for any trace of smugness. Did he do this on purpose? Did he want me to walk in and see his entire family? Did he want Carly—the mother of his child, the woman he cheated on me with—to see me?

I take in his expression, the tight pull of his lips, how he's frowning, how his blue-eyed gaze darts from me to behind me, where his entire family is sitting. I recognize that panicked look instantly. He's not smug. He's freaking out. And pissed.

"What do you mean, what am I doing here?" I struggle to keep my shrill, shocked tone under control. "You told me to come here. At six. To meet you so we could talk—"

"Fucking hell, Riley." He closes his eyes and pinches the bridge of his nose. "I meant for you to meet me outside at the entrance. I never meant for you to come inside."

I grit my teeth. "Then why didn't you say that?"

Instead of answering me, he rolls his eyes and looks off to the side. "Just wait for me outside."

No apology. No explanation. Nothing.

I scoff. "Fine."

I head back to the entrance of the pub but stop short of walking outside. It's raining even harder now. No way am I going to stand out there and get soaked when it's cold out.

I stand off to the side, near where the hallway to the bathrooms is, and take a second to collect myself. Leaning against the wall, I close my eyes. My heart is racing. My breath is ragged. I'm so lightheaded that if I don't plant both of my feet firmly on the ground, I'll lose my balance. Christ.

I was prepared to see Tristan and Portia. But seeing their whole family unexpectedly felt like a punch to the gut and a slap to the face at once. There's a tightness in my throat as I recall how sad and shocked Nesta and Roland looked. God, I miss them. I hate that this is how they're seeing me—without any warning, at what was clearly an intimate family gathering. And here I am barging in and interrupting like some jerk.

When I open my eyes, I catch my reflection in the massive horizontal mirror nailed to the wall opposite me. Under the dim lighting the dark eyeliner I'm wearing makes my eye sockets look hollowed out. I look like I'm channeling the creepy figure from Edvard Munch's *The Scream*.

I step to the side so I can stop looking at myself.

Out of the corner of my eye, I see movement.

"Tristan," I say when he starts to walk past.

He halts, pursing his lips at the sight of me. He walks over to me. "I told you let's talk outside."

"It's raining and cold."

Again he rolls his eyes. I clench my fist at what a dick he's being.

"Why the hell did you invite me here to talk on the same night that you're hosting your entire family?" I demand.

He glances behind him, probably to make sure that no one hears. When he looks back at me, he looks bored and annoyed. "I already had plans for tonight."

"Tristan." His name is a curse I push out through gritted teeth. "Are you out of your mind? Inviting me here makes no sense. I'm the last person your family wants to see right now."

"And they wouldn't have seen you if you had stayed outside."

"You never told me to stay outside!"

Tristan whips his head around to check behind him. "Christ, Riley. Will you keep your voice down? I don't need you to cause a scene."

A bitter laugh falls from my mouth. "You're a piece of work. You tell me to come to the same restaurant that your family is dining at, and you blame *me* for causing a scene? Okay, Tristan." My phone buzzes in my pocket. I check it and see a text from Poppy.

Poppy: Everything going okay?

Me: Nope. Just walked in on Tristan's entire family dining at his pub.

Me: He told me to come to his pub to talk to him . . . on the same night that he planned a massive family dinner. Can you believe that?

Poppy: WTF?!

Me: I feel like I've been ambushed.

"Riley, could you possibly tear yourself away from your phone so we can finally talk?"

"Nope. You can wait till I'm done texting," I say, my eyes still glued to my phone.

When I finish and look up, I take in the impatience in his tone and body language, how his hands are folded in front of him, how he keeps looking at his wrist.

I register the watch he's wearing. It's a vintage Cartier—the watch I gave him for our first wedding anniversary.

Why is he wearing it still? After the disastrous way our relationship ended, why would he want to keep anything from me? And why would he wear it around Carly? Does she know her boyfriend is wearing an anniversary gift from his ex-wife?

The longer I stare at that watch, the more the shock and confusion inside me shift to rage. This disaster unfolded all because of Tristan, because he either wanted to see me sweat in front of his family or didn't care that I'd be walking into an uncomfortable situation.

I catch myself biting my tongue to keep from saying what I really want to say. That he's a jackass. That he's nothing to me anymore.

And then I wonder why. Why am I holding back? He doesn't deserve for me to think about his well-being when he's made it clear he doesn't give a shit about mine.

My eyes burn when I look at him. "You're such a jerk, Tristan."

"What?" He has the nerve to look confused.

"You invited me here, with your entire family and your new girl-friend, knowing that it would make me feel uncomfortable. Only a truly vile person would do that."

His eyes widen slightly at what I've said.

I point at his wrist. "I gave you that."

His expression turns annoyed as he fiddles with the band. "Yes, I recall."

"Why are you still wearing it? We're not together anymore. Doesn't that piss off Carly? That you still wear the watch that your ex-wife gave you?"

"God, Riley. Why do you have to deflect?" His tone is tired, like he's sick of talking to me, of listening to me. "We're here to discuss my family's flat. I've got a baby on the way, and I deserve to raise him in *my* home. My family's home."

Inside I can feel myself snap. Actually, "break" is a better word. The audacity Tristan has to bring up his unborn baby to try to manipulate me into giving up the flat. The acid in my stomach curdles.

"No," I bite. "There's nothing to discuss. I came here to remind you that legally the flat is mine. I'm not giving it to you or anyone else in your family."

He scowls. "Technically that's not true. I believe my cousin is currently living there with you. So in a way it's still in our family."

His tone is low, but I don't miss the bite in his words. The longer I stare at Tristan's face, the less I recognize him. I can't remember him looking this smug, sounding this cruel. For a moment, I wonder if he's acting like this because he's stressed about the birth of his baby. But then I halt that thought the moment it materializes in my brain. That doesn't matter. That isn't an excuse for him to behave like an entitled jerk. That doesn't give him the right to treat me like this, to speak to me like I'm nothing, to order me around and demand that I give up something that's rightfully mine.

I look down at my trembling hands. All I feel is anger. It pumps hot inside me. I can feel it coursing through me with fury, like lava bursting from a volcano.

"That's fucking rich. You insinuate that I'm trashy for being with your cousin after we broke up even though *you* were the one who cheated."

I've stepped into Tristan's space. I'm crowding him, and judging by his wide-eyed stare and how his brows are hitting his hairline, he doesn't like this one bit.

"You broke us, Tristan. You destroyed us with your affair. You cheated on me for god knows how long. You got another woman pregnant behind my back. The whole time we were together, I was so happy. But it was a lie. *We* were a lie. Our entire relationship, our marriage, our life together was a lie. Because of you, Tristan. Fuck you."

I'm panting when I finish. And my throat is sore. That's when I realize I've been shouting. This time my hands are trembling so hard that I can't even curl them into fists.

When I look at Tristan, I'm stunned. That unflappable, unbothered facade has cracked. There's pain in those blue eyes as he looks at me.

"Riley, I—"

I move past him. "I'm done. Don't ever contact me again."

I head for the door.

"Riley, wait!"

I stop at the sound of Nesta's pleading voice. When I spin around, she's standing just a few feet away, looking like she's about to burst into tears. Before I can say anything, she pulls me into a hug.

I nuzzle that wild mass of copper-red curls. "I miss you," she says in a shaky voice. "I-I didn't know you were coming."

"It's okay. I . . . I miss you too." I sniffle.

Half of the tension riddling my neck and shoulders dissipates. I can feel in the tightness of Nesta's hug just how much she missed me—how much she still cares about me.

"Nesta, goodness. Get a hold of yourself."

My muscles go tense in an instant at the sound of Portia's voice.

"Shove it, Auntie Portia," Nesta says without moving from our embrace. I feel my body relax, comforted by the way she tells off Portia so easily. "I haven't seen my favorite cousin-in-law in months. I owe her a proper hug."

I smile despite the palpable tension infiltrating this space.

"I miss coming to your shop," Nesta says.

"You're always welcome. Always."

We pull apart, but Nesta keeps hold of my shoulders. "Really?" Her cinnamon-hued eyes glisten with unshed tears. "I just figured you wouldn't want to see me . . ."

I shake my head. "I always want to see you. And Roland. And Molly. I miss you all."

I clock Tristan and Portia in my peripheral vision. I don't care that they can hear us. I don't care that they're both probably annoyed and pissed that I'm trying to rekindle my friendship with their family member. Nesta means the world to me. I've missed having her in my life. And yeah, I know she eventually comes to see me. But that won't be for months. This is the last time I'll get to see her till she walks into my shop on a cold February day, her beautiful toddler in her arms.

"I know this isn't an easy situation," I say to her. "And I get it if you need some time. But you're always welcome in my life. Whenever you're ready."

She reacts with a shaky smile.

"Nesta, what on earth?"

We both twist around and spot Tristan's grandparents standing next to Portia, twin scowls on their faces.

Nesta rolls her eyes in full view of them.

"What are you doing speaking to her?"

Tristan's grandmother Agnes looks like she just downed a gallon of lemon juice, given the way her thin lips are twisted in pure disgust. The sight of me clearly repulses her.

"That woman is no longer part of our family," their grandfather Edward says gruffly. "No need to converse with her."

Nesta lets out a delirious laugh. "You two are beyond ridiculous. Riley has been nothing but polite and kind to you the years that she's known you. She's the one who gets cheated on by your pathetic grandson, and yet *she* is the one we should ostracize?"

Tristan flinches.

"You know what, I'm tired of this." Nesta wipes her nose on her wrist. I dig a tissue from the pocket of my jacket and hand it to her. She tells me a quiet thanks and wipes at her face.

She turns to Tristan. "You're an asshole for what you did to Riley, Tristan. I should have said it months ago, when we all found out about it, but I tried to take the high road and bite my tongue because Carly showed up pregnant with your baby, and they were going to be part of the family, and to be honest, I hadn't the slightest clue what in the world to do, because fucking Christ, it was an absolute mess . . ."

Tristan's shoulders slump, almost like he was anticipating this verbal dressing-down from his cousin.

"But screw it. I'm finally saying it because no one in our family has the stones to tell you to your face how angry we are with you for hurting your angel of an ex-wife."

Nesta lets out a bitter-sounding chuckle. "Except Milo. He's the one person in this family who had the guts to do what was right. To align himself with the right person." She pivots to me. "I'm sorry I never came to you, Riley. I should have. I was just so thrown at what happened. It was like whiplash. One minute we heard you two had split up; the next we heard that Tristan had gotten back together with his ex, who was about to have his baby . . . We put two and two together, and . . ." Nesta's lips quiver. "I'm ashamed to say that I was more concerned with keeping the peace in my family than doing the right thing and seeking you out, making sure you were okay."

My eyes burn as I take in how pained she looks as she explains herself. Her lip is quivering so hard, my own lips ache just seeing it.

"I get it, Nesta," I croak out.

"It doesn't make it right, though." She squeezes my hand.

"Well." Tristan's grandmother runs her palm along the front of her cream-hued blouse. "This is all quite embarrassing to see our family lose their composure so publicly. I'm quite ashamed of you, Nesta."

Nesta rolls her eyes and sniffles. "What else is new," she mutters. "I'm not ashamed."

I whip my head toward the entrance of Last One Standing and see Milo standing there in jeans and a jacket, soaking wet from the rain. When he steps to my side, a million water droplets fall from his dark-gray puffer coat onto the stone floor.

He aims his gaze at Nesta. "I'm proud of you for speaking your truth, Nesta. Especially in front of this bunch, who have all been fixated on maintaining a proper appearance despite all the fucked-up things so many people in this family have been doing for generations."

I notice the dazed look on his grandparents' faces as they gaze at him.

He turns to me. His deep-brown eyes shine with worry.

"You're here," I say, my voice a mix of dazed and unbelieving.

He offers a sad smile. "Nesta texted me what was going on."

I thank her.

"You haven't come to your senses yet, it seems." Agnes shakes her head as she looks at Milo. She narrows her gaze at her favorite grandson. "A shame, really. We'd give anything to have you back in the family, dear. Why you aligned yourself with your cousin's ex is beyond any of us."

"Speak for yourself, Gran," Nesta says.

Just then Roland walks in on us. His brown eyes go wide. "Oh . . . what did I miss?"

Nesta starts to say she'll catch him up right as Milo huffs out a heavy breath. He rolls his shoulders, like he's prepping himself for something.

"Okay, this ends right fucking now."

Everyone freezes at Milo's booming voice. Agnes looks like she just witnessed a demon stroll into the room. Her eyes are wide with shock.

"Gran. Grandad. You know I love you, but you two are some of the most problematic people I've ever met," Milo says. "You too, Aunt Portia."

Portia clutches at her pearl necklace like some uptight upper-class cliché.

"Uncle Weston too. But he's never around, since he prefers to spend his time traveling, doing who knows what instead of spending time with his own family, so I guess I can't really tell him that," Milo mutters. He turns back to his grandparents. "I know you don't like my mom because she's Portuguese and American. I know that you make an exception for me because my dad is your son. And that's beyond fucked. I know you come from a different time, but you live in the present day. It's not okay to treat people like shit because they look different from you or because they come from a different country. It's hateful. It's racist. It's bigoted. Shame on you for acting like that." He runs a hand through his damp hair. "And shame on me for waiting so many years to call you out on it."

When he takes a second to catch his breath, you could hear a pin drop, everyone is so quiet, so still.

Milo aims a steely stare at his grandparents once more. As the seconds pass, it softens. "It breaks my heart not to have you in my life. But I won't stand for you mistreating Riley. We're officially done."

The way Agnes grabs her hands to her chest worries me for the briefest second. Is she having a heart attack?

But then I see the pain as it flashes in her eyes. In Edward's eyes too. They're devastated at losing their grandson, at seeing him remove himself from their lives.

In the stress and chaos of this moment, I look at Milo. I take in his tall stance, the sure expression on his face. He looks like he's never been more certain than this moment, when he's defended me in front of his entire family.

I think back to the way Milo went off on Carly and her friends when we overheard them gossiping about me at that pub. How he defended me just like he is now.

How I was wrong to get upset with him then. I wasn't used to having a partner defend me. I am now, though.

Warmth courses through me. A familiar comfort hits.

I think of what he said that night when we fought on the sidewalk outside the pub.

I don't care who it is. I don't care how awkward it makes family dinners or gatherings or holidays or whatever. I'll always defend you.

Emotion surges inside me. He glances over at me, the hard look on his face softening as he gazes at me.

My voice is soft when I tell him, "Thank you." Emotion flashes in his eyes, his gaze on me focused and clear.

The dozen of us quietly stand around and process what's happened. I wonder if this is it, if this is what will jolt Agnes and Edward into doing the right thing—putting aside their dislike of me and Milo's mom for the sake of their grandson.

But neither of them budges. They just stay standing there, looking devastated, not saying a word.

Milo turns back to look at them. I take in his expression. He doesn't seem upset or fazed at all. He pivots his gaze to Tristan, who looks like he's about to shatter his own jaw with how hard he's biting down.

"You already know what I think of you," Milo says to Tristan. "I won't repeat myself. But I will say this: stay the hell away from Riley. Nothing she does is your business anymore. If you have an issue with the flat or some other bullshit, take it up with her lawyer."

When Tristan starts to step forward, I can feel the panic rising inside me. But then I see a small hand grab at him, keeping him in place. It's Carly.

I take in the stunned look on her face, how her body language reads uncomfortable and anxious and worried all at once. She stays behind Tristan and doesn't say a word. It's like she's too afraid to make a sound, to be seen and heard . . . to be the one this toxic group singles out as the new person to hate.

I was like that. Not anymore, though. Being welcomed and accepted by Milo's mom and her family has made me feel bolder, braver, stronger. I feel seen and heard in a way I never was with Tristan's mom and grandparents.

The longer I look at Carly, the clearer my thoughts are: I feel sorry for her. Yeah, when I first found out about her affair with Tristan—the first time I saw them at that Hampstead house with their son, kissing and embracing—I felt hate. For both of them. How could they cheat and hide and lie and sneak around? How could they smile and laugh and kiss and be affectionate knowing that their actions resulted in breaking someone else's heart? In ruining someone else's life?

But now I realize that I don't care about the answers to any of those questions. When I look at Tristan, I don't recognize him anymore. He's just someone from my past. A mistake. A prior heartbreak. When I look at him, I don't feel jealousy or longing. I just feel pain and anger.

And when I look at her, I feel pity. He's her problem now.

A crashing sound echoes from the back, where the kitchen is. Tristan darts off in that direction, but he doesn't make it more than a few steps before Poppy comes stomping out.

"Ah. Here he is. The cheating bastard. How are you, cheating bastard?"

Tristan's face ignites to a familiar shade of red. His gaze narrows, and I can almost feel the anger coursing through him.

"What the hell are you doing here?" he snaps.

She leans against the empty host lectern and flashes a taunting smile. "Just stopping by to tell you what a cruel and worthless cunt you are for ambushing my best friend."

As surprised as I am to see Poppy, I'm relieved too. It feels really, really good to see the people I love stand up for me.

Tristan glowers at me before he lets out a bitter laugh. "Of course you'd bring in reinforcements."

That anger from earlier simmers inside me once more. "Why shouldn't I? You have your family here. I have mine too." I stand tall as I say it, emboldened.

Just then Desmond stumbles from the hallway leading to the kitchen. "Poppy, why did you go in through the back . . . ?"

He trails off when he sees the dozen of us standing off in the pub's cramped entryway. He clears his throat, his expression sheepish. "I do apologize for us barging in like this."

Tristan rolls his eyes, grumbling. "Pathetic fucking lot," he mutters under his breath.

And then something happens that I've never witnessed before. Desmond glares. He turns to Tristan. "What was that?"

Tristan rolls his eyes and doesn't answer him.

Desmond puffs out his chest. "If anyone is fucking pathetic, it's you, Tristan."

Everyone goes quiet at the sternness in Desmond's voice. I can't remember him sounding this angry before. Even Poppy is staring at him in shock.

"I never liked you, you posh . . ." Desmond frowns and scrunches his lips, like he's working up the nerve to get out the words. "You posh prick."

Poppy stammers. Milo stares at him with his mouth half-open.

"All the money in the world can't buy decency," Desmond says. "You're a disgrace for how you treated Riley."

Desmond lets out a breath, his shoulders slumping. He gasps, like he's just finished sprinting. "Christ, I've been holding that in for ages."

It's a long moment before I can get the words out. "Wow. Thanks, Desmond."

He nods at me. Poppy walks up to him, her crystal-blue eyes dazed, and pats his arm. "That was fucking hot, Des."

He shakes his head, like he's snapping out of a trance. "Um, sorry for the colorful language . . ."

"Don't apologize," Milo says. "You're supporting your friend."

The worry on Desmond's face eases as he looks at Milo.

"Well, isn't this just delightful," Tristan mutters, glancing at each of us before settling on Milo.

Tristan closes the space between them in less than two seconds. As I stand off to the side and watch the two of them stare each other down, I can feel my entire body seize. Every muscle is tight with tension. I quickly glance down at their hands; they're both making loose fists.

I hold my breath in anticipation of who's going to throw the first punch.

The alcohol smell on Tristan's breath is somehow stronger than it was when he came up to me. "How does it feel, cousin?"

"How does what feel?" Milo says through gritted teeth.

An ugly smirk dances on Tristan's lips. "Dining on my leftovers. Does that make you feel special? Knowing that my trophy wife gets passed to you now?"

I flinch at Tristan's words.

He smirks at his cousin, his blue eyes taunting, defiant. "Does this feel as fun as the last time you—"

Milo shoves Tristan back so hard, he crashes into the nearby wall, knocking the wind out of him. Tristan quickly rights himself. He moves to charge Milo, but Milo socks him in the stomach.

My hands fly to my mouth, barely muffling the shriek I let out. Everyone is gasping and yelling around us. Déjà vu sets in. This fight happened, right here in this pub, between Tristan and Milo. Only this time Milo's the one to land a hit.

Just like before, it ends in a chaotic scramble. Carly and Portia run to Tristan. Nesta and Roland head to Milo. Desmond and Poppy stand off to the side, eyes wide and darting between Milo and Tristan, taking it all in. And I'm on my own, fighting off the weird fog that's taken over me. I can't seem to move or talk right now. All I can do is stand back and observe.

Tristan groans before standing up, brushing off his mother and Carly as they fuss over him. "You son of a—"

"Don't fucking start, Tristan. I'm ending this, right here, right now. If you so much as think about uttering another insulting word about Riley, I'll fucking end you."

Milo's threat booms loud against the walls of the entryway. Everyone falls quiet.

"You had her, Tristan. You lucky son of a bitch, you had her. She was yours, and you fucked it up. Like you always do."

The two of them scowl at each other, chests heaving, fists still clenched, like two posturing gorillas.

"Riley was always too good for you," Milo says. "You don't deserve to breathe the same air as her. And if you ever try to reach out to her again, I'll make sure you regret it."

Tristan opens his mouth. Milo takes another step so he's fully in his cousin's space. "Don't. You. Fucking. Dare."

Tristan closes his mouth, but I can tell by the crazed look in his eyes he's thinking, contemplating, wondering if he has it in him to see if his cousin will make good on his threat.

"Leave. Now." Tristan's growled demand has Desmond heading for the door. Poppy stays in place, though, her gaze bouncing between Milo and Tristan.

"What the—where did that smoke come from?" Roland asks.

I look up and see a black-gray cloud wafting from the hallway just as the fire alarm wails. Muffled shouting echoes from the kitchen. A moment later, someone comes sprinting out to the entryway. Maybe a busboy, based on his uniform.

"The kitchen's on fire!"

Screams shatter my daze. I shoot a look to Poppy. She was just in the kitchen. And she was smoking earlier. Add that to the fact that she's been champing at the bit to stick it to Tristan for what he did to me, and there's a strong possibility that she started the fire.

"What?" she says to me. Much to my surprise she looks utterly clueless.

More shouting around us. Tristan takes off to the back. Someone yells to grab the fire extinguisher. Someone else hollers to call the fire department.

The rest of us scramble out the front door into the rain. Milo grips my hand in his. I grab Poppy by the arm, shout for her to grab hold of Desmond, and pull her along with us down the block, away from where everyone else is crowding. Soon the black cloud of smoke grows bigger. Flames glow in the restaurant's interior.

Milo pulls me into a hug. "Are you okay?" he asks.

I close my eyes, savoring the warm, firm feel of his body. My heart rattles in my chest from the chaos of minutes ago. But in his embrace, I'm calm, I'm safe.

"Yeah. I'm okay," I whisper into his shoulder.

He squeezes me tight before releasing me. "I'm gonna check on Nesta and Roland. Stay here with Poppy, okay?"

I nod and watch Milo jog off down the block.

I turn to Poppy, who's gawking at the fire as it consumes the pub. I grip her arm.

"What?" She looks startled.

"Did you start the fire in the kitchen?" I'm careful to keep my voice down.

Her jaw falls to the pavement. "What the hell, Ri! Are you serious?"

"You mentioned you were smoking earlier, and I thought that maybe—"

She jerks out of my hold and crosses her arms over her chest. "Fuck no. God, how could you think that about me?"

She steps away from me. I shake my head, feeling like garbage for even thinking my best friend could do such a thing. "You're right. I'm sorry. I don't know what I was thinking . . ."

Her expression softens, and she steps back toward me. She pulls me into a hug. "Believe me, if I wanted to set fire to Tristan's pub, I'd show up with a flamethrower. I wouldn't use a pitiful little cigarette."

I let out a weak chuckle, feeling in that moment just how exhausted I am from what just went down. My neck and shoulders are sore from tensing the muscles in them as I watched Milo and Tristan's violent showdown.

Sirens blare in the distance. Poppy and I break apart right as a fire truck screeches to a stop in front of us. We all move farther out of the way for the crew and watch as they grab a hose and douse the restaurant in water.

I watch as the flames and fire eventually die down, leaving the brick exterior charred and black.

For a while we all stand there and look at the damaged building—Tristan and his family huddled together at one end of the street, mine at the other.

I blink, in awe of the damage. I hazard a look at Tristan, his mom, and his grandparents. They're all frowning at the ruined pub. I can't tell if they're more angry or sad.

After a second, I look away. As much as I dislike all of them, it feels intrusive to stare as they process the loss of one of Tristan's businesses.

A moment later I hear Tristan raise his voice. I look over and see him talking to one of the firefighters. He's gesturing like he's frustrated, then booms out the words "grease fire."

"A grease fire . . . ," I mumble to myself.

One of the other firefighters walking by looks back at me. "It was a good thing you lot got out when you did."

We all spend the next few minutes milling around, unsure of what to do. I watch as Milo checks on Nesta and Roland.

He catches my eye and offers a small smile. I return one of my own. Even that's tiring. All the muscles in my face ache.

I catch Poppy watching the two of us; then she aims a knowing look at me.

"What?" I tug at the belt of my trench coat.

"I think I'm starting to like Milo."

"Seriously?"

She nods.

"You missed him defending me earlier."

I fill her in on what he said to his grandparents. Her crystal-blue eyes are wide when I finish.

"Fucking hell. I had him pegged all wrong." She looks over at him as he offers Nesta his jacket.

"So did I," I muse. "But I think I finally see him for who he really is."

Milo walks over to us. "You guys wanna grab a drink? I could use one after tonight."

Desmond nods. "I think we should."

Milo points out a pub across the street. He walks over to Roland and Nesta again and asks them if they want to come too.

"I wish we could join, but we have to go home to Molly," Roland says. Nesta nods before turning to me. The look on her face is pained, like she's trying to hold back tears.

My heart sinks. I don't want Nesta to go. Or Roland. I miss them both so much.

I pull Roland into a quick hug, then turn to Nesta and pull her into my arms, holding her tight. People step around us on the sidewalk, grumbling about how we're in the way. I don't care. I need this hug to last. It's been so long since I've gotten to hug her.

She starts to pull away, and my heart sinks. I give her a quick squeeze, then release her. She holds me by both hands, her eyes teary as she looks at me.

"We're going away for the next few months," she says, her voice soft and shaky. "To France, to stay with Roland's grandparents so they can spend some time with Molly. When we come back, can I see you?"

I nod and flash a wobbly smile. I blink, and the memory of Nesta walking into my shop that February day flashes in my head. She comes back, and things between us end up okay.

"Thank you for what you said, for standing up for me in there. That meant everything."

She hesitates. "I should have done more, sooner."

"Nesta, no. This whole situation is beyond complicated, beyond fucked up. I understand why you didn't say anything."

Her eyes are teary as she smiles at me. "God, you're an angel. I love you."

I hug her again. "I love you."

We let go, and she walks off with Roland. Everyone says goodbye and waves them off. As I wipe my face, Milo walks up next to me. He touches his hand to my arm.

"Are you okay?" His brow is furrowed in concern, and his voice is soft.

I shrug. "Kind of. It was good to see Nesta. But I feel like I've just been hit by a truck, emotionally anyway."

He lets out a sad laugh before exhaling sharply. "Same."

"That makes three of us," Poppy says as she walks up to us.

"Four." Desmond shoves his hands in his coat pockets. He looks dazed and fatigued.

"Christ, I need that drink," Poppy mutters.

Desmond nods while Milo and I say "God, yes" at the same time.

Chapter 28

"Fucking hell, why did I let you talk me into Scotch?" Poppy groans as she twists around to look at Milo, who's walking behind her.

We just spent the last hour and a half at a gastropub drinking to decompress from the events of earlier this evening. We're all definitely tipsy, but Poppy had the most to drink out of all of us. The morning I witnessed makes a lot more sense now.

Desmond slinks his arm through hers. "It's all right, Pops. We'll get you some water, tuck you into bed, and you'll feel better. Promise."

She spins back around and snuggles into Desmond's embrace. "Thank you, my love."

I smile at the sound of Poppy going soft for her husband. She normally doesn't use that gentle, pleading tone unless she's sick or had too much to drink. And even though I feel bad that she drank too much, it's sweet to hear her go all gooey. It doesn't happen often.

Milo winces. "Sorry, Poppy."

She waves a hand in the air. "Eh, it's all right. You're forgiven for the way you told off fuckface and stood up for my best friend."

I peer over at Milo, who's grinning at the ground, hands tucked in his pockets as he walks. "That means a lot, Poppy. Thanks."

He looks up, and his eyes turn shy when he realizes I'm watching him. My chest squeezes at the sight of him so happy at winning my best friend's approval.

"Oh! What's that I smell?" Poppy straightens up, her blonde bob moving in a perfect swoosh as she pivots her head from side to side. "Kebabs! Fuck yes!"

She darts over to the food cart, Desmond trailing behind her. The line is three people deep, so while Poppy and Desmond wait to order, Milo and I stand off to the side.

"I owe you an explanation," Milo says out of the blue.

I glance over at him. "For what?"

He huffs out a breath, his shoulders sagging. "For that trophy wife comment I made all those years ago."

"Oh."

I let myself think about that moment, that night when Milo and I first met and I overheard him talking about me near the bathrooms. It doesn't cut like it did before. But I'm still curious as to why he said it, especially after he has admitted to liking me and having feelings for me.

For a long second he holds eye contact with me. "This is gonna sound like such a cop-out, but I swear it's the truth. It was more an insult to Tristan than to you." He pauses and glances off to the side for a moment. "Tristan used to joke about nabbing a trophy wife. Like that was his major goal in life. That always bothered me. It was shallow and sexist as fuck. Not to mention entitled, thinking he deserved some beautiful wife just so he could cheat on her . . ."

I hold up a hand. "Milo, wait. The trophy wife part didn't bother me as much as the rest of what you said."

He frowns.

"I mean, yeah, no one wants to be called a trophy wife. But when you said, 'What the hell is Tristan thinking? A guy like him and a girl like her?'"

My face heats as I say it. It catches me off guard just how much repeating those words bothers me.

"It really sucked to hear you say that. It felt like you were saying I wasn't good enough for your cousin."

Milo's jaw muscle bulges through his stubbled skin. A hard swallow moves through his throat.

He shakes his head. "That's not at all what I meant, Riley. I swear. That was a dig on Tristan. I couldn't believe a sack of shit like him was able to land a woman like you. Beautiful, sweet, smart, funny, kind . . ." He trails off before pulling his hand from his coat pocket and cupping my face. He steps closer to me. "I'm sorry, Riley. It was a shitty thing to say. If I could take it back, I would. But I swear it was never meant as an insult to you. You are the last person I ever wanted to hurt."

Milo's softly spoken words hang like a damp fog in the cold air. I stand there, quiet as I stare into his mahogany-brown eyes. My skin feels icy and on fire all at once.

"I'm sorry for hurting you, Riley."

My chest aches at the pained look on his face, the sincerity in his words. Yeah, he hurt my feelings. But everything he's said, everything he's done, more than makes up for it.

I pull him into a hug. "It's okay," I whisper into his chest. "We're good now. I forgive you."

He pulls back to look at me. "You mean that?"

And that's when I realize: this is what Milo was so concerned about. This is what he was talking about when he asked me if I meant what I said.

"Of course I mean it," I say, looking him straight in the eye.

He pulls me back into his chest. When I feel him relax against my embrace before squeezing me tight, I close my eyes and smile. So *this* is what it feels like to be with someone who's honest and owns their mistakes, who apologizes, who goes out of their way to make things right.

"Let's get a move on, lovebirds!"

We break apart at Poppy's slurred holler. When I look over at her, she's chowing down on a lamb kebab while walking arm in arm with Desmond.

"God, I'm fucking exhausted," Poppy says around a mouthful of kebab. "Don't think I'll be able to make it home in this state."

"You can crash at our place," Milo tells her.

"But the mattress in the guest room is too firm," she whines.

Desmond shushes her and apologizes to Milo, but he just laughs.

"It's either the bed or the sectional," he tells Poppy.

Poppy groans. "Bloody fucking sectionals." She takes another massive bite of kebab before reaching over and giving Milo an appreciative pat on the shoulder. "Fine. Thanks, big boy."

Milo and I chuckle and walk the rest of the way to the flat.

Chapter 29

May 10, 2024

When I wake up, I'm in a dimly lit airplane. Again.

I don't jolt up in my seat this time. This time, I stay lying down in my capsule / airplane-seat-bed thing. We must have managed to get first class again. I blink a few times before my eyesight adjusts to the dimness, and I look over at Milo, who's lying down next to me, eyes closed, breathing softly as he sleeps. I squint at the screen in front of me and see that we're flying over Canada. I tap the touch screen to see where we're headed. London.

When I swipe the screen left to see where we're coming from, my breath catches. San Francisco, California—where I grew up and where my family still lives.

I smile to myself. It's been so long since I've visited home, more than a year.

I hear the sound of fabric rustling. I peer over at Milo, who's stirring. He opens his eyes. When he sees me, he flashes a groggy smile.

"Hey there, Sleeping Beauty," he whispers.

"Hey."

"How long have you been awake?"

"Not long. Just a few minutes."

He leans up and stretches his arms in the air. The hem of his dove-gray Henley shirt rides up, revealing a peek of his toned stomach. A flight attendant walks by. I don't miss the way her gaze lands on Milo's exposed abs.

I hold back a chuckle as she stops to check on him.

"Any breakfast for you, sir?" she asks.

"Just some water would be great, thank you."

"You sure you don't want anything to eat?" she asks sweetly, her eyes bright as she stares at him. "We've got a cheese omelet or eggs Benedict on the menu. Or a smoked vegetable crepe if you're vegan."

Milo aims a polite smile at her. "I'm really okay. Thank you. I think my girlfriend would like a tea, though."

He gestures to me, and I try not to laugh when the flight attendant aims a tight smile at me. "Tea for you, miss?"

I nod. "Yes, please."

She walks off without another word.

Milo shakes his head. "Wow. A bit much, huh?"

"She was smitten with you. I can't say I blame her."

He grins and reaches out to swipe my hand in his. "How are you holding up after leaving your family?"

"I'm doing okay." I try to contain my smile. I can't wait to wake up the next day and hug my mom and brother.

But then I take in how Milo's expression shifts from soft to somber. "I'm so glad your mom ended up being okay. And that it all worked out."

He gives my hand a gentle squeeze. The tender gesture helps take the edge off the flash of panic that hits me. That must be why we went to California—something happened to my mom.

I nod and look away, hoping that the panic I'm feeling doesn't translate to my facial expression. I silently hope that when I see my mom, when I see whatever state she's in that warranted a last-minute flight home, it's not bad.

I look at him. "I'm glad too."

For the rest of the flight, I quietly hope that everything—my mom, my brother, my family, Milo—really is okay.

Chapter 30

May 9, 2024

When I wake up, I'm in my childhood bedroom, which is now a functioning storage room. I peer over at Milo, who's fast asleep next to me. Good. I don't want him to get up right now. I want to be alone as I go and check on my mom.

I slowly and quietly inch my way out of the covers. As I stand up, I hear the telltale noises of my mother in the kitchen: dishes softly clanking and the sizzling of the ancient coffee machine that she's had ever since I was a little kid.

My heartbeat eases from frantic to just speedy. That's her in the kitchen right now. She's well enough to go through her normal morning routine. That means she must be okay.

I shake my head. Of course she's okay. I've talked to her in my timeline—in the future, technically. I know she's fine. I shouldn't be so worried.

I can't help it, though. She's my mom. I love her more than anything, and even just the thought of her being hurt is enough to send me into a worry spiral.

I walk quietly around the cluttered room, somehow moving past the folding chairs, spare ottoman, and plastic bin of winter clothing without making a sound. Once I'm out of my bedroom and into the hallway, I head to the kitchen. My bladder screams for me to stop when

I pass the bathroom, but I ignore it. I'll pee in a minute. I need to see my mom first.

When I see her standing at the kitchen counter with her left leg in a cast, I'm hit with relief. A broken leg. Serious, for sure, but manageable. People break their bones all the time and recover.

When she turns around and sees me, she starts to smile. Before she can utter even a word, I pull her into a hug.

"Goodness, *anak*." She lets out a surprised laugh. "Good morning to you too."

"You're okay," I say quietly.

Another chuckle. "Of course I'm okay."

I give her a tight squeeze in my arms before breaking our hug. I grip her shoulders and glance down at her leg.

She pats my arm. "Oh, *anak*. You've been like this every day you've been here this week. I'm fine." She does a small kick with her injured leg. "See? Just fine."

When she grins, her carob-brown eyes light up. Two sets of faint crow's-feet flank her beautiful eyes. I feel my heartbeat slow as I take in her expression, how she's relaxed and happy all at once.

"You sure?"

She tilts her head at me and raises an eyebrow. Her signature mom look where she's silently saying, "You're the kid, I'm the mom. Of course I know better than you."

"Oh, *anak*. It's only a broken leg."

"Only?" I hold back a scoff. She hates it when I or Jordan scoff at her.

She steps out of my hold to pour herself a mug of coffee. "It was a clean break, remember? And remember when I told you that the doctor said I got lucky because of that? Right through the bone. He said the way I fell off that step stool was practically perfect."

I can't help but flinch. "Of course I do," I lie.

"I'll be just fine. The surgeon drilled screws into my leg. I'm like RoboCop." She chuckles and runs a hand through her shoulder-length jet-black hair.

I take a moment to absorb what she's said. *Surgery. Screws. Clean break. Right through the bone.*

Those are some jarring-as-hell words to process. But she's fine. She's standing in front of me, joking and smiling and laughing, going about her morning routine like it's a normal day.

I need to ease up.

"Just like RoboCop." I try to smile.

She winks at me and starts to offer me some coffee but stops herself. "Oh, wait, I forgot that you like tea more now."

I grab a mug from the cupboard. "That doesn't mean I've sworn off coffee completely." I pour myself a cup while she dumps a ridiculous amount of vanilla creamer into her cup.

I resist the urge to help her as she makes her way to the kitchen table. There's already a small plate of *pandesal* sitting out, her go-to breakfast. But when she pauses and grimaces slightly as she pulls a chair out, I rush over and do it for her.

She rolls her eyes. "I could have gotten it."

"I know, but I'm here. Let me help you."

"*Anak*, I've had nearly a week of you fussing over me," she grumbles. "I'm sad you're leaving tonight, but I won't lie. It'll be nice to be on my own again. I can take care of myself."

I shake my head, only slightly annoyed since I've heard her repeat that phrase my whole life. My fiercely independent mother hates being doted on. She's always been this way—strong willed and determined to do everything by herself, even in the most desperate times.

I think back to when I was in middle school and she and my dad divorced. It was then that he started traveling a lot for work, and we hardly saw him anymore. It was a rough transition—she went from having a partner to share the load of parenthood to having to do it all on her own. Supporting two kids on a single nurse's salary, picking up extra shifts, helping Jordan and me with homework, shuttling us to school and activities and appointments, taking care of us when we were sick, and a million other things. But she handled it all.

Even now as adults, when Jordan and I send her money to help out or try to talk her into dropping a shift at work now that she's close to retirement, she always rebuffs us. Always with her trademark phrase: "I appreciate that you care, but I can take care of myself."

I blow on my steaming coffee and choose not to challenge her on this. I've learned to pick my battles with my mom. This isn't worth an argument. So we sip our coffee in companionable silence.

I let the hot, bitter liquid coat my tongue. It's been months since I've had coffee. The flavor hits differently this time. It's not that it tastes bad. Just that it doesn't taste as good as I remember it.

She chuckles. "What, you don't like my coffee anymore?"

I shake my head. "It's not that. It's still good. But I guess I'm developing a taste for tea now."

She lets out a soft laugh as she sips. She swallows, then looks at me, her expression sober. "How are you doing, *anak*? Really."

I'm about to say that I'm doing well, but she keeps going.

"I can't believe Tristan did all that to you." Shaking her head, she mutters a Filipino curse word while gazing out the window. "What a snake. He had me fooled. I thought he was such a charmer. I should have listened to your brother."

She turns back to me and pats my hand. "I'm fine, Mom. Really."

Her deep-brown gaze studies me. "You sure? It's only been a few months since you found out what he did."

"I'm sure. I have a really good support system in place."

She sighs, then smiles slightly. "You mean Milo?"

Heat flashes across my cheeks as I take in my mother's knowing look. "Yes, Milo's been wonderful. So have Poppy and her husband. I'm good, Mom. Really."

She nods even though I know she wants to keep asking me to make absolutely sure I'm telling her the truth. I feel the slightest bit guilty. I need to cut her some slack. I fussed over her minutes ago when I saw her broken leg and wanted to make sure she was okay. She's doing the same to me right now, because she loves me and cares about me.

After a long sip of her coffee, she clears her throat.

"Don't hate me for saying this," she says. "But when I called you to tell you about my fall and that I'd have to have surgery and you told me you'd be on the first flight home . . . and you'd be bringing some new guy named Milo, I wasn't thrilled." She sighs. "And then when you told me he was Tristan's cousin, I got a bad feeling."

She sighs, her delicate shoulders lowering with the movement. "I owe you an apology for that. I shouldn't have been so distrusting of Milo. Especially after everything he's done for you and how he's helped you through the divorce."

I bite my tongue to keep from asking her for specifics. I just need to be patient and let this timeline play out. I'll find out soon enough.

"It's okay, Mom," I say instead. "Honestly, if you or Jordan or anyone else I cared about were in my position, I would have been suspicious too."

"Yeah, but I could have been nicer about it." She sighs, her gaze sad as she looks at me, then her coffee mug. She lets out a weak laugh. "I still can't believe he was so great when I demanded you put him on the phone to explain himself." She shakes her head, chuckling. "That's when he started to win me over."

"What do you mean?" I ask.

"When I realized how he was helping you, how he was going against his own cousin for your sake, I realized what a good guy he must be." She grins at me before cupping my cheek in her hand. "I'm so happy you brought him with you. The whole family is. They loved meeting him at the party the other day. Jordan needed a bit of convincing, though. Goodness, that boy. So stubborn. I don't know where he gets it from."

I start to laugh, then stop myself when she shoots me a look.

"I know, I know. Me. Of course he gets it from me," she says before her gaze on me turns sincere once more. "You've got a good man now, *anak*."

My chest warms at her heartfelt words. As the warmth dissipates, eagerness collides with my nerves when I think about the family party that will happen soon. I'm about to see how exactly things go down between Jordan and Milo, and I'm nervous as hell.

"Speaking of the devil." Mom looks past my shoulder and grins. I turn around and see Milo flash a groggy smile at me, then her.

"Good morning, Maria. How's your leg?"

"Just fine. Now come on, you know we don't do good mornings like that."

Milo's smile turns shy as he walks over and leans down to give Mom a hug. They break apart, and he offers to refill her coffee.

"So nice of you to offer, *anak*. Thank you."

Milo steps over to the counter and refreshes her mug.

"Creamer and a sprinkle of sugar?" he asks.

"Yes, please."

He sets it in front of her, and she pats his hand in thanks. He turns to me and presses a kiss to my cheek. "Want some tea?"

I nod. As he turns to the cupboard and fetches mugs for the both of us, all I can do is quietly take in the scene. Mom and Milo embracing like they've done this a dozen times before—which technically they have, at least in their timeline. How comfortable Milo is moving around my mother's kitchen. How happy Mom is to have him here.

It's weird and wonderful all at once.

Milo joins us at the kitchen table, and for a couple of minutes, he and Mom chat. She peers over at me, smiling. "This is nice, isn't it, *anak*?"

I nod, too dazed to speak at first. But then I smile at her and Milo. "It really is."

Chapter 31

May 5, 2024

I gaze around my mother's house. It's full of relatives chatting, eating, laughing, playing cards, and singing karaoke.

I spot Mom sitting at the dining room table with a couple of her cousins. I walk over to check on her.

"Everything good? You feeling okay? Your leg is elevated enough, right?" I reach down and adjust the pillow on the chair Mom is resting her foot on. "Did you get enough to eat? Here, let me get you a plate."

Her cousins laugh as she leans forward and gently swats at my hand. "Ay, *anak*, you've been fussing over me ever since you got here. For the millionth time, I'm fine. And I had two plates of food. I'm full."

She flashes a wide grin. I take in how bright and happy she looks, how she took the time to put on her nice makeup for today's family gathering: she's wearing her Mary Kay lipstick and mascara. She breaks them out only for special occasions. She's definitely feeling good if she went out of her way to do that.

"Your mom's right, *anak*," Auntie Betty chimes in. "I saw her scarf down her food in record time."

When Mom gently smacks her cousin's arm, they all laugh.

"We're looking after her, *anak*." Auntie Randi gently pats my hand. "You don't have to worry."

I soften as I look at my mom with her cousins. I give them all hugs.

Auntie Randi quirks her eyebrow at me and flashes a knowing smile as she looks past me. "Your boyfriend is so sweet. He's getting along so well with everyone."

I turn around and see him sitting on the living room floor cross-legged, playing *Mario Kart* with my cousin Elliot's son Nathan.

"You're too fast for me, buddy," Milo says to Nathan, who giggles as he expertly handles the controller. "Oh man, did you just pass me? Nathan! How could you?"

Nathan giggles even harder at Milo's exaggerated tone. Everyone watching them play laughs too. My insides go gooey at the sight of Milo charming my family.

"He said my pansit was the best he'd ever tasted!" Auntie Randi announces proudly.

"Did you know that he helped Uncle Wyatt set up the karaoke machine?" Auntie Betty adds. "Uncle Wyatt never lets anyone help him with electronics. I wish he would. Always takes him forever to set up anything, and half the time he breaks it." She mutters an Ilocano curse word before looking over at me again and schooling her features into a smile. "That means he really likes Milo."

Another burst of laughter and cheers comes from the living room. The four of us glance over just as Milo high-fives Nathan.

"That's how you know a man will be a good dad," Auntie Betty says matter-of-factly. "If he's this good with someone else's kids, he'll be amazing with his own."

Mom elbows her. "Ay, *manang*, don't say that. They just started dating. Don't put so much pressure on them."

Auntie Betty shrugs. "It's true, though." Auntie Randi nods along.

The three of them chat freely as if I'm not standing right there next to them, listening to everything they say. My skin heats as the nerves in my stomach crackle.

Kids.

I've never been baby crazy. The thought of having kids has never even occurred to me, not even when I was with Tristan.

But as I gaze over at Milo playing with my little cousins, I can't ignore that ache in my chest. No, it's not some magical change-of-heart moment. I don't suddenly want to birth five babies just because I witnessed my boyfriend doting on kids. But I'm open to it—I'm thinking about it. That's never happened before.

Mom asks me to refill her water. When I return with a full glass for her, I notice Auntie Betty and Auntie Randi are gone. She pats the chair next to her, and I sit down.

"Milo is a hit, *anak*. Everyone loves him."

She changes the subject and talks for a few minutes about something funny one of her cousins did when they were out shopping the other day. A familiar melody echoes from the living room. When I look over, I see Milo with a microphone from the karaoke machine in his hand sitting next to Nathan's older sister, Maizie, who's got a microphone in her hand too. She sways along with the beat of the pop song I don't know the name of but have heard a million times. Together she and Milo sing the lyrics. When Milo jokingly attempts a high note ridiculously off key, the kids fall into uncontrollable laughs.

"I'm really glad to hear everyone likes him," I say to Mom.

My mind flashes back to Tristan, even though I know it shouldn't. He should be the last person on my mind right now, but I can't help but make the comparison. I think back to the three times he traveled to the US to meet and visit with my family during our relationship. He was always polite and cordial. I could tell he was uncomfortable at how loud and touchy-feely my family was, though. The standard greeting among my relatives is a long hug and a kiss on the cheek, which was definitely not the norm for Tristan. I think I only saw him hug his own parents twice ever the entire time we were together.

But to his credit, he handled my family well, always hugging them back. Every time we went out to eat as a family or ordered takeout, he swooped in to take care of the check. But I could sense his discomfort. It was obvious in the way his smile didn't reach his eyes when he'd chat with my family, how he'd often slip out during dinners and family gatherings like this one, always on the phone for some work-related matter.

Or maybe he was talking to Carly. Or another woman.

My stomach churns at the thought. I glance back over at Milo, how this whole day he's been able to comfortably fit into the fun-loving chaos of my family's dynamic.

"You're thinking about Tristan, aren't you?"

I'm caught off guard by Mom's knowing tone and the inquisitive look in her eyes. Like she's studying me.

I shake my head. "Of course not."

"Oh, *anak*. No need to hide the truth."

I stammer, but she stops me with her hand on mine. "You're my baby girl. My only daughter. My firstborn. I carried you for almost ten months." She pats her tummy and chuckles. "I know you. I know that look you get on your face when you're hiding what you feel."

"What look? I don't do that," I say, my arms crossed over my chest.

Mom tilts her head at me. "Yes, you do. You've done it ever since you were little. It's pretty cute, actually."

She reaches over and cups my cheek in her hand, and I start to soften. Her expression turns tender when she pulls her arm away.

"It's okay that you're thinking of your ex, *anak*. It's completely natural."

I exhale. "Mom, we really don't have to talk about this."

She holds up a hand. "We do."

"This is supposed to be a happy, fun day with the family. We don't need to bring it all down by bringing up Tristan." I'm careful to keep my voice low. I don't want my family hearing what my mom and I are talking about.

Mom sighs. "We're not bringing anything down. It's okay to talk about your feelings, *anak*. It's healthy. And it's natural to think about your ex when you're only months out of a relationship—a marriage."

There's a blast of music as the song changes on the karaoke machine, drowning out our conversation.

"I thought about your dad a lot, too, when we broke up," she says when things quiet down.

I'm thrown by her mentioning Dad. They've been divorced for almost two decades. None of us have seen him in years.

"It's not like I wanted to," she says. "It's just that when you spend so much of your life with someone, you can't help thinking about them, even when they're gone. Even when you don't want to think about them." She taps her fingernails on her glass. "You know you're not supposed to, but it's like a reflex. And even though you shouldn't, you compare them to the people that you date afterward. For a little while, at least."

I'm quiet as I soak in what she's said, stunned that my mother is practically reading my mind.

She shrugs. "I'm sure not everyone does it. But we're all human. I promise you a lot of people do. And that's okay, as long as you don't do it forever—and as long as you don't let it consume you. If you spend the rest of your life comparing your new boyfriends to your exes, that's a recipe for disaster."

We're quiet for a while. And then I finally speak. "Okay, you're right. I was thinking about Tristan."

"That's okay," Mom says with a tender smile. "I like Milo. I know I don't know him well, but he seems like a sweet young man who makes you happy. And that's all that matters to me—your happiness."

"Really?"

She nods. "It doesn't hurt that he seems to fit into our family well. And what he's done to help you through your split with Tristan . . ." She goes quiet and turns her gaze off to the side. "I still can't believe it. He's got my respect, that's for sure."

Her gaze pivots to across the room. When I follow it, I see Jordan standing off to the side in the living room, next to a group of cousins who are chatting. Except Jordan isn't chatting. He's staring daggers at Milo. Milo is oblivious as he continues playing with our little cousins, smiling and laughing with them.

"It seems like your brother's gonna need some convincing, though," Mom says.

As I take in my brother's cold stare, I silently tell myself it's all going to be okay. Jordan and Milo eventually get on good terms. I think of when Jordan visits us in London, how he and Milo defend each other against Tristan, how they fist-bump in the taxi ride home, how they share that look of camaraderie—how they look at each other like they share a kinship, a brotherhood.

How the next time they meet, they treat each other as family.

That thought sticks with me, offering the slightest of comfort. But it evaporates the moment Jordan marches up to Milo and says, "Let's step outside."

Chapter 32

I clear the distance between the kitchen and living room in seconds. It's long enough for Milo to stand up and face my brother. To his credit, despite the outright aggression in my brother's demand and stance, Milo's expression and body language remain easy. His shoulders are relaxed and the look on his face is neutral.

"Jordan, what are you doing?" I say.

"Riley, it's all right," Milo says in a weirdly upbeat tone.

"I just wanna have a chat with my sister's new boyfriend. That's all."

I take in the tight smile on Jordan's face, his overly chipper tone. Yeah, this is complete bullshit.

I grab my brother by the arm and walk him to the hallway, away from the rest of the family, half of whom are looking over at us.

"What the hell are you doing?" I say in a low voice. "Are you seriously trying to start something with Milo in front of our whole family?"

He frowns and pulls his lips into his mouth before he sighs, his hard expression easing the slightest bit. "He's Tristan's cousin, Riley. I'd like to know why he thought it was cool to make a move on his cousin's ex-wife."

My blood boils. "Don't talk about me like I'm an object to fight over. I'm a person—I'm your older sister, and I can make my own decisions. I don't need my little brother policing who I choose to date."

He sighs, his shoulders slumping a little bit. "I just want to get to know the guy who's with my sister. That's all."

Footsteps echo behind me.

"It's okay, Riley. Really." I spin around to see Milo. "I'd like to get to know your brother too," he says.

"Good." Jordan claps Milo on the shoulder. I wince at the sound as it echoes in the hallway. That had to have hurt. Milo doesn't even flinch, though. It's like he was expecting it.

"Let's get a drink," Jordan mutters. Milo walks off with him.

They're headed for the garage. I go after them, but when I walk past the dining table, Mom reaches up to stop me.

"Let them have some time alone," she says.

"Mom, no way. Jordan's gonna try to pick a fight with him."

Mom sighs before hollering after him. "Jordan!" The entire house falls quiet at her go-to mom tone, that loud, sharp, no-nonsense voice that she's used on my brother and me our entire lives. Just the sound of our names spoken in that tone stilled us instantly. We knew she meant business.

Jordan stops dead in his tracks and spins around. "What is it, Mom?"

"You be nice to Milo. You hear me?"

Milo starts to smile before quickly reining in his expression. Mom tilts her head at Jordan. I don't miss the hard swallow that moves down my little brother's throat. That fiery look in his eyes is dialed back. Now he just looks more determined than pissed.

"Yes, Mom."

The two walk out the door.

"See, *anak*?" Mom smiles at me. "They'll be just fine."

My stomach churns. "I hope you're right."

~

"Why do you keep looking at the clock, *anak*?" Auntie Randi asks while I put a new liner in the trash can.

Before I can answer, Mom chimes in: "She's worried that Jordan and Milo will get into a fight. So silly."

"It's not silly," I say. "They've been in the garage for over an hour."

Mom waves a hand. "So? That must mean they're having so much fun together that they lost track of time."

If only. "I'm going to check on them."

"Oh, *anak*, just have some faith. It'll work out."

I ignore her as I walk off, my adrenaline pumping like hot steam from a teakettle. For the last hour I battled the urge to burst into the garage to see what they've been up to. Every time I started to walk in the direction of the garage door, Mom would stop me to ask for a refill on her water or to help her up so she could run to the bathroom.

But I can't take it anymore. My brother and my boyfriend might be beating each other to a pulp in the garage. I need to do something.

I push open the door and walk past my mom's car and out to the driveway, where there are lawn chairs set up. Mom always does that when family comes over, in case anyone wants some fresh air.

When I see Milo and Jordan sitting in the lawn chairs, their backs to me, a bottle of Scotch between them, I stop in my tracks. I'm about a dozen feet from them.

"Look, man," Jordan slurs. "I love my sister, okay? I know she's older than me and can take care of herself, but her ex was a dickhead. I mean, no offense, I know he's your cousin and all . . ."

Milo sways in his chair and shakes his head. "None taken. You're right. He's a dickhead."

The tension in my muscles eases. They're both drunk, but I can't detect an ounce of harshness in their conversation.

As quietly as I can, I step to the side so I can get a better look at their faces.

Jordan twists his head to look at Milo. "You really gave up your cousin to be with my sister?"

"Yeah." Milo says it while looking Jordan straight in the eye, without hesitation.

Jordan's gaze turns thoughtful as he nods, like he's processing the seriousness of what Milo has just told him.

"Your family must have been pissed," Jordan says.

"A lot of them are, but I don't care. Just because someone is related to you doesn't mean you should listen to them or be loyal to them. Decency is more important than blood."

My little brother's brow shoots to his hairline as he continues nodding, like that's the most profound thing he's ever heard.

A long moment passes where the two of them quietly gaze ahead. Jordan takes a sip from the Scotch bottle before handing it to Milo. He takes a swig too. They both wince.

"God, Scotch is nasty," Jordan mutters.

"You get used to it," Milo says.

"When does it stop tasting like shit?"

"Never."

Jordan laughs. So does Milo. I bite my tongue to keep from chuckling. That's when I realize how giddy I feel watching my brother and my boyfriend shoot the shit over a bottle of Scotch.

Jordan turns back to Milo. "I'm not gonna lie, man. Everything in me says not to like you. Which sucks because you're pretty cool to chill with."

Milo chuckles before quieting at the sight of my brother's frown.

"My sister deserves the best after what she's been through," Jordan says. "If you can't treat her well, you have no business being with her."

I take in the serious look on my brother's face, how his gaze is clear and focused despite the fact that he's intoxicated.

I feel myself soften. Yeah, this "protective little brother" act is obnoxious. But it's well intentioned. He's reading Milo the riot act because he cares about me—because he loves me and wants the best for me. For that, I adore him.

I look over at Milo, who's returning my brother's pointed, focused stare.

"I don't blame you for not wanting to like me, Jordan," Milo says. "You've got every reason not to. I'm dating your sister, for one. Brothers tend to hate the significant others of their sisters."

Jordan nods once. "Yup."

"Plus, I'm related to her ex. And I pulled a classic move from the slimeball handbook and made my interest in Riley clear to her pretty much the minute she became single."

I tense as I notice my brother clench his jaw.

"But there's a reason I did all that. Because I really, really like Riley. I have for a long time. Yeah, I didn't go about things the right way. I went about it in the messiest way possible, actually." Milo rubs the back of his neck, wincing. "But I'm not some smooth operator. I'm a guy who cares about your sister a hell of a lot and wants more than anything to make her happy."

Goose bumps flash across my skin at the conviction in Milo's tone, at how straightforward and honest and heartfelt his words are. I believe him.

I take in how Jordan stares at Milo without saying a word. I start to tense at my brother's lack of response.

But then he blinks. He holds his fist out to Milo. Milo stares at Jordan's hand for a long second before bumping his fist in return.

I can't help the smile that tugs at my mouth as I quietly turn around and walk back into the house, leaving Jordan and Milo to have this breakthrough moment on their own.

I walk up behind Mom as she sits at the dining table and drop a kiss to the top of her head.

"You were right, Mom. It all worked out."

Chapter 33

April 30, 2024

I wake up to a soft thud. My eyes fly open. I'm in my bed in my London flat. It's still dark out.

When I roll over, Milo's side of the bed is empty. He's here, though. The sheets are warm, and I spot his trousers and sweatshirt draped over the armchair in the corner.

I blink quickly until my vision adjusts to the darkness. I hear that soft thud again; then Milo whispers a curse.

I crawl out of bed and pad down the hallway. When I hit the kitchen, I flip on the lights. There's Milo standing between the dining table and the couch, wearing rumpled sweatpants and an undershirt. He's staring wide-eyed at me, holding an empty cardboard box.

I start to laugh at his expression. He looks like a little kid who's been busted for rummaging through the cookie jar before dinner.

"What are you doing?" I ask.

A sheepish smile is his answer. He tugs a hand through his messy black-brown hair. "I wanted to surprise you."

He nods his chin at the dining room table, where an empty vase sits next to a pile of baby-pink peonies.

"Early-morning flower run," he says. "I thought maybe having a fresh bouquet of your favorite flowers would soften the blow of this afternoon. I know divorce proceedings with Tristan this week haven't been easy."

He rubs the back of his neck before walking up to me. He starts to reach for me but seems to think better of it. I close the space between us, slide my arms around him, and hug him.

I close my eyes as I hold Milo tight against me. "This was so thoughtful of you. I love it."

I feel his body loosen against mine. He rests his chin on top of my head. "I'm sorry you've had to go through all this shit with him."

I can feel my body tense at the thought of going to battle with Tristan.

But then Milo's arms squeeze around me. The tension is still there, but there's comfort and warmth now too.

"I wish I could be in the room with you," he says.

"I wish that too." I sigh. "Probably best that you're not, though." I think of all the times that Milo and Tristan's conflicts have turned physical.

"You're right." He huffs out a breath. "It's way better to have Lara there with you. They don't call her Lara Barracuda for nothing."

He lets go of me and steps over to the kitchen and fills the teakettle.

"Lara Barracuda," I repeat.

Milo chuckles. "Hell of a nickname to earn in law school, isn't it?"

Lara Chan—*Lara Barracuda*—my divorce attorney.

Milo fetches two mugs from the cupboard and sets them down on the counter. He drops his special combination of tea bags in each one: one hazelnut black tea and one Earl Grey.

"I hope that this is the last day," he says as he pours hot water into each mug.

It *is* the last day, since I've lived the following days and haven't had a single meeting with a lawyer.

So this is it. Today is the legal end of my marriage.

Milo hands me my mug. As I wait for it to cool down enough for me to take a sip, I tense once more. This day is going to be hell.

Chapter 34

As I sit in the solicitor's office, my hands are shaking. I shouldn't be this nervous. I know what's coming, and it all works out in my favor. I keep the flat. I still have my car. My savings are intact. I'm okay.

I'm okay.

But it doesn't matter how many times I quietly repeat those words to myself. It doesn't change the fact that I'm sitting in a freezing-cold office not even three feet from Tristan, whose unreadable expression stings to even look at.

I'm not sure why. How do I expect him to look at me? With affection? Longing?

Just the thought makes me cringe.

I hazard a glance at him from across the table. He's frowning at a paper his lawyer has just put in front of him. His eyes cut to me, and his frown deepens before he glares back down at the paper.

And that's when I realize why this is all so upsetting. Because this man I used to be head over heels in love with, the man I thought I was going to spend the rest of my life with, now looks at me like I'm his worst enemy.

I don't know this man at all.

"Would you two excuse us for a few minutes?" Tristan's lawyer says. "We're going to step out for a moment."

I look at Lara, who's seated in the chair next to me. She says, "Sure."

Once they leave the room, she turns to me. "How are you holding up?"

"Okay," I lie.

She raises a perfectly arched eyebrow at me. I take in the sharp angles of her cheekbones, her flawless skin, how the natural makeup she's wearing makes her look lethal and stunning in equal measure.

I let out a breath. "I just want this to be over."

She nods, pursing her lips slightly. I notice Lara doesn't smile. We've been at this all day, and not once has her facial expression wavered from intensely focused.

"I understand. This has been really rough on you. But we're getting close. I can feel it." She rests a perfectly manicured hand on the stack of file folders sitting in front of her on the table. "They're grasping at straws."

"How can you tell?"

"They left the room. Very telltale 'strategy.'" She air-quotes with her left hand while sipping coffee from the tall paper cup in her right, like she can't be bothered to waste her energy gesturing with both hands. It's quietly dismissive, and I like it.

"They're struggling, so they want to regroup and come up with a plan," she says while thumbing through a file. "It won't change anything, though. You and your ex-husband had a good preregistration agreement. Everything was stipulated clearly and fairly. They're just trying to wear you down, see if they can get you to give anything up in the eleventh hour."

My adrenaline kicks up despite the fact that I've been sedentary for the past three hours.

The door opens, and Tristan walks back in with his lawyer. When they sit down, his lawyer clears his throat.

"Now then. About the flat," he says.

"What about it?" Lara asks.

A long silence follows while Tristan's lawyer ruffles pages in a folder. I hold my breath, feeling my muscles stiffen with each passing second.

"The Marylebone flat on Dorset Street legally belongs to Mr. Chase," he says, putting a document in front of Lara. I have to lean over to read it.

When I see that it's a copy of the deed without my name on it, my stomach drops.

What the hell . . . How did he even do that? My name was on the deed. He showed it to me the day after we got engaged.

I bite my tongue to keep from blurting out a string of curse words. When I glance over at Lara, I notice how she doesn't even flinch when she skims the document.

"As you can see, only Mr. Chase's name is on the deed of the home; therefore he's the rightful owner, and Ms. Ricci should vacate the premises immediately."

When I glance over at Tristan and see that smug, satisfied look on his face, I want to vomit.

"I see," Lara says, still studying the document.

I try to keep my hands steady as I sift through my folder of documents. I spot my copy of the deed.

"My name is on the deed too," I say, holding up the document to both Tristan and his lawyer.

"I have the original deed. My name is the only one on it. I don't know what that is." Tristan's voice is eerily calm as he gestures to the paper I'm holding.

For a solid five seconds I'm quiet, rendered silent by utter disbelief. He's lying. Straight to my face.

"If you'd like a moment to confer with your client, we're happy to give you that," his lawyer says.

"We would appreciate that," Lara says. "Thank you."

As soon as he and Tristan leave the room, I'm rambling.

"This is such bullshit," I mutter as I fly through the stack of papers, my mind racing. "My name was on the deed. I saw it with my own eyes. We met with a solicitor so I could sign all the paperwork to make it legal. That flat's mine. I swear. I-I don't know what Tristan is trying to pull . . ."

I still as clarity slowly sinks in. He must have consulted with one of his family's high-powered lawyers to figure out a way to forge a new deed. Yeah, it's illegal, but Tristan and his family are rich and powerful and ruthless enough to toss ethics aside when it comes to getting what they want. Rules and decency don't matter to them. I have zero doubt they'd do anything, even break the law, to get Tristan's flat back.

I frantically explain all that to Lara.

Lara frowns at what I've said. In the quiet moment that passes, I can hear my heartbeat thud in my ears. Sweat pricks along the back of my neck. I start to take off the blazer I'm wearing when Lara lets out a sigh.

"If what you're saying is true, if he pulled something that serious, that's illegal."

"Right . . ." Why doesn't she seem more upset?

She sighs. "Look, Riley. If that's the case, you definitely have a right to fight Tristan for the flat. But it could take a long time—and a lot of money. You'd have to take him to court. Even if that's a forged deed, it's designed to look like a legitimate document. He must have had some corrupt lawyers and advisers to pull that off. That wouldn't be an easy team of people to take on in court."

Lara's stern expression starts to fall.

My stomach drops. "Wh-what? But that's not right. He can't get away with that. It's illegal . . ."

She rests her hand gently on top of mine. The gesture is so soft, so nurturing, so completely in contrast with Lara's unflinching and sharp demeanor that it throws me off for a second.

"I'll happily help you fight it and bring along my toughest colleagues to join me. But I have to warn you: going against entitled rich guys like him can be soul crushing. It would likely be years of the courts system dragging this on and his lawyers fighting you every step of the way, making your life hell. Their goal would be to make life so miserable for you that you just give up your claim to the flat . . ." I don't even hear the rest of what she says, I'm too shocked.

How the hell can this happen? I end up with the flat—how can Tristan take it from me just like that . . . ?

And then I see it. In the haphazard mess of papers on the table, I spot the note he gave me that day.

This flat never felt like home until you moved in. It's my gift to you, Miss America.

"This is the note he gave me." I hand it to her. "The flat was a gift. You can't legally take back a gift, can you? And that combined with the fact that I have a copy of the current deed—the deed that he's pretending doesn't exist. That has to count for something, right?"

Something in Lara's stare shifts as she studies the card. A second later she looks at me. "He called you 'Miss America'?"

My face heats in embarrassment. I nod anyway. It's just now occurring to me how ridiculous that nickname was.

And then Lara does something I haven't seen her do all day. The corner of her mouth quirks up. She's actually smiling.

"This'll work," she says.

She stands up and opens the office door to let them back in. When they sit down, I don't miss the way they glance at the papers all over the table. They exchange a smug look that makes me want to slap them both.

"Mr. Chase, this is your handwriting, isn't it?" Lara says as she holds up the card to Tristan.

His eyebrows crash together. "Yes, but I don't see what that has to do with anything."

"You gave the flat as a gift to Ms. Ricci."

He shakes his head. "I didn't."

"According to this note you wrote, you did." Lara says it so resolutely, so firmly.

Tristan opens his mouth but hesitates. Lara grabs the paperwork I gave her minutes ago. His gaze cuts to his lawyer, who is frowning at the documents Lara is showing them both.

"Gifts aren't considered shared marital property; therefore you have no claim to them, Mr. Chase. Additionally, since Ms. Ricci has a copy of the deed showing her as co-owner of the flat, that means the deed you have must be forged. Which means you must have engaged in illegal actions to produce a fake deed with only your name on it, which means you've broken the law and could potentially be prosecuted for fraud."

Tristan's eyes go wide at Lara's stern words. His lawyer aims an incredulous look at Tristan. I'm guessing he wasn't the lawyer who helped him forge that deed, then.

Her laser stare doesn't budge from Tristan. "Unless you'd like to risk jail time, Mr. Chase, I'd suggest you drop this whole act and cede the flat to Ms. Ricci . . ."

The room is silent for what feels like a full minute. I wait for Tristan or his lawyer to say something, anything in response.

His lawyer finally clears his throat, breaking the silence. "We'd like to take some time—"

"Fucking hell, you just want to take everything from me, don't you?" Tristan blurts while glowering at me.

My jaw falls to the floor, jolted at his angry tone. "What are you talking about?"

His lawyer turns to him and starts to speak, but Tristan ignores him, his angry glare laser focused on me.

"That flat was mine, Riley. How dare you try to take it away, just like you did with everything else in my life."

I'm sputtering. My adrenaline has morphed into steam, leveling my insides, leaving nothing but fury and frustration behind.

"How the hell did I take away everything in your life, Tristan? *You* are the one who cheated. *You* are the one who lied. *You* are the one who deceived me for the entirety of our relationship."

I don't realize how loud my voice is until I look over at Lara and take in her shocked look. But I'm too angry to feel embarrassed. Not when my cheating ex is lashing out at me.

"You gave me that flat. You know you did. It's clear you regret doing that or wish you could take it back, but honestly? Join the club. I wish I could take back a lot of things when it comes to you."

The room falls silent once more. My chest heaves as I take a breath. I glance down at my trembling hands. I lost my cool. I got into a screaming match with my ex in a solicitor's office. And I'm weirdly proud about it. I didn't just sit there and let Tristan walk all over me, like he let his family do so many times when we were together. I stood up for myself. I always deserved that, but he never did it for me. So I did it for myself. Finally.

Lara and Tristan's lawyer converse in civil tones. Papers are straightened and stacked. Pens are handed out. I slash my signature along the solid line of the document that will legally dissolve my marriage. Lara slides the paper to Tristan's lawyer, who gives it to him. He does the same.

The table is cleared. The lawyers start to pack up. I watch it all in a daze.

Tristan and his lawyer get up to leave while Lara and I stay sitting. When they're out of the room, she turns to me.

"It's okay. I've seen way worse." I can't tell if it's her deadpan delivery or the stoic expression on her face—maybe it's both—but I start to laugh. Not a happy laugh. More like a tired chuckle that happens when you're emotionally drained and have no energy left.

"Thanks, Lara."

"Will you be all right?"

"Yeah, I just need a minute."

"Understandable. Tell Milo I say hello."

"I will."

She stands up, grabs her briefcase, and leaves. I take a few minutes to just sit and savor the silence around me. And then I stand up and leave the room. I head for the elevator and halt when I see Tristan standing there. Before I can turn around and head for the stairwell, he catches my eye. I freeze.

We're standing just a handful of feet apart. As we stare at each other, I take in the anger in his eyes as he looks at me.

Those crystal-blue eyes that used to mesmerize me. Those eyes I used to dream about.

All I see now are the eyes of a man I don't know anymore.

The elevator dings. The impossibly shiny stainless-steel doors glide open. He steps inside. "This isn't over, Riley."

He's right. I know he is. He isn't close to giving up, despite the fact that the flat legally belongs to me now. He's too stubborn, too petty, too selfish. He'll spend the next month plotting ways to get me to give it back to him. He'll text me to meet him at Last One Standing, and we'll have one of the worst arguments we've ever had. He'll resent me. He'll hate me.

And it doesn't stop until months after that, when I see his mother in Portugal with her lover and she concedes the flat to me.

But then he blinks, and his gaze turns pleading. It's so jarring, I almost flinch.

"I suppose what I said the morning after our anniversary didn't make a difference, did it?"

It's not a question. More like a defeated remark he's making to himself. He isn't even looking at me when he says it; he looked off to the side before he said a word.

For a moment I'm caught off guard. He sounds like the man I used to know. Caring, concerned, kind.

But when he pivots his gaze back to me, all I see is fury. And bitterness.

The elevator doors close before either of us can say a word. I stay standing there until someone bumps into me.

I mutter an apology as I snap out of the confused haze, then scurry down the stairwell.

I have no idea what Tristan is talking about. But I'll find out soon enough.

Chapter 35

April 14, 2024

When I wake up, I'm alone. The discomfort that washes over me is immediate. Like a side stitch when you're jogging or the feeling of a rock in your shoe.

I sit up, struggling to see in the darkness. Milo's not next to me, and I hate it.

There's movement at the foot of the bed. When I look down and see Coco lifting her head and aiming a sleepy stare at me, I feel the slightest bit comforted. At least she's with me.

She kneads her front paws against the bedsheets before yawning and falling back to sleep. I rest a hand on my chest, and for a second I just sit there and breathe.

I knew this was going to happen. In the two weeks that preceded the solicitor meeting, I saw Milo almost every day. He stayed with me almost every night. But there was a starting point before all that—the moment when he and I went from hardly ever speaking to friends to something more.

I swipe my phone from the nightstand and check the date. It's the middle of April, which means I'm two months away from Valentine's Day—the day before I find out that Tristan's been cheating on me.

The day before my entire life turns upside down.

I sit up in bed as a strange dip hits my stomach. Not excitement, more like anticipation. I know something big is about to happen, but there's a lot more left to see unfold.

I take a slow, deep breath and crawl out of bed, use the bathroom, then pad out into the living room. When I flip the lights on, I still. The decor in the living room and kitchen are completely different. No more tacky HELLO, BABES sign, no more chevron rug in the living room, no more KEEP CALM AND DRINK TEA sign, no more fuzzy throw pillows, no more sectional. The fireplace is stark white instead of the Mediterranean-style tile.

Most of the decor is gone completely. The only piece I can see is a trio of black-and-white framed landscape photos.

Tristan's artwork.

It takes several seconds for me to process the sudden change. I haven't redecorated the flat yet.

Even just standing there looking at the minimalist decor feels wrong. My skin pricks. All the muscles in my body stiffen. Even the air in the room feels off.

This isn't my flat. It wasn't even when I lived in it with Tristan. I just moved my stuff in. Everything else stayed the same. I added a couple of framed photos from our wedding, but that was it. Tristan never invited me to add my own pieces or try my hand at redecorating. It was his place, always. I just lived here.

I need to make it mine again, now.

I force myself to walk to the sink and chug a glass of water. Then I call Milo.

The sound of his groggy voice when he picks up snaps me out of my tunnel vision.

"Riley? Everything okay?"

"Yeah, I'm fine. I just . . ."

I hear the sound of fabric rustling. He's getting out of bed.

"I'm sorry, Milo. I woke you up, didn't I?"

"Yeah, but it's no big deal. Really. It's nice to hear from you first thing in the morning."

I can hear the smile in his voice. It softens me instantly. I start to smile too.

"I'm relieved to hear you say that."

"What's going on? Need me to run you over some tea since I've finally converted you?" He chuckles, which makes me chuckle.

I flip open the cabinet where I normally keep the tea and coffee, but all I see is coffee.

I close the cabinet. "I could definitely use some tea."

"Say no more." Milo lets out a soft groan, like he's stretching. I blink and in the darkness behind my eyelids picture how he looks. His wavy black-brown hair is messy, he's got a healthy sheet of stubble on his cheeks, and he's shirtless, wearing nothing but boxers.

My heartbeat kicks up. I miss Milo. I want him here.

"Hey, Riley. Listen." My stomach drops at the sudden seriousness in his tone.

"What is it?"

He sighs. "I'm not trying to pull one over on you, I swear."

"I don't think that at all. What would make you worry about that?"

He doesn't say anything at first. And then he starts to speak but stops himself.

"I guess I'm still worried about how everything unfolded with Tristan, the things that he said . . ."

I wait for him to say more, but he doesn't.

"Okay," I finally say.

I'm not sure what Milo is talking about. Does he mean me finding out about Tristan's affair with Carly? Did he and Tristan fight about something else too?

Before I even have to ask, he speaks. "I just don't want you to think less of me, Riley. I know I'm not perfect. I've messed up a lot, especially when it comes to you."

I think back to the night we met, when I overheard him on the phone, making that hurtful comment about me. But it doesn't hurt anymore. Milo explained himself and apologized. He doesn't know all that yet, not in this timeline, at least. But I know it. And I need to reassure him since he's clearly still upset with himself over it.

"I think the world of you, Milo. Here you are going out of your way to help me, the ex of your own cousin."

He exhales sharply. "Just because he's family doesn't mean I automatically side with him. I've never been like that."

"I know. And that's why I admire you. Other people wouldn't have the strength to go against their own blood, no matter how bad they are. You do. And you're a gem because of it."

"Damn," he says. "Hearing you say that . . ." He laughs lightly, like he can't believe what I just said and is struggling to process it. "That means everything."

"Just being honest."

A quiet moment passes. "I'm going to jump in the shower, grab some tea, and be over to your place," Milo says. "Give me an hour, tops."

I open my mouth to speak, but nothing comes out. I'm too overwhelmed, too happy, too relieved. Milo is such a sweet guy, so doting and caring and thoughtful. Willing to sacrifice a morning lie-in to keep his cousin's ex company.

"Thank you," I finally say.

"You don't have to thank me, Riley," he says. "I meant what I said. I'm here for you in whatever way you want me."

My heart skids at the firmness in his tone, how he sounds so certain about me.

"I need to redecorate the flat," I tell him. "I want to change it all. Today. I don't want to keep being reminded of . . ." I bite my tongue, not wanting to even say Tristan's name.

"I get it," Milo says. "Operation Redecorate will commence after teatime."

I chuckle, then exhale.

In that single breath my entire body starts to loosen. "I'm ready."

Chapter 36

April 3, 2024

"Why don't you take the rest of the day off, Ri?"

I glance up from where I'm standing near the register and see Poppy aiming a worried glance at me. She turns back to the table of lace thongs she's folding and pretends to straighten them, even though they're already in perfect order.

"Why would I need to take the rest of the day off?" I scan our store. A half dozen customers are browsing. I shake my head at Poppy. "It's been pretty busy all morning and afternoon. I don't want to leave you in the lurch."

Poppy walks over to me and rests a hand on my arm. I take in the concern on her face. I can look back at her for only a few seconds before my gaze drops. I'm not used to seeing my joking and snarky best friend look at me this way, with raw pity in her ice-blue eyes.

"It's really okay, Ri. If you need to take today off or the next day or a week or even longer, I completely understand. You're going through a lot right now, what with the divorce and dealing with Tristan. I've got this all handled." She flashes a sad smile.

A strange warmth courses through me as I take in my best friend's concern. That's something I've had to get used to in this backward timeline, the way everyone around me has been coddling me since we're just weeks away from them finding out about my split from Tristan. Mom has been calling almost every day to ask how I'm doing and whether I'm eating enough. My brother has been texting me just as often, asking if he can fly over here so he can kick Tristan's ass.

It makes sense. For them, my split with Tristan is fresh. But because I've been living life backward, I've had more time to process my feelings. I'm over Tristan. There's not an ounce of me that's sad about losing him after how he betrayed me and our marriage for so long.

I observe the raw emotion in Poppy's eyes, how much she cares about me and my feelings. A pang of guilt hits that I'm not half as upset as she is right now.

I wish I could explain to Poppy that I'm already over Tristan, that I've had an impossible opportunity to live my live backward, and that's helped me process my breakup.

But there's no way to explain that, not without sounding like I've lost it. I remind myself that I need to be careful of how I act right now. How strange would it be if I came off like I'm completely unbothered weeks out from discovering my husband's been cheating on me for years?

"Thank you, Poppy," I say gently. I give her hand a squeeze. "That means everything. Really. But the last thing I want to do is wallow alone. It's better if I stay busy with work. It's good for me to be around people right now. Especially you."

The way she smiles, she seems comforted by what I've said. That guilt burrows deeper in my chest, though. It feels like I'm performing in this moment, to make it seem like I'm coping when really I'm okay.

"I appreciate that you care about me so much. You don't have to coddle me like I'm made of glass, though," I say. "I guess I'm not used to seeing soft Poppy. I'm so used to cutthroat Poppy."

My attempt at turning things a bit lighter works, judging by the way her ruby-red lips turn up in a knowing smile.

"Oh, Ri. You know I'm cutthroat to the core."

She pets Gus, who's snoozing in his tiny bed next to the register. She rings up a customer before turning back to me.

"I've been making a list of inventive ways to ruin fuckface's life," she says nonchalantly. I burst out laughing.

Once I catch my breath, I shush her. A customer perusing the perfume collection across the store spins around to look at us. I clear my throat and murmur an apology. Poppy elbows me and smirks.

"Fuckface? Really?" I whisper.

She shrugs. "Seems like a more fitting name for him, don't you think?"

I cover my mouth to muffle my laughter.

"I could slash his car tires. Or dump a fresh coat of paint on the storefront of his poshest restaurant," she says. "Or start a rumor that he's so vile that he's contracted a new strain of herpes."

When I finally catch my breath, I wipe my eyes. "Now there's the Poppy I know and love."

I hug her.

"I've got loads more ideas," she says when we break apart. "Just say the word."

"Just the fact that you've thought all that up is enough. Thanks, Poppy." I pat her shoulder before turning back to the register.

Another customer approaches with an armful of clothes. I spot that kelly-green blouse in her haul. Poppy rings her up. She chuckles when she sees the blouse.

"Have you got a dinner with the in-laws coming up?" she asks.

The woman flashes a cheeky smile and nods. "Yup. This should get a rise out of their stuck-up arses."

The two of them laugh. I do too. I gaze around the shop and take in the items Poppy and I have decided to stock. Loads of naughty see-through, barely there lingerie. But there are just as many cozy pieces, like silk and satin pajama sets and onesies. Some pieces of our clothing are sexy, low cut, and tight; some are flowy and modest and sweet. The jewelry we carry is just as varied as our clothing and intimates: some gaudy and big, some delicate and understated.

They're all beautiful, though.

I take a moment to appreciate the kind of shop Poppy and I have curated, how we're a store that welcomes customers no matter their taste or background or preferences. We don't judge. Because it's clothing, makeup, and jewelry. It's all meant to be fun.

Something about that lands deep in the center of my chest. Maybe because for so long I spent so much time and energy trying to be accepted by people who never wanted me to belong with them. I realize now that my job—my store—was how I dealt with that rejection. My livelihood was one of the things they couldn't stand about me. But I held on to it. And it feels really, really good to know that I didn't give it up for them. No way would it have been worth it.

"You look different, you know," Poppy says to me after the customer leaves.

I turn to her. "What do you mean?"

She offers a gentle smile. "Don't take this the wrong way, Ri. But you don't look as polished as before."

She gestures to my legs. I look down at the skirt I'm wearing.

"Wrinkled as fuck. The polished princess would never let herself out of the house in this state. But you're rocking it. You look more relaxed. Happier."

I take a second to think about what she said. "I guess you're right. I don't think about how I look as much anymore. It feels good."

She smiles at me. "Honestly, Ri? You've always looked beautiful, but now it's effortless. It suits you."

I never realized just how much thought I put into my appearance when I was with Tristan. Some of it stemmed from my own desire to look nice. But I realize now that I did it, too, because I wanted to look good enough to be part of his family. It didn't matter how hard I tried, though. I was never good enough for them.

I breathe in, my body feeling looser, calmer. "Thanks, Poppy."

As I ring up a few more customers, my phone buzzes with a text. I finish up, check my phone, and smile at the text Milo has just sent me.

It's a photo of a package of bright-yellow marshmallow Peeps that's been ripped open.

I don't know how the hell you eat these things. They taste like sugary glue.

I bite my lip to keep from grinning too wide. Easter is just a few days away. That's the day Milo texts me to check up on me. That's the day I start to like tea.

That's the day things kick off for me and Milo.

I text him back, feeling the telltale drop in my stomach.

Me: You're wrong. Peeps are delicious.

Milo: Maybe it's an acquired taste.

Milo: Like tea.

Me: LOL

Milo: You like tea now, admit it.

Me: You're right. I love tea.

Chapter 37

Milo: Hey. Happy Easter.

I stare down at my phone as I cuddle in bed with Coco. She purrs softly as I pet her. I glance out my bedroom window. It's a typical cold, gray, and rainy London day in late March.

She paws at the package of half-eaten marshmallow Peeps sitting next to me in bed. I give her a chin scratch, and she purrs even louder. It mingles with the soft pitter-patter of rain against my window. Like a unique blend of white noise.

I stare at my phone screen, unable to text Milo back just yet. I'm too nervous.

Actually, "nervous" isn't the right way to describe how I'm feeling. It's more like butterflies mixed with an intense flash of emotion.

This day is technically the day I start to fall for Milo. But I'm already into him. I already like him. I miss him when he's not with me. I already care about him so much.

A familiar ache hits my chest. It's accompanied by a warmth, a comfort I haven't felt in a long, long time.

And that's when it hits me: I think I'm falling in love with Milo.

Gripping my phone in my hand, I stare at the screen.

I love him.

I love him and he has no idea. He likes me. He cares about me. He wants to check on me, to make sure I'm okay.

All I want is him.

Dread and sadness clash at the pit of my stomach. If I keep going back in time, things between us will change. I'll see him less and less . . . and his feelings for me will fade.

I sit there and stare at my phone, frozen with the realization that I don't know how to stop this. No matter what I try to do, this backward timeline always wins.

I just have to keep going.

I breathe in and type out the response I knew I'd type out the whole morning while waiting for him to text.

Me: There's nothing happy about the way I'm annihilating this package of marshmallow Peeps.

Milo: Damn, that's a blast from the past.

Milo: They'd go down easier with some tea.

I text back a string of vomit emojis despite the fact that I've been craving tea since the moment I woke up.

He texts back a laughing emoji.

Milo: I can make you love tea.

Me: No way in hell. Tea is gross.

Milo: Come on.

Me: Tea is gross.

Milo: Okay, hear me out: give tea one more try. If you hate it, I'll sign over my flat to you.

Me: That's quite an offer.

Me: Game on.

Milo: Are you free now? There's a cafe in my old neighborhood in Camden Town that serves the best cup of tea you'll ever have.

Me: They're open today? It's Easter.

Milo: Yup. They're open at the most random days. It's why they're my favorite.

Me: I can be there in an hour.

He texts me the name of the shop and the address.

Milo: See you soon, Riley ☺

Chapter 38

When I walk into the café, Milo is already there, sitting at a tiny table for two near the front. He grins at me and stands up. When I walk over to him, he starts to reach for me, like he's going to pull me in for a hug. But then he pulls his arm back and brushes his palm against the front of his gray Henley, like he's changed his mind. I'm instantly disappointed that I don't get to touch him.

His smile turns shy as he gestures to the empty chair across from him. "Saved you a seat," he teases.

I chuckle and tell him thanks. We sit down. For a long moment I stare at him, taking in how good he looks. His burnt-umber eyes are bright, like he's thrilled to be looking at me. He's got a healthy sheet of scruff on his cheeks.

"You look nice," I say.

His brow lifts the slightest bit, like he's shocked I've complimented him. "Thanks. So do you."

The tenderness in his voice melts me. I look down at the halfway decent outfit I managed to put together before driving down here. A forest-green sweater, black skinny jeans, and brown leather ankle boots.

"I look like a soccer mom," I mumble.

Milo chuckles. "You don't. Not that there's anything wrong with soccer moms. You just . . ." He hesitates, like he's searching for the right words. "You just look amazing, Riley. Like always."

My cheeks burn at the compliment. I glance around the long, narrow space of the café with a half dozen two-person tables. We're the only ones in the place, save the two hipster baristas with matching man buns.

"You think you're required to have a man bun to work at this place?" Milo says in a soft voice.

I chuckle. "I don't doubt that. So, um, no big Easter plans?"

He shakes his head. "If I were in Portugal with my parents, it'd be an all-day thing. Mass, then brunch, then dinner with all of my mom's relatives."

I think of the pool party Milo took me to, how his family was warm and welcoming, how they drowned me in hugs and food and made me feel like one of them after just one afternoon together.

"That sounds amazing, actually," I say. "You didn't want to go see them?"

"Not this year. I'm too busy with work. I took over my dad's real estate business here in London when he retired. I can't afford to be away even for a quick holiday. You didn't want to go home for Easter yourself?"

I shake my head. "Home is too far away to justify the cost of the flight. I FaceTimed with my mom and brother, though, this morning. We always FaceTime when we're apart during holidays and birthdays."

"That's really sweet. And where's home?"

"California."

He smiles. "I think you mentioned that before. NorCal, right?" He fiddles with a sugar packet on the table, like he's nervous to be chatting with me. It's cute and endearing.

"Yeah. Bay Area," I say. "You lived in LA, right?"

"Yep. I was one of those SoCal brats that you Bay Area folks hate so much," he jokes.

I chuckle. "You're not so bad." His stubbled cheeks turn rosy as he looks at me.

The barista drops off two teacups. Milo grins. "Are you ready to change your opinion of tea?"

"We'll see."

He chuckles at my defiance. "Give it a couple minutes to cool down. Then prepare for your life to change."

I laugh softly as I pick up a spoon and stir my tea. I breathe in the aroma. Hazelnut and that earthy-citrus smell of Earl Grey.

"This is a special blend," Milo says.

"I can tell. It doesn't smell like a standard brew."

"It's my own concoction. When I asked the guy to make it, he glared at me."

"What's that?" I ask even though I already know the answer.

"Half–Earl Grey, half-hazelnut. I figured hazelnut tea would be a good bet because you always drink hazelnut coffee."

I knew that was coming, but Milo's words hit hard when he speaks them. Because I didn't realize that he'd paid attention to my coffee order. All those times I was around Milo during family events, even though I hardly spoke to him, he had been paying attention to me.

"You know what kind of coffee I drink?" I say softly.

He nods, the look in his eyes sincere. "I do."

I grab the teacup and slowly raise it to my lips. I blow on it before taking a careful sip. The minute the warm liquid hits my tongue, I'm humming. It tastes amazing, just like I knew it would. Light yet flavorful. The richness of the hazelnut balances out the dankness of the Earl Grey into something milder, something pleasantly floral and citrusy instead of dirt tasting.

I swallow and smile up at Milo. He's gazing at me with the most expectant look, like he's watching me open a gift he's given me. It's so sweet, so endearing, that my chest goes warm and gooey.

"Okay, you win." I let out a satisfied sigh. "This is good. I like tea now."

He pumps his fist in triumph, and my head falls back as I laugh. We close down the café that Easter Sunday, ordering more tea and devouring half the pastries in the display case. We talk about our families, our jobs, what brought us to London. Some of it we already know from conversations we've had at Chase family events; some of it is brand new. It's all wonderful.

As the hours fly by, I know without a doubt that this is the moment I start to fall for Milo. This is where I get to know him—the real him. Not the cousin of my ex. But the guy who took over his family's real estate business. The guy who spends one weekend a month in Portugal, visiting his parents, and one whole month with them in the summer, because he hates living so far away from them. The guy who was deathly scared of dark water as a kid. The guy who crashed his car in a round-about the first time he tried to drive in London.

He's not afraid to tell me embarrassing stories from his uni days, how he got blackout drunk with his cousins in London when he was sixteen because he spent his teenage years in the US and hadn't drunk much at all. My cheeks hurt from smiling, and my stomach aches from laughing.

He listens intently as I tell him what it was like growing up in the Bay Area; how I was obsessed with the Bridget Jones book and movie series as a teenager, and that's what made me want to move to London; how I met Poppy at a sketchy modeling casting call when the casting director tried to coax the models into going topless, so Poppy spit in his face. We became instant best friends after that.

When the baristas tell us they're closing, we apologize for staying so late, grab our jackets, and head out of the café; then Milo walks me to my car down the street.

"Thanks for meeting me on such short notice," he says as he walks beside me.

"It was nice to get out. I probably would have just spent the day napping and stuffing my face with Peeps."

Milo's throaty chuckle makes my skin hot despite the wet chill in the air.

"So you're a fan of sleeping in on the weekends then?" he asks.

"Always. Who isn't?"

He shrugs. "I struggle to sleep more than six hours a night."

"Really? Because my dream would be to get at least nine hours of sleep a night."

"Jesus," he says through a chuckle. "Guess I should start calling you 'Sleeping Beauty' then."

My stomach flips. So this is when he gives me that nickname.

I bite back a smile. "If you want."

We stop at my car and turn to face each other. He lets out a breath through that beautiful grin of his. "Drive safe, Sleeping Beauty."

"Do you need a ride to your flat?"

He shakes his head. "It's just down the street." He gestures to the right.

For a second we're quiet.

"So, um—"

"Thanks again for—"

We both laugh. Milo clears his throat, and his expression turns serious.

"I know you said it's all okay, but I really am so, so sorry for the way things went down, Riley."

I take in the worry that flashes in his mahogany-brown eyes. His gaze is pleading and nervous, and I'm not sure why.

He must mean my breakup with Tristan. He feels bad for what I went through—for what I'm about to go through in splitting up with his cousin. But it's not like it was his fault. He shouldn't feel this bad.

I reach out and touch his arm. "It's okay, Milo. Really."

He breathes out, his shoulders easing to a more relaxed position. I feel him ease under my palm.

Our gazes lock. As we inhale and exhale, the air between us changes. It feels thicker, like there's an electrical current sparking between us.

Something inside me takes hold. I step forward, fully in Milo's space. I'm close enough to feel the heat from his body skim mine. I lean up and press a kiss to his lips. It's nothing wild, just my lips on his lips for a total of two seconds before I pull away. On a scale of passion, it's on the chaste end.

But something about it feels heavy. The softness of Milo's lips, how firmly he kisses me back, how he grips my waist like he has no intention of letting me go . . . it all leaves me dizzy.

When we break apart, I'm wobbly. I have to replant my feet on the sidewalk to steady myself.

Milo keeps a hand on my waist. "You okay?"

When I glance at him, I take in how dazed he looks too. And something about that makes me so damn happy. That means this two-second, PG-looking kiss rocked his world too.

I nod, smiling. "I'm great. You?"

He grins. "Fan-fucking-tastic."

We don't talk more about what we just did. But judging by the knowing look we exchange, we're both aware we've crossed a line. And we're both thrilled to be on the other side.

He opens my car door, making me promise to text him when I'm home. I tell him I will.

He closes my door, and I start the car. As I drive away, he stays in my rearview mirror, his eyes on me the whole time until I turn the corner and lose sight of him completely.

A wave of emotion hits; my chest aches. I think about how in this backward timeline, Milo won't remember this moment between us. Only I will.

That ache in my chest deepens. I have to take an extra second to breathe through it. With each day that passes backward, his feelings, his affection for me, will fade. And someday we'll be strangers.

A lump appears in my throat. I swallow through it. There's nothing I can do about that. I don't know how to stop this, how to turn this all around so that I can start living forward once again.

Dread simmers at the pit of my stomach. But I breathe through it. I refocus on the giddy feelings and joy from minutes earlier. That's all I can do. So I savor them for the rest of the day until I fall asleep.

Chapter 39

February 15, 2024

February 15 sneaks up on me quickly.

It's the morning after Valentine's Day. It's the day I find out that Tristan has been cheating on me—that he's fathered a child with another woman behind my back.

As my eyes adjust to my bedroom, I see the well-worn spot in the blankets on the other side of the bed—Tristan's side of the bed.

A boulder digs into the pit of my stomach. I'll be waking up with Tristan from now on. We were together for three years. That's three years' worth of mornings waking up next to him . . .

Just the thought of that makes me want to puke.

I swallow it back, along with the sudden surge of panic. I knew this was coming all along, but I didn't want to think about it. Now that day is here, and I have no idea how I'm going to handle it, handle this new normal of living life backward with someone I hate.

This is my worst fucking nightmare.

My breathing starts to kick up. My heart is racing even though I'm lying in bed. I take a handful of deep breaths to calm myself.

I wait for clarity to set in, for some magical solution to fall from the sky that will show me how I can avoid it all . . . but it never comes.

I keep breathing until that tightness in my chest eases.

It's not long before I figure out what I need to do. It's nothing magical. Not even close.

It's what I've done every day since I woke up in this backward world.

It's simple: live through it.

If every day I have to wake up with Tristan, then so be it. I'll do it. I don't really have a choice.

But I have a choice on how I spend each day. And each day, after I wake up, I'm going to tell him I know. About Carly, about the affair, about their baby. I'll tell him we're over. I'll kick him out of the house. And I'll spend the rest of that day without him, relishing the joy of it. Because when I wake up in the morning, I'll have to do it all over again.

The thought is daunting. Actually, more like fucking demoralizing. But this is my life now. If I have to fight with him and break up with him every day for three years, then that's what I'll do. It's my dignity. It's my happiness. And they're worth fighting for, every single day.

The faint sound of a low voice coming from the kitchen pulls me out of my thoughts. A second later I hear another low voice.

Milo's here. He's confronting Tristan about his affair.

I shiver despite the thick down comforter on top of me. I know what happens today, but I don't know the details. I don't know if Tristan and Milo get into another fistfight. I don't know if they get loud enough for the neighbors to hear and they end up calling the police. I don't know how bad it all gets.

Nerves crackle at the pit of my stomach. A cold sweat breaks out across the back of my neck. Through the crack in my bedroom door, I can hear Tristan's tone get angrier and louder.

I lean forward and strain my ears so I can hear him.

"You think you can barge into my home and ruin my marriage?"

"No one's ruining your marriage besides you, Tristan. You're the one who decided to cheat on Riley. No one forced you to do that. This is all on you, you selfish—"

A soft thud cuts Milo off. The anxiety inside me kicks up.

Live through it.

I walk out of the bedroom, down the hallway, barely glancing at Coco, who's sprawled on the back of the couch, a pink bow tied to her collar. She's the one good thing to come out of today's impending disaster.

I make it to the kitchen and see that Tristan has Milo by the collar of the sweatshirt he's wearing and is pulling him away from the wall. They both pivot their heads to me.

"What is going on?" I blurt.

Tristan releases his cousin and steps away from him. Milo tugs at the hem of his shirt, chest heaving as he breathes in.

Tristan's sky-blue eyes dart to Milo, then to me again. He forces a smile. "Nothing. Milo was just stopping by."

I look over at Milo, who's glaring at his cousin. When he pivots his gaze to me, he immediately softens.

"Riley, I'm so sorry to have to tell you this, on the day after your anniversary of all days, but . . ."

I catch Tristan balling both hands in his fists as he turns to Milo. "You fucking prat."

"Tristan is cheating on you," Milo says without even acknowledging his cousin's insult. "I saw him. I saw him with Carly the other day. I saw them kiss. I-I saw that Carly was . . ."

He hesitates. His face twists, like it physically pains him to get the words out.

"She's pregnant, Riley. With Tristan's baby." Milo makes a face like he's tasted something bitter. "I confronted Tristan and told him that he needs to come clean to you. But clearly he didn't."

Tristan starts to charge Milo, but I dart between them. "Tristan, stop!" I press a palm on his chest, and he halts instantly. He falls back, his eyes dazed as he looks at me.

"Don't believe anything this piece of rubbish says about me, love. He's clearly out to get me . . ."

"Tristan. Stop." Somehow my low, steady, firm tone is more compelling than when I shouted that same command a moment ago.

Tristan gazes at me, his eyes wide with panic. "Riley, don't tell me that you believe him."

I drop my hand from his chest and step back until I'm standing next to Milo and we're both facing Tristan.

I don't say a word. I stay quiet and observe the look of disbelief take over Tristan's face as I choose to stand next to his cousin over him.

As Tristan stammers, I glance up at Milo. I take in the pained look on his face.

"I'm sorry, Riley. I didn't mean to hurt you like this. I just . . . ," Milo says.

My chest aches at the emotions playing out across his face.

"You don't deserve this," he finally says. "I'm sorry."

He touches my arm. I close my eyes for a long second, savoring the comfort of his touch.

I turn back to Tristan, whose expression is now one of disbelief as he looks between us.

"Fucking hell," he mutters under his breath. His expression shifts to hard. Irate. I watch him ball his hands into fists. I tense, preparing to stand between the two of them again to prevent yet another fistfight.

But Tristan stays planted in his spot, just a few feet away from us. He glares at his cousin. "I fucking knew it. You've always fancied Riley. You fucking lowlife."

"Tristan . . ."

"You'll say anything to break us up, won't you?" he says to Milo, completely ignoring me. "So you can get your hands on my sloppy seconds?"

I flinch at the phrase, just like I have every other time he's said something like it.

Fury flashes in his eyes as Tristan glowers at his cousin. And then he punches Milo.

I scream when it happens, covering my mouth with both hands, instinctively. Milo hunches over for a second before righting himself, holding his left cheek in his hand.

I go to him. "Are you okay?"

He winces but nods anyway. "I'll be fine."

I spin to Tristan, anger raging inside me. "What is wrong with you?"

Instead of answering me or acknowledging me at all, Tristan looks past me. His eyes are alight with fury as he glowers at Milo.

"It didn't end up working out with Elena, so why not try with Riley, eh?" he bites. "A bit pathetic that you have to resort to stealing your cousin's women instead of finding your own, don't you think?"

My stomach plummets to my feet at the mention of Elena. I flash back to that pool party at Milo's family's house in Portugal . . . at how his grandmother called me Elena . . . at the conversation Milo had with his cousin Rafa . . .

"Really, Milo? Again? Is this a pattern with you?"

"Rafa. Stop."

"Look, man. I only ask because it's not a normal thing to do. To go after—"

"I didn't go after anyone."

I can feel my heartbeat throughout my entire body. "Thrashing" is a better word for it, actually. It feels like cannonballs are rocketing through me.

Tristan finally looks over at me. All I can register is desperation in his eyes. "Riley, listen to me. Milo has been gunning for you since the day he met you. He's been waiting in the wings like some opportunistic prick, waiting for the right time to swoop in and take you from me. He's willing to say anything to make you leave me."

"I wouldn't lie about something like this," Milo says, his tone hard and pleading all at once.

I glance between them, dazed as I struggle to take in everything Tristan says.

Milo evidently has a pattern. And that's to go after his cousin's partners.

A wave of nausea hits, but I cough it back.

Tristan grabs my hand, turning me toward him. "Elena, my uni girlfriend, cheated on me with Milo."

I open my mouth, but I can't speak a word. I pull out of Tristan's hold. When he reaches for me again, I wave him off.

"Don't," I bark. He jolts back. So does Milo.

For a long moment I just stare between Tristan and Milo. I know for a fact that Tristan has been cheating on me. There's no way I'm taking him back, no matter what he says.

But to discover this about Milo is a jolt to my system. I feel like I've been electrocuted.

This marks the second time that Milo's set his sights on his cousin's romantic partner. My skin crawls. I can't decide if I want to scream or vomit. God, that's so creepy and sleazy, so unlike who I thought Milo really was.

He's been so kind, so caring and considerate. I thought I was getting to know him—the real him. Yeah, he's no angel. He was a jerk to me when we first met all those years ago. But he apologized. He sounded so sincere. He admitted to me that he's been the other man in a relationship before. But he was honest with me—at least I thought he was. Until now.

I think of all the early-morning cuddles in bed, how he remembered my favorite flowers, how he helped me through my divorce, how amazing he was with my mom, my brother, my entire family . . .

I let my guard down. I let myself start to like him, care about him, fall for him . . .

I started to fall in love with him . . .

This whole time he's been lying to me.

He lied and cheated. Just like Tristan.

"Clearly you've got a type," Tristan says through a sneer.

Milo steps into his space. "It's not like that."

"You're so full of shit, Milo. Why don't you try meeting women on your own instead of waiting around for my scraps?"

Milo shoves Tristan, and he bumps into the refrigerator.

I'm in a haze watching the two of them shove one another, acting like two gorillas pounding their chests as they gear up for a brawl.

I start to feel dizzy and wobble.

Milo spins around to me. "Are you okay?" he asks in a soft voice.

But I don't answer. I can't, not when another wave of nausea pummels me.

I glance at the two men staring at me.

Liar. Cheater.

The words bounce around in my head, growing louder by the second.

Liars. Cheaters.

I swallow back the hot bile creeping up my throat.

Liars and cheaters. That's all I seem to be capable of attracting.

Milo reaches his hand to me, but I jerk away. I dart toward the front door, grabbing my coat along the way. I slip on my boots; then I sprint down Dorset Street as fast as I can.

Chapter 40

I end up sitting on a random bench outside some random brick-front building I don't recognize.

I don't even know where I am or how far I ran. But I'm covered in sweat and panting and need to sit down for a second.

And go to the bathroom.

I realize now that in this morning's chaos, I haven't even peed. So I stand up and scurry into the pub nearby. I catch my reflection in the glass front. My hair is a rat's nest. I'm wearing silk pajamas, a trench coat, and knock-off UGG boots. I look like I'm sleepwalking.

Thankfully the half dozen patrons are more interested in the soccer game on the TV than in the disheveled woman walking past them.

When I finish and walk back out the door, I hear my name.

"Riley."

I spin around at the sound of Milo's voice and see him standing down the block.

I don't move as he walks over to me. Part of me wants to run off, but the other part of me is too exhausted.

"Riley," he says through a breath. His chest heaves. I register the worry in his stare as he looks at me.

He jerks his arm slightly, like he wants to reach for me but thinks better of it.

"Are you okay?" he asks after a minute of us standing on the side-walk, staring at each other while people walk around us.

I almost laugh. "No, Milo. I'm not okay. I found out that my husband has been having an affair with his ex-girlfriend. I found out that he got her pregnant. And then I find out that not only do you have feelings for me, but that Tristan's ex cheated with you. What the hell is this, some weird kink of yours? Do you only go for women your relatives have dated?"

I ignore the stares of the people passing by. I don't blame them, really. I'm sure this looks like a scene straight out of a soap opera.

He sighs, his shoulders sagging. "I know how bad this looks. I know I'm coming off like a sleazy piece of shit."

I hold up a hand, cutting him off. I feel the beginnings of a tension headache gripping the base of my skull.

"I can't stand here anymore." I walk back to the bench.

Milo stays standing for several seconds before walking over to me. "Can I sit?"

I sigh and shrug. "It's a public bench. I can't stop you."

I have to bite my tongue to hold back the rest of what I want to say. I think back to the conversation I overheard between Milo and his cousin Rafa at their family pool party in Portugal. This is why Rafa was so critical of seeing me and Milo together—because Milo pulled a similar move with Tristan's uni girlfriend.

I think back to asking him who Elena was after the pool party, how he admitted that the start of their relationship was essentially an affair since she was still with someone else . . . how he left out the fact that the other relationship was with Tristan . . .

In his timeline I already knew; our fight already happened.

I think back to how I reassured Milo, how I told him it was all okay, how I wasn't mad anymore.

The urge to let out a feral, bitter laugh hits, but I swallow it back. If only I had the full story then. I would have left Milo in Portugal and taken the first flight out.

As angry as I am, I can't bring any of that up to him now. It wouldn't make any sense—he hasn't lived the same timeline I have.

He hasn't yet taken me to Portugal to meet his family. We haven't yet started a relationship.

The ache in my head intensifies with how confusing this all is. I press a fist to the base of my skull, closing my eyes as the tension slowly starts to dissipate.

"You have every right to be angry with me, Riley," Milo says.

I open my eyes and look at him. He's resting his elbows on his knees and gazing down at the ground.

He twists his head to me. "Tristan is right. I had a thing for you pretty much the moment I met you. But I ignored it. I was enough of a sleazebag, being the guy who dated my cousin's girlfriend years ago. I didn't want to be the piece of garbage who went after his wife too." A hard swallow moves along the length of this throat. "It was easier if I was a jerk to you both. I know that's fucked up. Beyond fucked up."

He scrubs a hand over his face, then tugs at his hair. He turns to me. "But what Tristan said about me trying to break you two up so I can have a shot at you isn't true at all. I told you about his affair because you deserve to know what he's been doing behind your back."

The weight of his words hangs in the air between us.

"Did he cheat on Elena too?" I ask.

Milo is quiet before nodding. "Yeah. A lot. Look, I know what I did was wrong, but this is the full story. We all went to the same university in London. I knew Elena because Tristan brought her to a lot of family events. I liked her; she was sweet and nice. We'd see each other at family stuff from time to time and became friends." He huffs out a breath. "When Elena found out that Tristan was cheating on her, she was so upset. She came to me and told me everything. I was so angry for her. And I was pissed at Tristan. I tried to comfort her . . ." He blinks, and his gaze turns shy, like he's embarrassed. "In the heat of the moment, we kissed."

Milo's cheeks go fire-engine red, like he's mortified to admit all this to me.

"We slept together. And then one more time after that, while she was still with Tristan. I knew it was wrong, but I didn't care. I was sick of seeing my cousin treat his girlfriends like shit. I was sick of seeing his parents and most of our family treat him like a golden boy when he was doing so many dishonest things in his personal life. Elena wanted to keep hooking up in secret, but I told her that she needed to break up with Tristan first. So she did. She told him about our hookup to make him mad and jealous. Tristan and I fought over it." Milo exhales and looks down, like he's ashamed. "When Elena ended it with Tristan, we tried to make it work. We lasted almost a year before we finally broke up. We weren't compatible long term. And we both had major trust issues, given the fact that our relationship started out as an affair."

For a few seconds he's quiet. He frowns slightly, like he's in pain. "My relationship with Tristan was never great. But that was what broke us for good. Yeah, I'm a piece of shit for sleeping with his girlfriend behind his back, and so is he for cheating on her in the first place."

Milo is quiet again. For a few minutes all we do is watch as cars and buses whizz by on the street in front of us.

He turns to me, the look in his eyes tender and sorrowful. "I'm sorry for everything, Riley. Look, I don't know what you'll decide to do when it comes to Tristan, but I just hope you know that you deserve better than any of this."

He stands up and walks in the direction he came from, down Dorset Street. I stay sitting on the bench, processing everything he's just told me.

I wait for the surge of anger and frustration and hurt to surface once more. But it doesn't. For a few minutes I sit there, confused. But then it hits me: Milo was honest with me. He admitted what he did wrong, apologized for it, and seemed genuinely regretful for the pain he caused.

And that's when I realize how wrong I am to lump him and Tristan together. Yes, they both lied. But Milo took responsibility for what he did wrong. He admitted it right away. He came after me to make sure

I was okay and so he could explain himself to me, without any expectation from me whatsoever.

Tristan didn't do any of that. He lied to me again and again. And then he made up lies about Milo to avoid admitting fault.

That's the difference between these two men. And my feelings for both of them are crystal clear now.

I jolt up from the bench and run down Dorset Street. I weave around slow-moving pedestrians and strollers and kids and dogs until that familiar tall, lean form with thick brown-black hair comes into view.

I shout Milo's name so loud that everyone around me jolts.

I mutter "sorry" as I speed ahead, hoping I can catch him.

"Milo!"

He stops in front of a crosswalk, his eyes wide as he spins around and looks at me.

"Riley, what—"

"I was wrong," I huff out between gasps. "You and Tristan aren't the same. Not even close."

His brow furrows, like he's confused. "Okay . . ."

I take a few seconds to steady my breathing. "You were honest. You admitted all the things you did wrong, no matter how bad they made you look. You're no saint, that's for sure. But no one is. We all fuck up. What matters is that we can admit it when we do. And apologize. And make things right and try to be better. That's what you did."

He takes a second before speaking, like he needs a moment to process what I've said. "Yeah, I mean, I'm trying to do all that."

"I'm leaving Tristan. I'm going to divorce him."

He looks stunned. "You are?"

"Yeah. I can't be with him anymore, not after what he did."

Milo nods, the look on his face dazed. "I have a lawyer friend I can refer you to," he says after a moment. "She's brutal. She'll make sure you're protected, no matter what you decide to do."

"Thank you, Milo."

For a second we just stand there and look at each other. He opens his mouth to speak, but then a truck turns the corner while blaring the horn. We both jump at the noise.

When he looks at me again, his eyes are shy. Whatever he was building up the nerve to say, the moment's clearly gone.

"I'll get you her number," he says. "Do you need me to come back with you to the flat?"

I shake my head. "Tristan and I need to talk alone."

Milo nods. His gaze on me turns focused and intense. "I'll see you around, Riley."

He starts to walk off. My stomach churns as I watch him make his way down the block.

"Milo, wait!" I jog after him for the second time this morning.

He stops under a nearby street sign. When I catch up to him, I notice it's the Dorset Street sign. And then without another word, I hug him. It takes him a second before he slides his arms around me and holds tight. That twist in my stomach disappears. Now there's nothing but warmth.

I lean back and look up at him. "Can we be friends?" I blurt.

His mouth curves up in the most beautiful smile. "I'd love that."

We leave with a promise to text each other. I already know what happens. Texts about marshmallow Peeps and tea and Easter. We meet up at that café by his house. It feels like friendship, but different. Better.

Something new, something wonderful, develops between us. And it all kicks off today.

I walk back to my flat and open the door to see Tristan standing in the kitchen, frowning at his phone. He starts to smile, but it fades as I walk up to him. Probably because I'm not smiling back.

"Tristan, I need you to listen to me. I know you're cheating on me. I know you got Carly pregnant."

His mouth falls open. He closes it quickly and swallows. His blue eyes turn focused as they scan my face, like he's silently scrambling to think of another lie, of someone else to blame.

"Riley, I'm not sure what—"

"We're done. I want a divorce."

He looks like I've punched him in the gut. His eyebrows crash together as he clutches a hand to his stomach. "Riley, you can't be serious."

"I'm dead serious. I don't want to be with you anymore."

He shakes his head, like he doesn't want to accept what I've said. "Riley, this can't be the end of us. Please."

"It is, though. You've been fucking your ex behind my back for who knows how long. And you got her pregnant. We're done. So fucking done."

His chest heaves with the breath he takes. His gaze flits off to the side. He's frowning out the window, like he's confused and upset and mystified all at once.

It's strange . . . the longer I look at him, the more I realize I don't feel angry or hurt or sad.

I'm more curious than anything.

"What exactly was your plan, Tristan?" I finally ask the question swirling around in my head. "Did you really think you could go on like this? Did you really think you could be married to me and have an affair with your ex forever? Did you think you could have a secret family on the side and still be with me?"

He whips his head to me. His blue eyes are wide, like he's shocked I could ask him such a thing.

He says nothing. He just looks at me, his mouth a straight line. He blinks quickly, and his gaze turns shy. Like he's embarrassed.

After a while his gaze falls to the floor. "You want the truth?"

"Yes."

"I don't know." He lets out a weak breath. "I don't know what I was thinking. I just . . . did it."

I almost laugh. That's such a nonanswer, such a cop-out.

I let out a soft scoff and shake my head. "I don't buy that. There's gotta be a reason. I thought we were happy. I was happy, at least."

I'm surprised at how detached I sound. There's not an ounce of pleading or longing in my tone. I just want to know why.

"I was happy too," he says. He clears his throat. "I ran into Carly at one of my restaurants a while ago. We got to catching up, and um, well. Things escalated . . . it was just meant to be one time. But then things got out of hand . . ."

A hard swallow moves along his throat. The skin on his neck and cheeks is cherry red. I can tell this conversation is making him want to crawl out of his skin. I don't care.

He shoves his hands in his pockets. His shoulders slump. His gaze bounces back to the floor. It's striking just how adolescent he looks right now. His stance, his posture, his eye contact are all reminiscent of a teenager in trouble.

"I just wasn't thinking, Riley." He sighs, presses his eyes shut, and pinches the bridge of his nose before looking at me again. "Growing up, I watched my dad run around with other women constantly. I know it's wrong, but that's what was modeled to me as a kid. I kind of don't know any better. I know you probably don't want to hear that, but it's the truth." He shrugs.

This time I actually laugh. I should have known this was what he would say. No apology, just blaming someone else for what he did wrong.

And that's when I decide I don't care about what Tristan has to say anymore. I just want him gone.

"Leave. Now."

His brow hits his hairline, clearly shocked at what I've said. "What?"

"I want you to leave, Tristan."

He starts to speak.

"Don't," I say, my tone calm but firm. "You need to pack your things and leave."

He opens his mouth, but I cut him off, too angry and frustrated to hear him speak another word.

"You're pathetic, Tristan."

He looks stunned at what I've said. But I don't care. If he wants to stay, if he wants to draw this out longer, then it's happening on my terms. He's going to listen to everything I have to say.

"You're selfish. And arrogant. And you never truly cared about me. You never defended me. You were never really on my side. The way you let your family disrespect me all these years shows that. Because you're weak, Tristan. You refuse to accept responsibility for your actions. You refuse to stand up to your family, even when they're in the wrong. Everything good about you was a sham, a facade, a way to make you look good. You're nothing to me anymore. And nothing you could ever do or say will ever change my mind. Now I want you to leave."

For a long moment he just looks at me, his soft blue gaze wide, like he's stunned at what I've said.

It takes a few seconds for my heartbeat to slow after the adrenaline rush of saying all that. But when it does, I feel calm. I feel in control despite the chaos of everything that's happened.

Tristan hesitates for a second before he purses his lips and walks off, disappearing into the bedroom. For the next hour the sounds of suitcases zipping and fabric rustling are all I hear as I sit with Coco on the sofa.

When he wheels his bags to the door, he stops and looks over at me. "Riley, I just . . ."

"There's nothing more to say, Tristan. Get out."

He clenches his jaw. "This isn't over, Riley." He glares around the flat.

"I know that. I still want you to leave."

He scoffs before stomping out of the flat, slamming the door behind him.

Coco's ice-blue eyes go wide at the noise before she nuzzles against my arm in a bid for more pets. I'm scratching under her chin, and she's purring happily when my phone buzzes with a text.

Milo: Hey. Sorry to text so soon, but how are things going right now?
Me: Tristan just left.

Milo: Are you okay?

Me: Yeah.

Milo: You sure?

Me: Positive. Thank you for checking on me.

Milo: Of course.

Warmth surges through me before worry starts to creep in. When I wake up in the morning, it'll be Valentine's Day—the day of my wedding anniversary, the day of that disastrous party at Tristan's restaurant.

I'll wake up to Tristan surprising me with coffee in bed. He'll have no memory of what happened between us today. Neither will Milo. No one will. They're all living a different timeline than me, and I'll have to start over. I glance down at Coco, who's yawning. She won't be here when I wake up.

The thought of continuing this backward, nonsensical timeline makes me want to curl into a ball. How long will this be my life? How long will I have to keep living backward, waking up next to a husband I no longer want to be with? How can I change it so I can start moving forward in time—so I move on for good?

The questions swirl in my head until I'm dizzy. I press my eyes shut and exhale. I have no idea how to do any of that.

So I stay sitting on the couch, Coco cuddled in my lap. It's the only thing I want to do right now, the only thing that feels calming and right in this backward chaos that is currently my life.

That and one more thing.

I pick up my phone and dial Milo's number. He answers on the third ring.

"Hey. You okay?"

I'm heartened that he cares enough to ask me that again. "You already asked me that."

"I wanted to hear you say it this time."

I smile. "Yeah, I'm okay. Are you busy?"

"Not at all."

"Just wanted to chat with a friend for a bit."

"Well, then, I'm your guy." I can hear the smile in his voice. It makes me feel instantly at ease.

When I wake up in the morning, it won't be like this—Milo and I won't be friends. It'll be like this day and this conversation never happened. We'll have to start all over again.

A knot forms in my stomach at the thought.

"What do you want to chat about?" he asks.

I think for a second. "I don't know. Just something to take my mind off things."

He's quiet for a second. "Wanna watch TV together?"

"While we're on the phone?"

"Yeah. It'll be fun, I promise."

I smile at the lilt in his tone. "If you say so."

"You've never done that before? Like when you were younger with your friends?"

"Can't say that I have."

"I used to with my long-distance friends. It was great. We'd pick out a show or a movie and watch it together while on the phone."

That's such a cute thing to do. And it's exactly what I need right now. "Okay. What should we watch?"

"You're putting me on the spot. Let me think for a sec."

When he doesn't say anything for a bit, I say the first show that comes to my mind. "*Daria*."

"The MTV cartoon?"

"Yeah. Didn't you watch it? It's an American classic."

He laughs. "Damn, that's a blast from the past. Of course I watched it."

"It was my favorite as a kid. I was a sucker for an angsty, no-BS female protagonist."

Milo's low chuckle rumbles against my ear. "Me too. *Daria* it is."

I pull it up on the TV and wait for Milo to do the same.

"Wait, we gotta get snacks. And drinks," he says.

I hop up, grab a bag of chips from the pantry and a bottle of water from the fridge. "I'm ready."

"What are you eating?"

"Chips and water. You?"

"A sandwich and soda."

"What episode should we start with?"

"I say we kick it off with the original. Season one, episode one."

Emotion bubbles in my chest at the simple joy of this.

I'll keep living this backward timeline. I don't know when it will stop . . . *if* it will ever stop. That's why this time with Milo is so special. In the chaos and instability of all that, I'll think of sitting on my couch, watching TV with him on the phone, the peace of it, how fun it was, how right it felt.

And the happy memory of this moment will help power me through everything else that will happen.

I select the episode on the TV. "Let's do it."

Chapter 41

I wake to the smell of something dank and wet. And citrusy. And floral.

Eyes still closed, I breathe in. It smells like freshly brewed tea.

When I try to open my eyes, I can keep them open for only a moment. My eyelids feel so, so heavy.

A strange feeling hits me out of the blue. It feels like I've done this before.

After a few seconds, I finally manage to open my eyes.

When I do, I still.

I should be waking up in bed next to Tristan on the morning of our one-year anniversary. But I'm not. Instead, I'm in the passenger seat of my car.

I take in the dark finish of the door as it materializes in my sleep-blurred vision.

I shift slightly and gaze at the road ahead, swathed in early-morning sunlight.

When I twist toward the driver's seat, I see Milo. He turns to look at me and flashes that handsome smile I love so much.

"Morning, Sleeping Beauty."

He gestures to the cup holder next to the center console before focusing back on the road, just like I knew he would. There sits a tall disposable cup of tea, steam wafting from the opening in the plastic lid.

"Stopped by the tea shop down the street from the flat while you were snoozing and got your favorite," he says. "Half–Earl Grey, half–hazelnut black tea. The tea smith working there actually scowled at me when I ordered it. Again. Does he do that to you, too, whenever you order from him?"

He chuckles.

I don't say anything. I can't. I'm too stunned.

Because somehow, someway, after living an entire year backward, I've been launched forward in time.

I clear my throat, unable to speak for a long stretch.

"Damn. You're usually chattier than this in the morning Must have been an extra-hard sleep."

I try to smile as I dig my phone out of my purse. "Something like that."

My screen illuminates, and I still once again when I see the date.
February 14, 2025.

I'm back where I started.

My head spins as I try to make sense of what just happened. How did this happen? How am I all of a sudden moving forward in time after almost a year of moving backward?

It feels like my head is in a cloud as I try to make sense of what has happened—what is *still* happening.

I don't know how long I stare at my phone in utter shock, but it must be a while, because I hear Milo repeating my name.

"Riley?"

I whip my head up and look at him. "Yeah?"

"Are you okay?" Concern is etched in the lines of his frown.

That skidding feeling intensifies. It feels like my chest is swollen with emotion.

I think about living the past year in reverse with him . . .

The year where I ended one relationship and started another.

The year where I learned the truth about two men I thought I knew.

The year where I left behind the man I thought I'd be with forever.

The year where I forged a bond with a man I couldn't stand.

The year I fell in love with Milo.

Love.

He glances back at the road. I stare at him, that tidal wave of emotion consuming me from the inside out.

I think back to the last thing I remember before falling asleep and waking up in my car. How Milo and I stayed on the phone the whole day while watching *Daria*. How we chatted and laughed and joked late into the night. How I fell asleep on the phone.

And then I remember how this day unfolded the first time I lived it . . . how terrified and confused I was when I woke up and saw him driving my car. I remember the affection in his eyes when he looked at me. I remember the concern etched in his expression when he saw me at my flat. I remember the warmth of his body when he hugged me tight. I remember the texts he sent me when I ran off to search for Tristan, asking if I was okay.

My chest goes tight. I swallow back the wave of emotion pummeling me.

"I'm okay," I finally say. "Sorry, I just had some weird dreams when I was asleep."

He smiles at me. "Yup. Definitely napped too hard."

I laugh with him, relishing the ease and comfort coursing through me as I relive this day.

"Where are we going?" I ask.

"It's a surprise, remember?" he says, smiling at the road ahead.

"Right."

Chapter 42

I'm quiet for a long stretch as my brain tries to process the impossibility of this moment. Why did it all unfold like this? Why did I wake up a year into the future one day and start living life backward? Why am I living it forward now? Why did any of this happen?

But the answers never come. I don't know why I expect them to. An experience like this, where my entire reality and sense of time have been turned upside down, can't possibly have an easy explanation.

I glance out the car window and focus on the soft hum of the engine as we fly across the speedway. The noise is a calming distraction for the endless thoughts and questions tumbling around my brain.

I try to look at the grass alongside the road, but I start to feel dizzy at how I can't focus on any visual, given how fast we're going. It's just swipes of green whizzing by. I press my eyes shut for a moment to steady myself. When I open them, I relax my gaze, focusing on nothing in particular. A minute later I twist my neck to look at the landscape behind us now, and that's when the scene comes into focus: an emerald-green hill dotted with bright-yellow flowers and fence posts, against a cornflower-blue sky.

I see everything so clearly, looking back at it.

And then something clicks in my brain. Maybe that's the point. Maybe I had to live my life backward to truly see everything and everyone for what they really were.

I saw Tristan's true colors. Milo's too.

For a few minutes I reflect on the thought.

Is it really that simple?

Maybe.

It's enough to calm the swirl of thoughts and questions. In this moment it feels like enough.

When Milo pulls off into the Kent countryside, just over an hour outside London, I gaze at the endless rolling green hills and winding country roads. He slows down and turns left onto a side road. We get to an open wooden gate that leads to a lush green hillside. I squint at the massive wooden sign off to the side.

"Beautiful Blossoms Farm," I say. Next to the pretty cursive writing is an illustration of pink and white flowers.

It takes a second before it registers. "Peonies?"

When I whip my head around at him, he's smiling.

"You guessed it." He eases the car to a stop in the dirt parking lot, next to a massive hillside with endless rows of tilled dirt.

He kills the engine and turns to me. "We're a couple months early from when the flowers bloom. We'll come back for that." He nods toward the dirt rows. Those must be where the flower bulbs are planted. "But there's something I want to show you now."

We get out of the car and walk toward a small wooden building near the fields. When he scoops my hand in his, my skin goes warm instantly. I glance around us, taking in the view of the farmland, which glows with shades of bright green and rich brown in the golden sunlight.

My heart thuds at the thoughtfulness in the day trip that Milo has planned for me. A day that was supposed to be a remembrance of my heartbreak is something different. Something better.

When we walk inside the little wooden shop, a small older woman with a lovely warm smile greets us.

"You must be Milo and Riley?" she asks.

"That's us," Milo says while I nod.

"Greta. Good to meet you."

We shake hands with her.

She grabs a coat and slides it on before focusing on me. "Well, my dear. Let's head out and take advantage of this sunny February day. Don't get many of those in England."

She chuckles and bends down to grab a small wooden square with wire attached to it.

I look up at Milo. "What is all this?"

He grins. "You'll see."

We follow Greta out the back door and head along the fields. Milo chats with her while we walk. She tells us that her family has run this farm for three generations.

A small gust of cold wind breezes around us, but the sunlight above counters it with warmth so that the combination feels pleasant.

Greta stops at the head of one of the tilled rows and opens her arms, like she's presenting the entire field to us.

She looks at me. "Your bloke called and said he'd like to reserve a row of peonies for his special lady. So you, my dear, get to choose your row."

I make a soft gasping noise as I look at Milo.

"Are you serious?" I ask.

His smile is warm and giddy all at once. "Completely serious."

I rest my palm against my chest as I catch my breath, blown away at the sweetness of this surprise Milo's arranged for me. That wave of emotion crashes through me once more.

I lean up and press a kiss to his mouth, careful to keep it quick and PG since Greta is here. "I love you," I murmur to him.

I take in the dazed look in his eyes, how he looks like he could topple over, he's so shocked at what I've said.

And that's when I realize this is the first time I've said this to him.

The first time we've said this to each other.

I remember the first times I said "I love you" to past partners. I always felt rattled, like my nerves were crackling inside me.

But I don't feel any of that right now. All I feel is warmth and calm as I gaze up at Milo.

He blinks, revealing a brightness I haven't seen before in his rich brown eyes.

"I love you too," he whispers before kissing my forehead.

Greta gazes adoringly at us before looking back out at the field. I glance down at the row right next to my feet.

"This one," I say.

Greta beams at me. "You've got it, my dear." She pulls a black marker from her coat pocket and scribbles something on the black wooden square in her other hand. When she sticks the wire legs into the ground, I read what she's written.

"Riley's Row," I say through a smile.

"I like the sound of that," Milo says, sliding his arm around me.

Greta says she'll leave us to explore the property.

"I'll put on the kettle," she says. "You two can come in and have some tea when you're done."

She walks back to the building. Milo and I stroll along the edge of the field.

"This is the most thoughtful gift, Milo. Thank you."

"It's my pleasure." He squeezes my hand in his. "We'll come back in June and pick a bouquet for you to take home. We could invite Poppy and Desmond. And Nesta and Roland too. Molly will be running by then, I think. It'll be fun to see her explore this place."

He smiles out at the farmland. Something inside me swells, intensifies.

It feels like a mix of hope and hesitation.

After living life backward for so many months, I've gotten used to not thinking about the future. But I can't help the excitement that simmers within me. I think of coming back here to Beautiful Blossoms

Farm when it's sunny and thousands of peonies in every color are in full bloom.

I think of warm weather. I think of the days getting longer and longer.

I think of outings with Poppy and Desmond, and Nesta and Roland. I gaze at the emerald-green hills surrounding us in every direction and picture Molly running around.

I think of living this life with Milo. Forward or backward, it doesn't matter. It's perfect as long as it's with him.

My heart swells in my chest. "I can't wait."

Acknowledgments

This book was a wild idea that I never thought would see the light of day. But it's here and I couldn't be happier, and I have so many people to thank for that.

Stefanie Simpson, thank you for reading the earliest draft of this book, when it was a certified mess. You were so supportive and urged me to keep working on it, and I owe you everything for that.

Rebecca Chase, thank you for beta-reading and offering your brilliant insights.

To my editors Krista, Alexandra, and Erin: thank you for believing in this story and helping me shape it into the book it is today.

To everyone on the Lake Union marketing and publicity team: thank you for putting this book into the world and helping readers find it.

Thank you to my family and friends for supporting me, loving me, and being proud of me.

To my mom: Thank you for everything. For life, for your love, and for encouraging me to follow my dreams. I wouldn't be doing this without you.

And my biggest thanks goes to you, my amazing readers. Thank you for taking the time to read my words. It means more than you know.

ABOUT THE AUTHOR

Photo © 2015 Jessi Reiss and Nick Zielinski

Sarah Echavarre is the author of *Three More Months* and *What We Remember*. She has worked a bevy of odd jobs that inspire the stories she writes today. When Sarah's not penning tear-jerking women's fiction, she writes sweet and sexy rom-coms under the names Sarah Echavarre Smith and Sarah Smith. She lives in Bend, Oregon, with her husband. For more information visit www.sarahechavarre.com and follow her on Instagram at @sarahechavarre.